O9-AHT-180

Deadly Delights

Also available by Laura Jensen Walker

The Bookish Baker Mysteries

Murder Most Sweet

The Faith Chapel Mysteries

Hope, Faith, & a Corpse

Phoebe Grant Series

Dreaming in Black and White

Dreaming in Technicolor

Getaway Girls

Daring Chloe

Turning the Paige

Becca by the Book

Other Novels

Reconstructing Natalie

Miss Invisible

Deadly Delights

A BOOKISH BAKER MYSTERY

Laura Jensen Walker

NEW YORK

This is a work of fiction. All of the names, characters, organizations, places and events portrayed in this novel are either products of the author's imagination or are used fictitiously. Any resemblance to real or actual events, locales, or persons, living or dead, is entirely coincidental.

PUBLISHER'S NOTE: The recipes contained in this book are to be followed exactly as written. The publisher is not responsible for your specific health or allergy needs that may require medical supervision. The publisher is not responsible for any adverse reaction to the recipes contained in this book.

Published in the United States by Crooked Lane Books, an imprint of The Quick Brown Fox & Company LLC.

Crooked Lane Books and its logo are trademarks of The Quick Brown Fox & Company LLC.

Library of Congress Catalog-in-Publication data available upon request.

ISBN (hardcover): 978-1-64385-592-9
ISBN (ePub): 978-1-64385-593-6

Cover illustration by Rob Fiore

Printed in the United States

www.crookedlanebooks.com

Crooked Lane Books
34 West 27th St., 10th Floor
New York, NY 10001

First Edition: June 2021

10 9 8 7 6 5 4 3 2 1

In loving memory of my parents, David and Bettie Jensen, and the bookish, bakery childhood upbringing they gave me in Racine, Wisconsin, unofficial kringle capital of the world and home to the best Danish bakeries in America.

My fond growing-up memories include going into the West Racine bakeries with my mom, dad, siblings Lisa, Todd, and Tim to pick up a kringle or Seven Sisters—seven Danish pastry rolls baked together to form a round coffee cake with luscious custard filling and almond paste. (My sister and I always fought over the center piece.) On special occasions we would enjoy Danish layer cake with its ribbons of raspberry and custard filling and thick buttercream frosting. Yum.

The daughter of a book-loving father, I devoured books more than I did Danish pastry. My love of words began when Dad drilled us at the dinner table on the *Reader's Digest* "It Pays to Increase Your Word Power" section. This word love continued once I started school and received a constellation of gold stars for reading the most books in Miss Vopelensky's first-grade class—a hundred and three. That's when I determined to someday become a writer. A favorite Racine childhood pastime was our biweekly visits to the bookmobile where my sister, Lisa, and I would each check out the maximum number of books allowed (six or eight, as I recall). We would race through our books and then swap stacks. Another favorite childhood memory was receiving the latest Trixie Belden mystery hot off the press from the Western Printing factory in town where my aunts worked. My love of mysteries was born thanks to Trixie Belden.

It wasn't until we moved from Wisconsin when I was a teen that I discovered that the delectable Danish pastries and mouthwatering baked goods I had grown up with as a normal part of everyday life did not exist anywhere else in America. Definitely not in dry, dusty Arizona.

What? No more kringle or Seven Sisters as a special treat on weekend mornings? No more napoleon kringle with its rich custard filling at wedding showers and baby showers? And, worst of all, no more delicious Danish layer cake with the fat buttercream roses the grown-ups gave me at every birthday party and wedding? Sacrilege.

These Bookish Baker mysteries are my love letter to my Racine childhood.

Chapter One

I bent over to pick up my embossed rosemaling rolling pin that had rolled off the table onto the ground, and as I did, someone whistled and pinched my butt. Instinctively I whirled around and smacked the pincher with the rolling pin, which sent him staggering.

"Ow! What'd you do that for?" said Lester Morris, rubbing his polyester-suited arm.

"Keep your hands to yourself, Les." *You disgusting pig and sorry excuse for a human being.*

The aging lothario was the town lech—Lester-the-molester we'd nicknamed him years ago in high school—who fancied himself quite the ladies' man. A fancy none of the women in Lake Potawatomi returned.

Unfortunately, Les Morris, CPA and the president of the chamber of commerce, also happened to be the head judge of our annual baking contest. Every August our small southern Wisconsin town holds its version of *The Great British Bake Off*, with local bakers—including, this year, yours truly—gathering in a large white vinyl tent in the park competing to win the title of Best Baker of Lake Potawatomi.

"I thought you'd be flattered," Les whined. "I mean, since you don't have breasts anymore, I figured you'd be happy to know you still have some womanly *ass*ets men find appealing." He gave me a flirtatious wink beneath his bushy white brows and licked his ancient lips.

Is this guy for real? What century is this Neanderthal from?

Remember? They dug him out of that time capsule from the sixties, along with copies of Playboy *and pictures of Barbara Eden in her harem costume from* I Dream of Jeannie.

Pushing my flyaway dark-brown curls behind my ears, I raised my distinctive Norwegian rolling pin and took a step toward the scrawny senior with the ill-fitting silver hairpiece. "Lester," I said in an even, measured tone, "you need to shut up and move away before I knock that bad rug off your miserable bald head. Right here. Right now."

A couple women outside the end of the open baking tent tittered, and Lester flushed.

"Attagirl, Teddie," said white-haired Fred Matson, one of my cookie fans, punching the air with his cane. "You tell 'im!"

More titters and chuckles came from the crowd gathered in the park for the first day of the annual competition.

Unbelievable this guy can still get away with this crap. There had been complaints to the chamber and City Hall over the years, but Lester's influence—he owns several commercial properties in town—and wealth always made them disappear.

"Les, honey," his long-suffering wife Patsy called from her table in the center of the tent, "can you come here, please? I need your help."

"Sure, sweetie. I'll be right there." He hurried away from my baked-goods display table, glowering at me as he left.

"Way to put Lester in his place," said my best friend and bookstore owner Char Jorgensen as she high-fived me, "but you can kiss that first-place baking trophy good-bye."

"Not necessarily," said Sharon Hansen, co-owner with her husband Jim of the Lake House Bed and Breakfast and the third member of our fortysomething girlfriends-since-grade-school group. Our teacher had dubbed us The Three Musketeers, and it had stuck. "Lester's not the only judge in this competition."

"True," Char said, tossing her red ponytail. "But didn't you have to sign something about being an impartial judge, Blondie"—she used Sharon's high school nickname—"and not letting personal relationships with the contestants influence your decision-making?"

"Yes." Sharon lifted her chin. "And I *will* be impartial. My judging will be based solely on taste and presentation."

"Too bad Lester's won't," said white-haired Bea Andersen, the third and final Bake-Off judge and longtime owner of Andersen's Bakery, as she joined our conversation. "Patsy Morris has won the competition every year for the past nine years."

"That's what happens when you sleep with the head judge." Char waggled her eyebrows at me in Groucho Marx fashion. "Maybe you should reconsider your Lester aversion."

I shuddered. "Not in this lifetime." Adjusting the boho-cotton scarf around my neck, I straightened my three-tiered dessert stand of peanut-butter blossoms. "My cookies can stand on their own."

"Yes, they can," my fellow Musketeer Sharon said. "And they will, if I've got anything to say about it."

"Teddie, how come you haven't entered the contest before now?" Bea asked.

"I was too busy with my job, and then the cancer and treatments took me out of commission for a while."

Five plus years earlier, I'd been diagnosed with breast cancer, requiring a mastectomy and chemotherapy followed by a second mastectomy less than a year later. The cancer was a wake-up call—it made me realize life is short, too short for me to be stuck in a boring government job rather than pursuing my passion. I took early retirement, did some traveling, and followed my lifelong dream of becoming a writer. Since then I've had four Kate and Kallie mystery novels published, including the recently released *A Dash of Death*—my first *USA Today* and Amazon best seller.

"I've finished the first draft of my book and am letting it rest a while before I come back to it with fresh eyes to slash, burn, and rewrite," I said, "so this was the perfect time to enter the contest."

Char filched a cookie from the bottom tier and took a big bite. "Yum. You've definitely got my vote."

"*You* don't get to vote, Charlotte Jorgensen," said Sharon. "Only the judges." In a gesture well honed from being the mom of college-age twins, she placed her hands on her hips and shook her head at our freckled friend. "I can't believe you just did that."

"Yeah," I said, adjusting the cookies to cover the empty spot left from Char's cookie theft. "Hands off the goods, Cookie Monster, until after the judging."

"Sorry. My bad."

Brady Wells arrived and snaked his arm around Char's waist. "What's my girl gone and done now?"

"You need to arrest her, Sheriff," said Sharon, only half joking. "She stole one of Teddie's cookies before the judges even had a chance to sample each contestant's entry."

"Is that true?" Brady asked, giving Char a mock-stern look.

She held up her hands. "Guilty as charged. I've been a bad girl. Guess you better handcuff me and take me away," she said playfully.

Brady blushed above his uniform collar.

"Get a room, you two," I said. "Although it would be nice if you could wait until after the judging."

That judging commenced half an hour later. Sharon, Bea, and Lester stopped by each of the top-ten contestants' tables inside the spacious tent to taste-test the first entry of the competition: cookies. Contestants had been instructed to bake their favorite cookie using an original recipe of their own or one handed down through family generations.

I'd had a hard time deciding which cookie to enter, so a couple weeks ago I had enlisted Char, Brady, and (reluctantly) my mother to do some taste-testing in advance. Char wasn't much help. She'd never met a cookie she didn't like.

"You definitely need to make your peanut-butter blossoms," she said, after inhaling three. "I mean, peanut butter and chocolate? What could be better?"

"*Fattigman bakkels*," said Brady, brushing the powdered sugar from one of the fried-dough cookies (they're pronounced *futtymon buckles*) off his uniform shirt. "You know I love your *fattigman*."

"My grandma's *fattigman*," I corrected him. "She got the recipe from *her* grandmother, who brought it over from Norway. The name translates to poor man's cookies, because back in the day, after buying all the ingredients, it left the baker poor. Happily, that's no longer the case."

Brady popped another one of the airy confections into his mouth. "I don't care what they're called or what they cost. I like them because the inside reminds me of doughnuts."

"Careful," I teased, "or you'll turn into the pudgy doughnut-loving-cop stereotype."

Char patted her boyfriend's flat stomach. "No worries there. My guy is lean and mean." She bit into a chippy chunk cookie—my version of chocolate-chip cookies with extra chocolate—and moaned with pleasure. "I changed my mind. These are my favorite."

"You said that about the oatmeal-raisin too," I reminded her. "I need a consensus here."

"I vote for the lemon-sugar cookies," interjected my mother (the mother who doesn't have an ounce of fat anywhere on her slender seventy-three-year-old frame). "They're lighter and less fattening."

In the end, I decided on classic peanut-butter blossoms topped with a Hershey's kiss—Char was right; the combination of peanut butter and chocolate is hard to beat. The judges apparently agreed, because I'd wound up in the final top five.

The remaining winning entries also included Sophie Miller's granola clusters, Jeffrey Hollenbeck's gluten-free chewy chocolate-chip cookies, Barbara Christensen's snickerdoodles, and Patsy Morris's coconut macaroons. (Wilma Sorensen's sugar cookies had made it to the top ten, but Wilma, the town gossip, had been disqualified when it was discovered she'd used store-bought refrigerated cookie dough.)

"Congratulations to our finalists," squawked Lester Morris into the microphone at the gazebo bandstand, where all the contestants had assembled. "The judges and I had a hard time picking the final five—and almost came to blows doing so," he said with a fake laugh, sending a pointed glance in Bea and Sharon's direction, "but it all worked out in the end." He motioned for the finalists to step forward. "As you can see, this year we've got a man in the Bake-Off, our newest resident and latest member of the chamber of commerce, Jeff Hollenbeck. Jeff here is an artist. He moved to town a few months ago and set up our new local arts collective."

The head judge grinned at the good-looking gray-ponytailed male finalist wearing a Grateful Dead T-shirt, cargo pants, and Birkenstocks. "Never thought I'd say this, Jeff, but those healthy cookies of yours are mighty tasty—nice and chewy. Can you tell us why you made them gluten-free?"

Jeffrey took the mike from Lester's outstretched hand. "My daughter Willow was diagnosed with celiac disease when she was six, so I learned to make gluten-free meals and desserts for her. Over time, I realized that going gluten-free was healthy for me too, and since I love chocolate-chip cookies"—he chuckled—"I determined to make the best gluten-free chocolate-chip cookies possible."

"And you succeeded," piped fellow judge Bea, giving Jeffrey a thumbs-up.

"Yep," Sharon agreed, sending him a congratulatory smile. "You sure did."

Lester, who fancied himself the American Paul Hollywood—although he had a good twenty-five years on the *Great British Bake Off* judge—scowled at the other two judges for stealing his thunder and plucked the microphone back. "Thanks, Jeff. Let's hear from the other contestants now." He cast an appreciative glance at Barbara Christensen, an attractive silver-haired widow in crisp white linen slacks and a red top. "Ah, the lovely Barbara . . . would you like to tell us about your snickerdoodles, pretty lady?" He sidled up to her.

Barbara, distinctly uncomfortable, took a small step back from Les. "They were my husband's favorite, and my grandchildren love them," she said. "Simple as that."

The head judge then moved on to Sophie Miller, the granddaughter of my older neighbor, Margaret, who has Parkinson's. Sophie, who is five feet tall and maybe a hundred pounds, sported a turquoise streak in her long blonde hair, courtesy of her BFF and stylist Lauren. Sophie moved back home last year after losing her job and now lives with her grandma as her caregiver.

"Let's have a round of applause for our youngest contestant," Les said.

While the crowd clapped, the lecherous judge leaned down, apparently forgetting about his mike, and whispered something inappropriate into shy twenty-year-old Sophie's ear.

Sophie blushed furiously and slapped him in the face.

* * *

"Well, that was an exciting first day of competition," Sharon said as we gathered around the island in the Lake House kitchen later that afternoon.

"I'll say." Char scarfed down one of my leftover cookies. "I can't wait to see what happens tomorrow. Maybe one of the contestants will smash a pie into Lester's face." She sent me a hopeful look.

"I'm not wasting my grandma's classic cherry pie on that jerk," I said, thinking of the intricate lattice-and-leaf design I still had to painstakingly create when I got home. "Besides, custard-cream pies are the usual pie-in-the-face fare."

"That's right," Jim said. "Cream pies are what we used during our fraternity food fights." Sharon's forty-five-year-old husband and co-owner of the Lake House smirked at the memory. "I'd be happy to resurrect my college pie-smashing skills on Les. That guy is a piece of work."

"Tell me about it," Brady said. "I still can't believe he wanted to file assault charges against Sophie."

Char gave her boyfriend a quick hug. "I'm glad you set him straight, babe."

"How exactly did you manage that?" I asked. "I was busy packing up and missed it."

"I simply informed Les that everyone at the park heard his comments, so Sophie had plenty of witnesses to back up her sexual harassment claim—*if* she decided to file one. And was that something he wanted in his position as president of the chamber of commerce?"

"That's my boo." Char kissed him on the cheek.

"Patsy sure hustled Les out of there pretty fast," Jim commented.

"Poor Patsy." Sharon sighed. "I don't know why she puts up with that pig."

Char reached for another cookie. "She's old-school and doesn't know anything else. Patsy did the traditional fifties and sixties housewife thing: cook, bake, keep house, and ignore her husband's indiscretions. Haven't they been married like fifty years or something?"

"Fifty-one," Jim said. "They had their fiftieth-anniversary party here last year, arranged by their son, remember, Sharon?"

"How could I forget?" She grimaced. "Les got drunk and started hitting on every woman in sight, right in front of Patsy. It was awful. She was completely humiliated."

"I'd have decked him and walked out," I said. "But then, I'd have left years ago. No man would treat me like that and get away with it."

"That's for sure," Char said with feeling. "Speaking of men"—her tone turned sly—"how's your man Tavish?"

Hot and cuddly, thank you very much. "He's good. Busy working on his new book. We're Skyping tomorrow morning."

"I still can't believe you let that gorgeous Brit go back to England without you," Sharon said. "What if one of those pale English roses over there snatches him up?"

"Not gonna happen," Char said. "Teddie and Tavish are kindred spirits."

That we are. Something I'd never expected when the famous suspense author came to town a few months ago for a book signing. We bonded after his ex-fiancée was found strangled behind the bookstore with one of my scarves and I had to prove my innocence. When another woman was killed and suspicion turned toward Tavish, I sought to clear both his name and mine. In the process, we fell for each other—drawn together by our mutual love of dogs, books (both reading and writing them), and sweets. (I bake them, he eats them.)

"He had family and work commitments across the pond," I said. "Besides, we'll see each other in a couple months. Until then, we text, call, and Skype."

"How romantic," Brady teased.

"Says the king of romance." Char bussed him on the cheek.

* * *

Pulling into my driveway an hour later, I saw my mother in a crisp white blouse, black pencil skirt, and her ubiquitous black high heels—the ones that show off her slim, well-defined legs—scurrying to the car parked beside her sleek mother-in-law cottage.

I released a long, slow whistle. "Wow. Where are you off to all dressed up? Got a hot date?"

She smoothed a strand of her silver bob into place. "Don't be silly. I'm meeting Cheryl and some of my book club friends for an early dinner." Mom glanced at the vintage Rolex Dad had given her for her fiftieth birthday more than a couple decades ago. "Goodness, I'm late. Must dash." She slid into her pearl-white Lexus, buckled up, and backed out, giving me a slight wave as she left.

When I opened my back door into the kitchen, Gracie, my American Eskimo, welcomed me with her usual greeting—standing on her hind legs and pawing at the air rapidly with her front paws, her creamy tail wagging furiously.

At last! You're finally home, Mom.

I knelt down, and my canine daughter leapt into my arms and licked my cheek as I hugged her. "Did you miss me, Gracie-girl? I've only been gone a few hours."

Yeah, but it feels like forever. She licked my nose, then jumped down, an expectant look in her dark eyes.

"Yes, yes, Mommy will take you for walkies now." Thanks to Tavish, I'd adopted the English slang for walking the dog, which Gracie seemed to prefer. I clipped on her leash as she strained toward the door. We headed down the street, passing some neighbors on the way.

"Congrats on making it to the top five, Teddie," Joanne LaPoint said from her front yard, where she was watering her dahlias. "Not that I'm surprised. I think you're going to win the whole darn thing."

Not if Lester Morris has anything to say about it. "We'll see," I said. "Lots of good bakers in town."

Gracie pulled me forward. We jogged around the park and then returned home, where we ran into Mom's stylish friend Cheryl in yoga pants and a fitted short-sleeved workout T-shirt.

Cheryl Martin from book club? The same Cheryl that Mom is supposedly meeting for dinner?

"Hi, Teddie, nice to see you," the uber-fit, recently retired Cheryl said. "I just dropped by on my way to the gym to drop off the book your mom loaned me. She's not home, so I set it on her doorstep."

I murmured a distracted thanks. "I'll make sure she gets it." *What are you up to, Mom?*

"Congratulations, by the way. Your peanut-butter blossoms were absolutely delicious." Cheryl patted her flat stomach. "Between those and Sophie's yummy granola clusters, though, I really need a good workout."

I nodded, half listening, and made the obligatory niceties as Cheryl took her leave.

Where are you, Mother, and why did you lie to me?

Chapter Two

Two hours later, after I had applied the intricate latticework topping to my cherry pie now cooling on the counter top—my second attempt; the crust hadn't turned out the first time—a knock sounded at the back door. Gracie barked her happy bark, and I opened the door to find my fellow contestant and neighbor Sophie standing on the stoop in the dusk.

I flicked on the porch light, which shone on the stripe of turquoise in her hair that always reminded me of the Mediterranean Sea. "Hi, Sophie, what's up?"

"Mom's over visiting Gram, so I thought I'd go back to the tent and decorate my table while she's here," she said. "Gram has a doctor's appointment first thing tomorrow morning, and I won't have time to get all set up and decorate before the judging begins."

"Sounds like a good plan."

"Would you mind going with me?" she asked hesitantly. "I'd rather not be alone inside the tent after dark—it's kind of creepy."

"Sure. I can get my table ready in advance as well—then I won't be so stressed tomorrow morning." Making two pie crusts had already stressed me enough. Pies are *not* my forte. Especially crusts. Cookies, cakes, and muffins are more in my baking wheelhouse.

We loaded up our supplies and drove to the nearby park, Gracie sitting on Sophie's lap making goo-goo eyes at her as my young neighbor rubbed her belly and told her she was a pretty girl. Inside the white vinyl party tent, I flipped on the jury-rigged light and clipped Gracie's leash to the bottom of the metal tent pole so she wouldn't go rushing off after skunks and other nighttime critters. The chamber of commerce had funded Lake Potawatomi's bare-bones version of the *Great British Bake Off* tent five years ago after a sudden thunderstorm destroyed all the desserts that year, effectively ruining the event.

Our tent didn't have ovens, refrigerators, or individual prep stations like the fancy one on TV, simply sturdy card tables that each held one dessert entry, baked at home. Each baker decorated their table to complement the day's sweet offerings.

For pie day, Sophie had chosen a tropical theme, complete with pineapples, coconuts, palm branches, and colorful plastic leis, to offset her coconut-cream pie. I decorated my table—the one nearest the tent entrance—with my grandma's vintage white cotton tablecloth dotted with cherries, topped by a delicate glass vase of retro red-and-white mini carnations, a milk-glass pedestal candy dish that I would fill with plump red cherries tomorrow, and ruby-red Depression glassware goblets so the judges could enjoy a glass of milk along with their cherry pie. As a final decorative touch, I set my Norwegian rolling pin beside the glasses at an angle.

As we decorated our tables, Sophie sent me a timid look and said, "Teddie, do you mind if I ask you something?"

"Not at all. Fire away."

"It's kind of personal."

"That's okay. I don't mind personal."

She took a deep breath, then blurted out, "How come you decided not to get new breasts after your cancer? Especially since you're single. I don't mean to offend you or anything, but weren't you afraid it would be a turnoff to guys? They're so visual." She blushed to the roots of her pale-blonde hair.

"Actually, I had reconstructive surgery," I said. "My male surgeon recommended it for psychological reasons, since I was only in my late thirties. When I researched all my options, I discovered that most women under sixty choose the reconstructive route, so I followed their lead." I winked at her. "Honestly? I didn't want to deal with the lopsided factor of only one boob. I thought it would be easier to have a standard matched pair like I was used to."

Sophie stole a glance at my flat chest adorned with a sunflower-print scarf. "So . . . what happened?"

"My implant burst."

"Oh. My. Gosh." Her brown eyes grew wide. "Did it hurt?"

"Not a bit. I didn't even know it happened until later when I was showering and I suddenly noticed a flat tire where my fake boob used to be." I switched the vase of mini carnations from the upper right corner of my table to the left. "Apparently it popped when I hoisted a heavy ice cooler and rested it against my chest for a few minutes."

"Wow. Then what happened?"

"Luckily, it was a saline implant, so the saline simply absorbed into my body, but my doctor had me come in for an ultrasound and MRI to confirm the rupture." I sighed, remembering. "That's when they discovered I had several precancerous lumps in my other breast, which meant eventually I would get cancer in that one too. Since I didn't want to live in constant fear, wondering when the cancer would return, I decided boobs just weren't worth it. I chose to go flat instead."

"You're so brave," Sophie said. "I don't know if I could have done that."

"You'd be surprised what you can do when your life's at stake."

Sophie placed the multicolored leis on her card table. "Well, it doesn't seem to have hurt you any in the romance department. Are you still dating that English author?"

"Yes I am." Thinking of Tavish Bentley made my heart do a Simone Biles double backflip with three twists. "Tavish is a great guy."

"And hot. For an older guy, I mean."

"He certainly is. I'm a lucky girl."

In addition to our mutual love of reading, writing, England, and Jane Austen quotes, the fact that Tavish doesn't give a damn about my lack of breasts—a rarity among men—is icing on the Nipples of Venus cupcakes. I smirked, remembering those perfectly named white cupcakes with vanilla icing and a cherry on top that I had made and served to my fellow Musketeers at my Bye-Bye Booby party the night before my second mastectomy.

After we finished decorating—and Sophie had pronounced our tables "lit"—we closed and secured the tent flap door and took Gracie on a quick walk around the park before heading back home. As we walked, we chatted.

"How do you like being back home again, Sophie? Do you miss Chicago and your roommates?"

"Not really." She wrinkled her nose. "Amber and Amanda were both really into clubbing and partying. That's not my thing. I definitely don't miss my barista job—although it did teach me how to make a killer cappuccino."

"A necessary skill. Never underestimate the importance of a good cup of coffee."

"That's what my dad says."

"Smart man."

"My dad's cool. We get along great. Unlike my mom and me." She frowned.

"Sounds familiar," I said. "What is it with mothers and daughters?"

My mom and I have butted heads my entire life. She's into fashion and designer handbags from high-end stores. I shop at thrift shores for my myriad scarves and boho chic style. Mom likes kale smoothies, seeds, and salads. I prefer a great steak, potatoes, and anything sweet—which is why I bake. She likes her stark, industrial, stainless-steel kitchen. I love my bright and colorful vintage kitchen full of kitschy clutter and hand-me-downs from my grandma. Mom and I have nothing in common except the same blood and a mutual love for my deceased dad. Most of the time she drives me crazy and vice versa, but after two murders rocked our town earlier this summer, leaving me a prime suspect, Mom and I came to a better understanding of each other and started to see past our differences.

Which was why her lying to me earlier bugged me.

Sophie's voice cut through my mother musings. "I really like living with Gram. I'm grateful she asked me to move in with her—Mom and I would have killed each other if I'd stayed there any longer," she said wryly.

"I hear ya. In an effort to keep the homicide numbers down, adult mothers and daughters should never live together."

Sophie giggled as Gracie scampered to the car and we headed home. "Thanks for going with me, Teddie. I hope I didn't embarrass you earlier."

"Not at all. If you ever have any more boob or other body-part questions, this flat-and-happy woman is delighted to answer them."

She giggled again. "You're the best. I hope I can be like you someday." We pulled into my driveway and exited the car. Sophie gave me a brief wave as she crossed the grass to her grandma's house.

Aw. Bet you never expected to be the role model for millennials. Or is it Generation Z? I can never keep them straight.

Model for the Betty Crocker fan club, maybe. Guess I should get into TikTok and start saying, "I can't even . . ."

After eating leftover roast chicken and streaming some *Gilmore Girls*, I tried waiting up for Mom to grill her about where she'd gone earlier looking so hot, but I fell asleep before she got home.

Could it be that my seventy-three-year-old mother has a date? I wondered as I drifted off. *And if so, how do I feel about that?* I'd have to discuss it with Tavish during our Skype date in the morning.

Chapter Three

Tavish's handsome Colin Firth–ish face filled my laptop screen promptly at seven thirty. "Hello, lovely. Nice to see your beautiful face. I miss you. And I miss playing with those gorgeous curls of yours too." He cast me a seductive glance. "Among other things."

Down, girl. You'll ruin your laptop by slobbering all over it.

"I miss you too." I blew him a kiss. "How's it going over there? How's your family?"

"They're well, although Felicity's seeing someone Mum doesn't like."

A dog yipped. Tavish reached down and picked up his spaniel Scout, depositing him in his lap.

"Hi, Scout," I said. "Are you being a good boy?"

The caramel-colored dog gave a happy yip and wagged his tail, causing Gracie to come running over to me, barking excitedly.

Hey, Mom, I wanna say hi to Scout and Tavish too. Can I? Can I?

My Eskie jumped into my arms and batted her front paw at the screen. Scout and Gracie exchanged happy woofs.

"Good morning, Gracie," Tavish said in that great English accent of his. "Has your mummy taken you for walkies yet today?"

First thing, Tav. I have her well trained.

We chatted about our respective book projects—I'd finished my first draft of *Suffocating in Soufflé* a couple weeks ago and had set it aside so I could take a breather and return to it with fresh eyes in another week or so. At that point I would read it from start to finish, then likely ask myself, "What was I *thinking* when I wrote that?" at least once or twice before slashing an implausible plot point or two, rewriting and adding entire scenes in the process. I would check for clichés, rabbit trails, an overuse of certain words (*just* is always a culprit), and any inconsistencies—such as two different names for the same minor character (sometimes I have to pick a new name if I discover my original choice is too similar to another character's name, but it's easy to forget I changed it). Then I would read through the manuscript again, cover to cover, out loud, with a critical editorial eye out for improper punctuation and misspelled words. Misspelled words are my biggest pet peeve. (I'm the former Lake Potawatomi Spelling Bee Champ.)

"So, what do you think about Felicity's new boyfriend?" I asked Tavish. "Is he good enough for your baby sister?"

"I think so. He seems a nice-enough bloke and treats her well, which is a marked improvement over the last two tossers she's dated. The problem is he's eighteen years older than her."

"Whoa. That's quite an age difference. I can see how your mother might be concerned."

"Too right," he said. "How's everyone there? Your mum?"

"I think she might be seeing someone."

"Good for Claire. It will be nice for her to have someone in her life."

"I guess. Although I don't know why she needs to be so secretive about it."

Tavish gave me a gentle smile. "Perhaps she's concerned about your reaction, knowing how close you were to your father."

As an only child, I was daddy's little girl. Dad and I were always much more in sync than Mom and me, with our mutual love of baking and cooking. My father's death devastated me, leaving me without my anchor and the biggest cheerleader of my writing. It devastated my mom too, leaving her alone and missing her longtime partner and the love of her life. But she stayed active and filled her days and nights with yoga, shopping, Bunco, book club, and lunches and dinners out with girlfriends. Wasn't that enough?

Would it be enough for you?

Oh, shut up.

"Or maybe it's early days yet," Tavish continued, "and there's nothing to tell."

"Possibly." I frowned. "But she didn't need to lie to me."

"Right. It's not as if you've ever lied to your mother about *your* dates."

I recalled my first two dates with Tavish. At the time I was trying to keep things on the down low and had engaged in some subterfuge and told my mother a variety of little white lies to keep her in the dark. "That's different. She was on a mission for me to find Mr. Right and kept nagging me about it. I wasn't about to—" A loud clap of thunder startled me.

Gracie jumped down and raced to the window, barking loudly. I followed her, laptop in hand, and saw rain coming down in sheets. "Sorry, I have to go. We got a sudden thunderstorm and the rain is insane. I need to go check on the baking tent. I'll text you later."

Tavish and I said a quick good-bye, and I grabbed my yellow rain slicker from the backdoor hook.

Gracie stood on her hind legs and pawed the air with her front feet. *Can I go, Mom? Please?*

"Sorry, Gracie-girl. It's raining buckets out there and Mommy's in a hurry." I patted her head and tossed her a peanut-butter dog treat before racing out beneath the ever-darkening sky.

I made it to the park in less than five minutes. Pulling into the parking lot, I watched the wind rip away the tent's flimsy door flap that I'd secured last night, causing a torrent of water to stream inside through the now-open doorway. I put up my hood, jumped out of the car, and raced, slipping and sliding across the wet grass of the deserted park to the big white tent now being buffeted by gusts of wind and driving rain. The squall sliced through me, pushing the hood off my head and whipping my wild curly hair across my face. Heavy rain pelted down, drenching my jeans and tennis shoes.

I entered the dusky tent, made dim by the dark sky, and flipped the light switch. Nada. As I pushed my wet hair away from my eyes, I saw that my milk-glass dish and red tumblers had fallen off the table but thankfully hadn't broken—cushioned by the grass. The delicate vase of carnations wasn't so lucky. It had shattered.

As the deluge continued unabated with water now sleeting through the open doorway, I gingerly picked up the broken pieces of the glass vase and threw them away, along with the drooping flowers. I lifted up the drenched card table, still covered in my grandma's now-soaked vintage tablecloth, and carefully moved it farther back into the shadowy tent, away from the entrance. I returned to the open doorway and peered outside, searching for the missing door flap, hoping I could find it and somehow reattach it, but the blinding rain made it impossible to see anything.

I turned back inside and hurried over to my table, where I removed the sodden tablecloth and carefully wrung it out. As I did, I noticed in the dim recesses of the tent that Sophie's decorations had also fallen to the ground. And then I noticed something else. A dark shape covering her tabletop. *What is it? Some kind of cloth? Blown off another contestant's table, perhaps?* I pulled out my iPhone and turned on the flashlight, following the pale-blue light to my young neighbor's table.

As I drew closer, I saw that the dark shape was a man.

And not just any man. Lester. The head judge. Facedown in Sophie's coconut-cream pie.

I approached cautiously. "Lester? Can you hear me?"

Is he passed out in a sugar coma?

I touched his shoulder and noticed that his silver hairpiece was askew. And then as I looked closer, I saw that his bad rug was stained with something dark. Blood? My stomach roiled. "Les, it's Teddie."

No response. No movement. I knew what that meant. But I put my hand on his neck to make sure.

Suddenly, as fast as the freak thunderstorm had started, it ended. A shaft of sunlight broke through the entrance, allowing me to see the head judge more clearly.

No doubt about it. Lester Morris was dead.

Not again. I don't believe it.

What is it with you and dead people? Maybe you should stay inside and hibernate for the rest of the summer. Fall. Winter . . . my inner snark suggested.

More sunlight filtered in through the open tent flap as voices punctuated the stillness.

"Thank goodness the rain stopped. I hope there's not too much damage," judge Bea Andersen said as she entered the vinyl structure. She gasped as she took in the tableau before her: Lester facedown in Sophie's pie, my hand on his neck.

Patsy Morris, following behind Bea in her lime-green capris and carrying her renowned chocolate-cream pie, saw me and shrieked. "What are you doing?" The pie dropped from her hands. She flew my direction, flailing and swatting at me. "Get away from my husband!"

I stepped back, feeling sick.

"Les! Les, honey," Patsy sobbed, falling to her knees beside her husband and stroking his arm. "Speak to me."

Bea stared at me openmouthed. I shook my head.

Then Patsy stiffened, and I realized she'd seen the dark stains on his silver hairpiece. As sunlight flooded the tent, we both saw it at the same time: my distinctive, embossed rolling pin on the ground at Lester's feet, bloody at one end.

Are you kidding me? I gaped at my grandmother's rolling pin. *What the actual hell?*

"Oh my God." Patsy wailed. "You killed my husband!"

"Say what?" Brady entered the tent, followed closely by Sharon and Char, and strode past me to Sophie's table. Patsy began sobbing uncontrollably.

"He's dead. He's dead!"

Bea enfolded Patsy in her arms and murmured soothing words to the grief-stricken new widow as Brady knelt down beside Lester's chair to check his pulse.

My Musketeer pals hurried to my side. "What the hell?" Char said.

"That's what I said," I murmured.

"What in the world happened?" Sharon asked, her cornflower-blue eyes round as dessert plates.

"No idea. I found him like that."

Char slid a discreet glance to the dead judge at Sophie's table. "Looks like Lester got his pie in the face after all," she said sotto voce.

The same thought had run through my mind, but I hadn't voiced it. I stared at the surreal scene before me, shaking my head and trying to take it all in. But something didn't make sense. "Wait . . . what is Sophie's pie doing here? It wasn't here when we left last night."

"You were here last night, Ted?" Brady straightened and shot me a sharp glance. "What time?"

"I *told* you!" Patsy broke free from Bea. Her thin chest beneath her floral polyester-blend blouse heaved as she pointed a finger at me. "She killed my husband! Arrest her, Sheriff."

Here we go again.

You really need to check into that hibernation thing.

Brady signaled Char and Sharon with his eyes. They joined him as he approached the bereaved widow and gently led her to a nearby chair. Sharon pulled a water bottle from her tote, unscrewed the cap, and handed it to Patsy. "Here. Take a drink."

My fellow contestant accepted the bottle with trembling hands and took a sip.

"I'm so sorry, Patsy," Brady said. "I'll find out who did this; I can promise you that. I'll be conducting a full investigation."

"No need." She glared at me as tears streaked her drawn cheeks. "The murderer's standing right there!" She jabbed her finger at me. "Your friend, Teddie."

"I didn't kill Lester," I said quietly.

"Yes, you did! Everyone saw you hit him yesterday with your fancy rolling pin. And that's your rolling pin beside him, covered in my poor husband's b-blood." Patsy wept anew.

Sharon embraced the distraught baker and Bea murmured comforting words as Brady motioned for me to follow him. Char joined us as we moved a few tables away.

"I need to ask you a couple questions, Ted," Brady said, using the nickname he'd given me in high school. "But first I need to call Augie and the coroner. Back in a sec." He pulled out his phone and stepped outside the tent.

Char glanced at Lester and said in a low voice, "So, bestie, what is it with you and dead bodies?"

"I know, right?" I looked over at the head judge face-planted in the coconut-cream pie and frowned. "This doesn't make sense," I said in a pensive tone. "Why is Sophie's pie here?"

"I was wondering the same thing," Brady said as he rejoined us and pulled out his notebook and pen. "What were you doing here last night, Ted?" he asked. "Did you see Lester?"

"No. I haven't seen him since yesterday's judging. Sophie and I were the only ones here last night. She asked me to come with her while she decorated her table for today." I explained about Margaret's doctor's appointment and Sophie not having the time this morning to set up afterward.

"What time was that?" Brady asked, pen poised over his slim notebook.

"Let me think." I flashed back to last night and the making of my cherry pie. I'd taken the pie out of the oven to cool around six forty-five and Sophie had shown up at my back door a few minutes later. "About ten minutes to seven, give or take."

"How long were the two of you here in the tent?"

"Half an hour, maybe. Forty minutes tops."

"And what did you do during that time?"

"Decorated our tables and chatted."

"What did you talk about?"

"Breasts. Tavish. Coffee. And mothers," I said, wondering again if my mom might be dating someone.

Brady looked at me. "You didn't discuss Lester and his inappropriate behavior?"

"No."

"Then what?" The sheriff scribbled in his notebook.

"Then we went home."

"Did Sophie put her pie on the table before you left?"

Char and I snorted in unison. "No way." I sent Brady a skeptical look. "It's coconut cream—needs to be kept cool. Besides, leaving food lying around outside would attract all kinds of critters. Squirrels would have made mincemeat of Sophie's pie before you could say *Lake Potawatomi*."

The entire time Brady was questioning me, I could hear Patsy sniffling in the background and Sharon and Bea murmuring to her. Then Augie Jorgensen, Brady's deputy, who happens to also be Char's younger brother, arrived, along with the coroner, Frank Cullen. At the sight of Frank and his black medical bag, Patsy let out a fresh wail.

Char exchanged a glance with Brady, then hurried over to Patsy and, along with Sharon and Bea, led the sobbing widow out of the tent.

Augie released a long, low whistle at the sight of the head judge facedown in Sophie's pie. The middle-aged coroner was more eloquent. "I know it's not right to speak ill of the dead, but it looks like Lester Morris finally got his just desserts," Frank said.

Frank's wife, Belinda, who owns the local ice cream shop, Cullen's Creamery, had been another frequent target of Lester's come-ons over the years. Belinda had always laughed off Les's inappropriate remarks until the day he targeted her pretty teenage daughter, Lauren. That's when she told the town lecher where he could stick his ice cream cone. She also warned him to stay away from her daughter if he knew what was good for him.

As Brady accompanied Frank to Lester's body, he said over his shoulder to his young deputy, "Get hold of Sophie Miller and tell her we need her to come to the baking tent. Now."

"So-Sophie Miller?" Augie stammered.

"That's right. And don't tell her what's happened here either."

I stared at Brady's retreating back. *You've got to be kidding me. Does he really think sweet, shy Sophie killed Lester-the-molester?*

Well, someone did. And it is *her pie, after all.*

Augie punched in a number on his phone. "Sophie?" he said hesitantly, his ears reddening. "This is Augie Jorgensen. Uh, Deputy Jorgensen. Sheriff Wells asked me to call you. We need you to come down to the baking tent ASAP." He listened for a moment, the discomfort obvious on his face. "Sorry. I can't disclose that. We need you to come over here right away, please. Thanks. See you in a few." He ended the call, looking miserable.

Ah . . . someone has a crush. "Sophie's a really nice girl," I said.

"Yeah." Augie tugged at his uniform shirt collar.

"So sweet to her grandmother," I continued. "Sophie has a big heart. Not many girls her age would step up like she has to take such good care of their grandma."

"I know." His face flamed.

"She's really pretty too, don't you think?"

Augie nodded mutely, unable to meet my eyes.

"Hey, Augs, how's it goin', bro?" The returning Char slung her arm across her baby brother's shoulders.

"Good." Augie's eyes skidded to his boss and the coroner huddled over Lester. "I can't believe we've got another murder in Lake Potawatomi again," he said in a stage whisper. "I mean, what are the odds?"

"About the same as lightning striking the same place twice," Char said. "Or the same Musketeer who found the first body discovering the latest dearly departed."

Augie's head swiveled in my direction, his eyes huge. "*You* found Les's body?"

"Guilty as charged."

"I told you, Sheriff!" Patsy yelled at Brady, picking that auspicious moment to return to the tent with Bea and Sharon. "Theodora St. John killed my husband. She just confessed. I heard her. *Now* are you going to lock her up?"

Better watch what you say there, Slim, or you'll find yourself back in the pokey again.

A couple months ago, during the investigation of Lake Potawatomi's first murder, I had spent the night in jail after being falsely accused of attempting to strangle a young woman with one of my signature scarves. Brady had no option but to arrest me when the victim accused me of the attempt on her life. When she later recanted, I was released. No harm, no foul. Not an experience I cared to repeat, however.

"Patsy," Char said gently. "You misunderstood. We were talking about something else. Teddie didn't kill Lester."

"No, she didn't," Sharon said, coming to stand beside me in solidarity. "Teddie's not a killer."

"Well, obviously *you* wouldn't think so," Patsy said. "The three of you have always been thick as thieves. What do they call you around town—The Three Musketeers?" Her eyes narrowed. "Maybe you're all in it together."

Char snorted. "You've gotta be kidding me. What do you think we are? Some kind of fortysomething gang?"

"I wouldn't put it past you," Patsy said, eyes flashing. "You girls today are always so quick to take offense. A man can't give a woman a harmless hug or pay her a compliment without getting into trouble these days. My Les was a great one for giving compliments. He always liked to encourage folks."

I stifled a *ha. Is that what you call it?*

Patsy brushed wispy gray hair from her eyes. "But a man can't do that anymore or he gets accused of sexual harassment or assault."

Hate to bring you into the twenty-first century, Pats, but grabbing a woman's butt is assault. I didn't say that aloud, however.

Sharon, the lone mom among our Three Musketeers, said gently, "Patsy, you've suffered a terrible loss and shock. Why don't you let me or Bea take you home?"

Before the grief-stricken wife could respond, Sophie Miller entered the tent, wearing shorts and a turquoise tank top, her hair scraped back into a ponytail. "What's going on?" She looked from me to Augie and the rest of the group, bewildered. "What's everyone doing here?"

Brady strode over. "Sophie, thanks for coming. I'm afraid there's been an, ah . . . incident, and I need to ask you a few questions."

"An *incident*?" Patsy screeched. "My husband's murder isn't an *incident*, Sheriff."

Sophie blanched. "Murder?" Then she saw the coroner. And Lester. Facedown. In her pie. "Oh my God." She fell to the ground in a dead faint.

Chapter Four

Augie raced over to the object of his hidden affection but slipped on Patsy's dropped chocolate-cream pie and fell, landing beside Sophie, his arm across her chest. As he blushed and scrambled to right himself, Brady gently placed Sophie on her back while Char and I scurried over to help.

"Raise her legs above heart level," Brady instructed.

I plopped down at Sophie's feet and replaced one of her flip-flops that had fallen off. "Let's put her legs on my thighs—that should give us the necessary height." Augie's face flushed as he lifted one of Sophie's tanned legs and rested it on my Amazon thigh while I positioned the other one. Char brushed the young contestant's hair away from her face, and Sharon rushed over with a bottle of water.

"Sophie?" Brady said gently as he leaned over her. "Sophie, can you hear me?"

Her eyelids fluttered, and her baby browns opened. "Wh-what happened?" she asked, starting to rise.

"Don't try and sit up yet," Brady said. "Just lie there a few minutes."

"You're okay." I patted Sophie's ankle. "You fainted."

"I did? I've never fainted before."

Sharon—whose twins, Josh and Jessica, are the same age as Sophie—raised the bottle of water in her hand and sent Brady a questioning look. He nodded. Sharon squatted beside Sophie and lifted her head slightly. "Here, sweetie, take a drink of water."

As Sophie sipped, I stole a glance at her small, slender hands, wondering if those hands had blood on them. Was it possible my sweet young neighbor had killed Lester Morris with my rolling pin?

I gave myself an inner shake. *Sophie doesn't have it in her to murder someone.*

That's what they always say about the shy, quiet ones.

Not Sophie. Unless it was self-defense? Maybe Lester attacked her and she fought back, I reasoned with my inner self.

Patsy's voice intruded on my internal argument.

"Sheriff, I know you're preoccupied with this pretty young girl, but what about my dead husband?" she snapped. "Are you going to arrest Teddie St. John or not?"

"Arrest Teddie?" Sophie jerked upright to a sitting position and stared at me with wide eyes.

It's okay, I mouthed. I gave her leg a reassuring pat.

Brady straightened up. "Patsy, why don't you let me take you home now?" he said in a soothing tone. "We can call your son on the way so he can come over to be with you."

Patsy's hand flew to her mouth. "Oh no! Stephen! How am I going to tell my baby boy his poor daddy's dead?" She sobbed anew on Bea Andersen's shoulder.

Baby boy? Stephen Morris is two years older than me.

"I'll tell him for you." Brady pulled out his phone.

She stiffened. "You most certainly will not, Sheriff Wells." She swiped at her eyes and squared her shoulders. "That's *my* job. I'm his mama." Patsy turned to Bea. "Would you mind driving me home and waiting with me until Stephen comes?"

"Not at all," Bea said. "Whatever you need." She glanced at Brady uncertainly. "But what about the sheriff?"

"The sheriff needs to stay here and do his *job*," Patsy said, shooting a scathing look at Brady.

Ooh, watch out, Patsy. You do not want to dis my friend, especially in front of his girlfriend. I stole a glance at Char, whose fists were clenched at her sides, her mouth set in a thin line. A thin line that started to open.

Before Char could tell Patsy off, Brady took the more diplomatic approach. "Bea," he said, "you go on and take Patsy home, and I'll follow in a bit."

Bea and Patsy headed out of the tent, but as they left, Patsy shot daggers at Sophie and me.

Sophie shivered and rubbed her arms.

"Are you okay?" Augie asked.

"Yes. Thanks, Augie." She blushed. "I mean, Deputy Jorgensen."

Char gave me a knowing wink over the potential young couple's heads as "Matchmaker, Matchmaker" from *Fiddler on the Roof* began playing in my head.

"Sophie, you think you're okay to get up now?" Brady asked.

"Yes. I'm fine." Her fair skin flushed. "I can't believe I fainted." She glanced in the direction of her table and, upon seeing the coroner crouched by the dead Lester, quickly looked away. Her eyes sought mine. "I—I just can't believe this. It's so awful."

Yes, it is, I thought. Lester might have been a pig of the first order, but his wife had clearly adored him and was shattered by his death. No one should die like that.

Brady helped Sophie up and led her to a nearby chair as Augie hovered close by. "I'd like to ask you a few questions, Sophie, if I might."

"Sure." She looked up at me and my fellow Musketeers. "But can Teddie stay with me?"

"That's fine," Brady said. "I'd actually like to talk to both of you together." He inclined his head to Char and Sharon. "We don't need an audience, though, so if you two wouldn't mind making yourselves scarce, I'd appreciate it."

"No problem-o," Char said, linking her arm with Sharon. "We can take a hint." As they left, she mouthed at me behind her boyfriend's back, *Call me later.*

I sat down next to Sophie as Augie started to pull up a chair.

Brady shook his head at his young deputy. "Augie, I think Frank may need your help."

Augie glanced at the coroner, who was motioning him over, and swallowed hard. "Sure, Sheriff." He shot a departing look at Sophie. "See ya, Soph."

"See ya, Augie," she said, following him with her eyes.

The "Matchmaker" earworm started up again. Char and I needed to figure out a way to get these two together . . .

"Teddie, you still with us?" asked Brady, interrupting my cupid-playing contemplations.

"Yep. Sorry. Fire away."

The sheriff turned his gaze to my young neighbor and pulled out his notebook. "Sophie, Teddie said the two of you came over to the tent last night to set up your tables. Is that right?"

She nodded and repeated what I'd told him. I cut my eyes to Brady. *See?*

"So how did your pie get here?" Brady asked.

Sophie swallowed. "Before I went to bed last night, I suddenly realized there wouldn't be enough time to pick up my pie after Gram's appointment—she's moving slower these days, so things take longer than usual. Which is fine," she added hastily, "I'm not complaining. But it takes advance planning to allow for that extra time, and sometimes I forget things. Like the pie. That's why I came back to the park again last night—to bring over today's entry."

"Alone?" Brady, whose head was bent over his notebook, didn't see Sophie's face flush, but I did.

"Uh-huh."

Sophie, what aren't you saying? I wondered.

"What time was this?"

"Around eleven o'clock—maybe a few minutes before."

"And did you see anyone else in the park when you returned?"

She shook her head.

Brady looked up from his notebook and pinned Sophie with his penetrating sheriff's eyes. "From what I understand, coconut-cream pie must stay cold. Weren't you afraid your pie would be ruined staying out all night?"

Sophie shook her head again. "I put it in the ice chest to keep it nice and cool until I got here. It's a Yeti Tundra," she said proudly. "Gram and I saved up and bought it for Gramps a few years ago for camping and fishing."

That explained it. Yetis are the Ferraris of coolers. Any Lake Potawatomi angler or rugged outdoorsy type worth their salt who can afford one owns a Yeti. I've got Dad's old one in the garage that we always used on our father-daughter fishing excursions to keep the beer and sandwiches cold.

Brady has one too—the latest-and-greatest hard model to keep his Pabst on ice. "And where's your Tundra now?" he asked Sophie.

Her eyes skittered reluctantly to the corner table where Les still sat face first in her pie and where Frank and Augie were now talking quietly. "Under the table."

Brady and I both looked at the card table covered by a floor-length yellow cloth.

"Augie!" Brady bellowed.

The deputy jumped. "Yes, boss?"

"Check under that table and tell me if you see anything."

Augie lifted the yellow cloth with his gloved hands and peered beneath it. "Yep. There's a really slick ice chest under here."

"Okay," Brady called back. "Thanks. I'll be over in a minute. Don't touch it until I get there." The sheriff turned back to Sophie. "Let me get this straight. You came here around eleven last night, *alone*, with your coconut-cream pie in the ice chest and placed the cooler beneath your table. Is that right?"

"Yes, Sheriff."

"How long did you stay?"

"Seconds. Long enough to slide the Tundra under the table and get out of there." Sophie shuddered. "I don't like being in the park alone at night."

"Why's that?"

"I lived in Chicago for the past year," she said, "in not the best neighborhood. You learn early on not to venture out at night by yourself, especially if you're a woman."

"Smart girl." Brady gave her a nod of approval. "Chicago's got a high crime rate. But you're back home in sleepy Lake Potawatomi now. We don't have crime like the big city."

"Except for those two murders earlier this summer," I reminded him.

The sheriff sent me a look. "Right. Except for that."

"And now this one," I added.

Brady released a sigh. "Ted, could you let me finish questioning Sophie, please? You'll get your chance to talk."

"Sure. My bad. Sorry."

"So," Brady continued, "was it the idea of being out alone at night in the dark that creeped you out, Sophie, or being alone in the park?"

"Both," she answered immediately.

"What is it about the park that frightens you?"

"All the animals." Sophie shuddered again. "Skunks, squirrels, raccoons, possums . . . I've heard people have even seen rats sometimes too."

Now it was my turn to shudder. The way Indiana Jones hated snakes is the way I hate rats. Worst. Rodent. Ever. They're dirty, filthy creatures, and their long, slimy tails gross me out. Watching the movie *Ben* with Char in her basement family room when we were ten didn't help—especially when her dad trapped two rats in the basement the following week. I'm known for being a strong, independent woman (Tavish even dubbed me Wonder Woman when I came to his physical rescue soon after we met), but when it comes to rats, this strong, independent woman turns into a quivering mess.

"Did you see any animals in the park when you were here last night, Sophie?" Brady bent over his notebook.

"Nope, but I heard them."

The sheriff's head snapped up. "What did you hear?"

"A rustling in the bushes."

"Where?"

Sophie angled her head. "By the gazebo."

"How do you know it was an animal?"

"What else could it have been?" She scrunched up her forehead.

"A person, maybe," Brady said. "You're sure you didn't see anyone?"

She shook her head.

I cast my eyes to the head judge's slumped-over body. Had Lester perhaps arranged a late-night assignation in the park? Or could it have been the murderer lying in wait, hanging around until Sophie left?

Chapter Five

Char and I debated those questions over cherry pie and ice cream in my kitchen half an hour later, after Brady finished questioning Sophie and me and sent us both home.

"You think the murderer was hiding in the bushes last night when Sophie was there?" Char asked.

"Could be," I said. "Although that means whoever it was must have followed Les to the park." I shook my head. "What in the world was Lester doing in the park at that time of night anyway? It doesn't make sense."

"It does if he was meeting someone on the sly and didn't want anyone to know about it," Char said. "Maybe he was having an affair with someone and that was the only place they could meet where they figured they wouldn't be seen." She grimaced. "Although who would want to be with that dirty old man?"

I winced. "Impossible to even imagine," I said as I refilled our coffee mugs. "I feel bad for Patsy, though. If it comes out publicly that her husband was having a fling with someone, what will that do to her?"

Char forked up another bite of pie—my contest-entry pie, since the contest was now on hold and likely to be canceled—and shook her head. "Maybe it wasn't a fling. Maybe it was just a little hanky-panky fumbling."

"I don't even want to go there. Let's move on to the more important question."

"Which is?"

"Who killed Lester?"

My back door flew open and my mother clickety-clacked into the kitchen in her red mules, causing Gracie to run for cover to the living room. "Theodora St. John! You found another dead body? What is *wrong* with you?"

"Hi, Mom. Want a piece of pie?"

"No, I don't want a piece of pie." She sat down at the table and crossed her slim legs, now clad in crisp gray linen pants. "I want to know what in the world is going on."

"Hi, Claire," Char said. "Nice to see you. You're looking good as usual."

During our childhood days, Sharon and Char had always addressed my mom as Mrs. St. John (manners are still big in our small Wisconsin town), but once we went off to college, my mother insisted all my friends call her Claire.

"Thank you, Charlotte. So are you—that green really suits your complexion." My mother looked askance at my colorful boho blouse, tie-dyed scarf, and crinkled broomstick skirt—snagged from the thrift store—but refrained from commenting.

Wise move, Mom. I held up the coffeepot. "Want some coffee?"

"Yes, thank you." She smoothed down her silver bob as I poured her a cup of French roast. Mom took a sip, then said, "Well, Teddie, I'm waiting."

"For what?"

She puffed out an exasperated sigh. "For you to tell me what happened to Lester Morris and how it came to be that you, of *all* people, found him dead."

"Well you see, Mom, it's like this." I raised my hand to my forehead and struck a dramatic pose. "Les and I have been having a hot, steamy affair for weeks now, but last night when we met in the park for our usual late-night rendezvous, he dumped me. Said he'd met someone else. Someone with *breasts*! I was so upset that in a moment of passion and sheer blind rage, I grabbed my rolling pin and hit him over the head with it."

Char sprayed out her coffee as she howled with laughter.

"Very funny, Theodora." My mother sent me an icy look. "Now would you care to tell me the truth, please?"

I sighed. The truth is, I was already tired of repeating the story. In this case, Les was less than interesting. He was dead. I rushed through the particulars, knowing my mother would read about it in the *Lake Potawatomi Times* anyway.

She homed in on one detail, though. "When did you say Bea and Patsy arrived?"

"The very moment I was checking Lester's neck for a pulse."

Mom dropped her head into her hands. "No wonder Patsy's spreading it all over town that you killed her husband."

"Patsy's in shock and grieving," I said. "She's upset and not thinking clearly."

"When will you ever learn, Teddie?"

"Learn what, Mom?"

"To stay away from dead bodies! You're getting quite the reputation, you know."

"Claire," my best friend said reasonably, "how was Teddie to know that Lester would be dead inside the tent? It was simply bad luck that she was the first one there. Anyone else in town could have stumbled on his body. Bea and Patsy, for instance, or one of the other contestants. Even you."

"*Me?*"

"Yeah, Mom," I said. "Speaking of reputation . . . exactly where were *you* last night?"

She stared at me over the top of her coffee cup. "At dinner with Cheryl and my book club friends—I told you that as I was leaving."

"I know you did," I said. "Funny thing, though." I scratched my cheek absently. "Cheryl showed up shortly after you left to return your book. She was on her way to the gym and wearing workout gear, not all dolled up like you. Maybe *you're* the one who was having the hot affair with Les Morris," I teased.

My mother slapped her mug down, causing coffee to splash on the pine table, scraped back her chair, and stood up, eyes blazing. "Don't be disgusting. Where I go and who I see is none of your business, young lady. I am seventy-three years old. I don't need to explain myself to you or anyone." She stalked out of the kitchen, mules furiously click-clacking against my yellow-and-black checkerboard floor, and slammed the screen door behind her.

Char let out a slow whistle. "Someone touched a nerve."

"Ya got that right." I stared after my mother's retreating figure and sank down in my chair. "So . . . my mom's seeing someone, right?"

"Definitely."

"The question is, who, and why is it such a big secret?"

"Guess we've got two mysteries to solve now, Sherlock," my best friend said. "Question is, which one comes first?"

Gracie barked, followed by a frenzied knocking at my front door. I hurried to the living room and opened the door to find a distraught Sophie on the porch, her pale face red and scrunched up with tears.

"Sorry to bother you, Teddie, but Wilma Sorensen just called Gram and said that I k-killed Lester," Sophie said, weeping.

I put my arm around my young neighbor and led her through the living room into the kitchen, Gracie following hard on our heels. "Wilma Sorensen is the town gossip, always stirring up trouble," I said. "Don't pay any attention to her. No one does."

Gracie nudged Sophie's hand with her head and laid her creamy paw on the distressed girl's leg. *It's okay. Gracie's here.*

As Sophie petted Gracie and Char murmured words of comfort, my fists clenched as I thought about Wilma Sorensen, the nosy octogenarian who was always spreading tales and causing grief. Wilma had started tongues wagging when I discovered Kristi Black, Tavish Bentley's ex-fiancée, dead behind Char's bookstore two months earlier, my scarf wrapped around her neck. Wilma initially focused her rumors and innuendo on me, but when that didn't work and a second murder occurred, she turned her attention to Tavish. Then, when the best-selling author and I started seeing each other, she sent the rumor mill into overdrive.

Gracie nudged me. *Earth to Mom. Earth to Mom.*

I returned my attention to Sophie in time to hear Char say, "Teddie's right. No one pays any attention to Wilma."

"Some people do," Sophie said, sniffling. "After Wilma's call, two of Gram's friends from bingo called and asked who's going to take care of her now, since I'm sure to be arrested for Lester's murder." She burst into fresh tears. "I didn't kill him! I didn't. I couldn't do something like that."

"Of course you couldn't," Char said, hugging a shaking Sophie and rubbing her back. My best friend looked at me and mouthed, *That bitch.*

I nodded. *Someone needs to teach the town gossip a lesson. Maybe it's time to start a rumor about Wilma.*

About her and Lester, maybe? Since Les may have been meeting someone in the park last night, what if we point the finger at Wilma?

Wilma's a bit old for liaisons in the bushes, my logical self argued. *Besides, she's always turned her nose up at Lester's crude come-ons, calling him coarse and ill-bred.*

Exactly. Which would make a rumored dalliance with Lester all the more embarrassing.

Could I actually go through with it, though? That would be a pretty twisted thing to do.

Sophie blew her nose. "It's not only that people think I'm a murderer, but how could someone be so mean as to call my eighty-two-year-old grandmother and say those terrible things to her? She was so upset and frightened." She hiccupped. "I told Gram I wasn't going anywhere, and she said I'd better not; it was too hard to get good help." Sophie smiled through her tears. "Luckily, Joanne LaPoint stopped by to show Gram the latest pictures of her granddaughter, and while they were looking at pictures, I slipped out and came over here."

She swiped at her tears. "Sorry to dump all this on you, Teddie. I didn't want to upset my parents. Especially my mom. You know how she gets." Her eyes filled again. "I don't understand why Wilma is so awful and hateful. It's almost like she takes delight in causing other people pain."

That's all I needed to hear. Time to start putting Operation Teach Wilma a Lesson in place.

Chapter Six

The next morning I decided to do some baking. *Fun* baking. No troublesome pie crusts for this girl today.

I pulled out sugar, flour, baking soda, salt, and vanilla from the baking cupboard. Then I grabbed oatmeal, coconut, chocolate chips, butterscotch chips, and cereal and set them on my vintage-tile countertop. Everything but the kitchen sink. That's what I'd named these cookies: Everything but the Kitchen Sink, or sinkers for short.

Back when I was still working in government cubicle world, every Christmas my office did a cookie exchange. One year my coworker Molly brought some cookies I absolutely loved, full of heaps of yummy things including chocolate chips, oatmeal, and Rice Krispies. What I didn't love as much was what she called these delectable treats—garbage cookies. Yuck. I asked for the recipe, then changed it up to make it my own. And the first thing I changed was the name.

When I made my first batch of sinkers, I used Raisin Bran in place of Rice Krispies. It was the only cereal in the house, so I improvised. That's the great thing about this recipe—you can change it up with whatever you have on hand.

I pulled out my mixer and began creaming together the butter and sugars. As the mixer whirred, my thoughts returned to the events of yesterday.

As Char and I were leaving the tent after Sophie's questioning, we'd overheard Frank Cullen tell Brady that although he couldn't give an exact time of death yet, he estimated the head judge to have been dead approximately eight to ten hours. Since I'd arrived at the tent around seven fifty, give or take, yesterday morning and Les had been dead as a doornail, whoever killed him had likely done so sometime after eleven the night before. Sophie had told Brady she'd returned to the tent with her pie at about eleven o'clock and stayed only a few minutes. *Is it possible she just missed the killer? Or is Sophie lying about what time she arrived at the park that second time? And if so, why?*

I recalled how distraught my young neighbor had been last night after Wilma's malicious phone-call insinuations to her grandma, followed by the thoughtless calls from Margaret's bingo buddies prompted by Wilma's gossip. I'd assumed Sophie's distress was due to Wilma's spite and all-around nastiness, but now I wondered: could it have been something else?

Last night, after Char and I calmed Sophie down and she returned home to her grandmother's house, I had told my fellow Musketeer my idea of giving Wilma a dose of her own medicine. Char loved it. Then we brainstormed how best to execute Operation Wilma. Since Char owns and runs the

Corner Bookstore, she comes into daily contact with many of Lake Potawatomi's residents and is well positioned to drop a casual comment into the conversation. People were bound to be buzzing about Lester's death, and Char said it would be easy enough to offhandedly remark, "I heard he was having a rendezvous with someone . . ."

Then when people began speculating who that someone could be, Char would casually drop Wilma's name into the mix. Bam! Thus would begin the Wilma-and-Lester rumor.

Although . . . thinking about it now in the cold, clear light of day, it seemed mean. Yes, it might pay nasty Wilma back, but what would such a rumor do to poor Patsy Morris? I turned off the mixer and quickly texted Char.

Me: *Hey bestie, please tell me you haven't started the Wilma rumor yet. I'm having serious second thoughts.*
Char: *You mean about Patsy and how it would affect her? Yeah, me too. That's why I haven't said anything. That and the fact that the bookstore doesn't open for another two hours yet* ☺
Me: *Whew. Great minds. Glad we're on the same page. To echo one of our favorite people, 'When they go low, we go high.'*
Char: *Preach it, sistah. Now I'm going to catch some more Z's. Later, gator.*
Me: *Oops. My bad. Sorry.*

Char's not a morning person. Unlike me. I love mornings. I do some of my best work early in the day—after I've had my first cup of coffee. I finished off my coffee and ate a piece of peanut-butter toast before getting back to the sinkers.

After beating in the eggs and vanilla, I added salt, baking soda, baking powder, and flour and mixed it all thoroughly. Then I measured in the oats, chocolate chips, butterscotch chips, coconut, and Raisin Bran. At the last minute I tossed in some pecans for extra crunch. The brilliance of this recipe is that you simply throw in five cups of stuff—any combination.

Gracie looked up at me hopefully.

"Sorry, girl. This isn't good for doggy tummies. You know that."

She flattened her ears and adopted a mournful look.

I turned off the mixer. "Would someone like one of her peanut-butter treats?"

Gracie wagged her creamy white tail that curved up over her back.

Who's the alpha female in this house? That dog has you wrapped around her little paw.

Don't I know it. But she's so cute, I can't deny her anything.

My dad had gotten Gracie for me a couple months after Atticus, my beloved spaniel mix and the first dog I'd ever had, died. Mom hadn't allowed me to have a dog growing up. "They shed and leave hair everywhere. Too messy." After college, when I moved into my own place, I went to the pound and promptly got a rescue dog—one who'd been on a kill list; my darling Atticus. We had more than a dozen happy years together before cancer took him.

I blinked back tears as I remembered my sweet boy. After Atticus died, I vowed to never get another dog again—it hurt too much. But my dad knew better. One day he showed up in my kitchen—this very kitchen—with a little white ball of fur.

I tried to resist, but the moment I saw Gracie's big dark eyes against all that white fluffiness, I was a goner.

Gracie gave a yip, interrupting my reverie. *What are you waiting for, Mom?*

"Sorry, girl." I squatted down beside my canine daughter and ruffled her head before extending the treat to her. "Here you go."

She wagged her tail and promptly took her treat over to her dog bed in the corner and began munching on it.

I washed my hands and finished mixing the rest of the ingredients together. Then I dropped tablespoonfuls of dough onto the first cookie sheet, popped it into the oven, and set the timer. As I started spooning out the next batch onto the second cookie sheet, I heard my mother's car start up. I glanced at the clock above the sink. Seven forty-five. *Seriously? The woman who rarely gets up before nine and thinks scheduling appointments before eleven o'clock is barbaric?* I glanced out the kitchen window in time to see her Lexus pulling out of the driveway.

Where are you going so early, Mom?

To have breakfast with her mystery man, perhaps?

Why was my mom keeping this guy such a secret, anyway? Was he fresh out of prison or something? Was she pulling a Madonna with a thirty-year-younger boy toy? *My mother the cougar.* I tested the sound on my tongue. Nah. Not in this universe.

Then a terrible thought struck me. *Oh God, please tell me he's not married. Please don't let him be married.*

You better find out so that if he is, you can nip this in the bud. Think. What would Kate and Kallie do?

Kate Kristiansen is my single B and B owner and accidental sleuth heroine. Kallie is her intrepid canine crime-solving companion in the cozy mystery series I write.

Maybe Gracie can help me solve the puzzle of my mother's mystery man. I glanced down at my Eskie munching contentedly away on her treat. *Yeah, not gonna happen.*

The timer dinged, and I pulled the cookies out of the oven and slid in the next batch. As I removed the sinkers from the hot cookie sheet and placed them on the cooling rack, I made up my mind.

Mother dear, you leave me no choice. The next time you sneak away to meet your boo, guess who will be following? Discreetly, of course.

Chapter Seven

An hour later, feeling like Little Red Riding Hood in my red cotton dress and basket of goodies, I set off to deliver cookies and pick up some chatter. I dropped by Andersen's Bakery first, jingling the bell at the top of the door.

Fred Matson looked up from his customary bacon and eggs at the counter. "Teddie! Whoo-boy, you really gave it good to Lester with your fancy rollin' pin, didn't you?" The old-timer cackled. "Remind me never to get on your bad side."

"Fred!" Bea Andersen smacked his age-spotted arm with the *People* magazine she was reading behind the counter.

"What? I'm only sayin' what the whole town is talkin' about."

"Well then the whole town can take a flying leap," Bea said. "You know Teddie. She's lived here her whole life. She's no murderer."

"It's okay, Bea." I set my basket down on the table opposite the counter and turned the coffee cup right side up. "I knew my name would be on everyone's lips today."

"Well, it shouldn't be on the lips of anyone who really *knows* you." The plump white-haired proprietor of the local bakery bustled over and poured me a cup of coffee.

"Teddie knows I was only joshin' her," Fred said, with an aggrieved air. "Jeez, some people can't take a joke."

"Some things aren't funny, Fred." Bea turned her back on her regular customer to face me. "Now what can I get you, honey? Your usual cheese Danish?"

"You know me so well." We swapped smiles. "But before you bring me that delicious pastry, tell me, how's Patsy? And her son? Were you there when she told Stephen about his dad?"

Bea nodded. "Stephen took the news pretty well, all things considered. But then again, Patsy was a complete wreck, so he was busy comforting her." She tilted her head to one side. "Although . . . he didn't seem too broken up about his daddy's death, now that I think about it. Or even all that surprised, to tell you the truth. I'd say more like relieved."

My ears stood at attention. "Really?"

She glanced back at Fred, who suddenly affected an absorbed interest in his eggs, and leaned in and said quietly, "When Patsy went to the little girls' room, Stephen said, 'That bastard finally got what was coming to him. Now my mother can hold her head up again without him humiliating her all the time.' "

I released a low whistle. "Wow. No love lost there."

"You can say that again. I don't blame Stephen, though. That Lester was really a piece of work."

As Bea left to get my Danish, I thought about what she'd said. Could Stephen Morris have killed his father to put an end to the disgrace Lester had heaped on Patsy over the years?

Fred's voice intruded on my thoughts. "Teddie-girl, I'm sorry I teased you earlier."

I looked up to see the longtime retiree beside my table, leaning on his cane.

"That's okay, Fred." I gave him a wry smile. "I'm sure you won't be the last."

"Ya gotta admit, though, it's kind of funny the way you keep trippin' over dead bodies," he said with a chuckle.

"Fred . . ." Bea gave him a threatening look from the pastry case.

"Funny strange, I mean," he added hastily.

"You're right." I sighed. "It's definitely strange."

Fred's eyes shifted to the basket on the table. He sniffed the air. "Whatcha got there? Some more of your great peanut-butter blossoms?"

"Nope. Today's cookie offering is kitchen sinkers."

He licked his lips. "The ones with the chocolate chips and Rice Krispies?"

I nodded. "Except this time I used Raisin Bran instead of Rice Krispies." I reached into the basket and handed one of the plastic bags of cookies to him. "Here you go. Enjoy."

"Gee, thanks!" Fred's smile faltered. "And I'm sorry for teasin' you earlier; I didn't mean nothin' by it."

"I know." I patted his arm. "It's okay."

The bell over the bakery door jangled. I looked up and smiled when I saw Barbara Christensen enter. Barbara is a sweetheart. She and her husband Robert used to bring their golden retriever, Duke, to the park to play fetch, where Gracie and I would frequently run into them. Gracie and Duke would run and play together as their humans chatted and swapped recipes and book recommendations. Like me, Robert was a huge reader. Besides my dad, he was one of the few men in Lake Potawatomi who read my cozy mysteries. And then Robert got cancer. Sadly, he passed away last year, and his broken-hearted golden followed a month later, leaving Barbara bereft of both her beloved husband of fifty years and their adored fur baby. Luckily, her daughter and grandkids spend a lot of time with her.

My smile at seeing Barbara quickly faded when tightly permed gray-haired Wilma Sorensen, the source of Sophie's distress last night, materialized behind my fellow Bake-Off contestant.

Barbara hurried over to my table, concern etching her lovely features. "Teddie, how *are* you? Are you okay? That must have been horrible finding Lester like that."

"It was." *Although at least this time I didn't have to see the open staring eyes of the dead body.* I flashed back to the awful sight of Kristi, Tavish's ex, lying on the ground with my scarf wrapped tightly around her neck and shuddered.

Wilma's sickly sweet voice punctured the painful recollection. "It must have been even more horrible for you to find your bloody rolling pin on the ground at Lester's feet. Wasn't that your Grandma Florence's rolling pin that her mother brought over from the old country? Such a shame," she clucked. "I don't know how you'll ever be able to use it again. I know I certainly couldn't." She shuddered. "Poor Patsy. I'm not sure how she'll ever recover from this." Wilma's voice dripped with fake sympathy. "She was so devoted to Lester. They've been together since high school. I wonder who could have committed such a horrible crime. Do *you* have any idea, Teddie?" Her eyes glittered with malice.

I have plenty of ideas, Wilma, but none that you would like. I was sorely tempted to needle her with the Lester assignation rumor as Char and I had planned, but refrained, for Patsy's sake. It wasn't easy, though.

Good girl. My conscience gave me a pat on the back.

Bea rammed my plate of Danish into Wilma's back as she approached.

"Ow!" Wilma whirled around and glared at her. "What are you *doing*?"

"Oh, excuse me," Bea said. "I didn't mean to bump into you. I was just trying to deliver my customer's order, but it's gotten a bit crowded in here."

Fred cackled.

"Well, I never!" Wilma huffed.

Barbara's eyes twinkled behind her gossipy pal's back.

"Thanks, Bea," I said as she moved past Wilma to set my cheese Danish on the table. I handed the bakery owner one of the packages of cookies. "And here's some sinkers for you."

"Trying to buy one of the judges now, are you?" Wilma said with a sneer. "Some people will do anything to win."

"Not at all." I pulled another goody bag from my basket. "The cookie portion of the contest is already over. Remember?" I delivered an innocent look to the town tattletale. "That was the part where your store-bought entry was disqualified." I extended a baggie of sinkers to Barbara. "I'm simply delivering cookies to my friends."

* * *

I dismissed Wilma Sorensen from my thoughts as I crossed the street to the sheriff's office. Halfway across, a hot flash suddenly erupted, which, combined with the humidity of the August day, made me want to rip off all my clothes, run naked through the center of town, and jump into the lake bordering the park. Or at least the ornamental pond in front of Bud's Hardware, which was a lot closer. I refrained, however, and kept things G-rated by flapping my red-white-and-black scarf in front of my sweaty face.

Bill and Beverly Price looked at me askance as our paths crossed on the sidewalk. The Prices were relative newcomers in town, having moved here from Milwaukee a couple years ago when Bill retired from the marketing world, seeking a quieter life.

I smiled at them as I continued flapping my scarf. "It's a hot one today, isn't it?"

Beverly averted her eyes, and Bill took his wife's arm and pulled her aside to give me a wide berth as they scurried away. When I glanced back over my shoulder, I saw them stopped in front of Bud's Hardware beside the also-retired George and Kathy Henderson. Both senior couples shot suspicious looks in my direction.

Here we go again. I blew out a sigh, puffing up my bangs as I continued on my way. Then I stopped. *Nope. I'm not playing that game.* I turned around and lifted my basket high. "Hey, Bill, hey, George," I called, "fancy a nice coconut-cream pie?"

The men blanched and their wives gasped.

"Not to worry, Kathy. Beverly. There's plenty for you too." I sent them my sweetest smile. The women grabbed their husbands and scuttled into the hardware store.

Ha! Serves you right. I lowered my basket and turned around to discover Brady leaning lazily against the doorway of the sheriff's office. He regarded me with a frown. "Ted, what do you think you're doing?"

"Trying to win friends and influence people. Can't you tell?"

"You sure picked a funny way of doing it."

"We all have our methods, don't we?" I brushed past my friend, eager to enter the air-conditioned haven of the historic brick building. Once inside, I dropped my basket on the bench in front of the reception counter and raised my face to the blessed AC vent. "Ahhhh. Heaven."

"Hiya, Teddie," Augie said from his desk behind the counter. "How ya doin'?"

"Much better now that I'm inside."

"Whatcha got in the basket?"

"Apparently it's a coconut-cream pie," Brady's voice behind me interjected. "Isn't that what you said, Ted?"

"Could be." I lifted the basket onto the counter. "Or . . . it could be that I baked some Everything but the Kitchen Sink cookies and brought some to share with my two favorite lawmen." I pulled out two baggies and tossed one to the sheriff and one to his deputy.

"Thanks, Teddie," Augie said. "You rock. I wish you could teach my sister how to bake. She only buys store-bought."

Augie lives with Char in the family home left to them when their dad died. Char, who's the same age as me—forty-three—and Augie, seventeen years her junior, had the same dad but different moms, both of whom divorced their dad and left. Which is one of the reasons my BFF has such a dim view of marriage.

Brady chuckled. "That ship has sailed, buddy. Your sister told me years ago that if I wanted Martha Stewart or the Barefoot Contessa, I should look elsewhere." He scarfed down a sinker.

Char, who worked as a librarian in Cleveland for several years after college, moved back home more than a decade ago to buy and run the Corner Bookstore when it came up for sale. Less than a year later, her dad died of lung cancer, leaving twenty-nine-year-old Char to finish raising her half brother, who was only twelve at the time.

"Face it, Augie." Brady dropped some paperwork into the in-box on his deputy's desk. "Cooking and baking are not your sister's thing. Why do you think I barbecue so much?" He bit into another sinker. "Good thing her best friend's a great baker, though, huh, Ted? You'll keep us supplied in cookies and sweet stuff."

"Maybe . . . but I'm not the only baker in town." I shot a sly glance at Char's younger brother. "Sophie's a really good baker too, don't you think, Augie?"

He choked on his sinker.

Brady slapped his deputy on the back. "You okay there, buddy?"

Augie nodded, grabbed the water bottle on his desk, and chugged it down.

"Actually"—I turned my attention to Brady—"Sophie's one of the reasons I'm here. Did you know Wilma Sorensen called Margaret Miller last night and said her granddaughter killed Lester Morris?"

"What?" Augie shot up from his chair, fists clenched, a thunderous expression on his face. "That bi—"

"Careful." Brady cut him off. "Dial it down a notch, Deputy."

"Sorry."

"It gets better," I said, grimacing. "Two of Wilma's bingo cronies then called Margaret and said Sophie will likely be arrested for Les's murder."

"Are you *kidding* me?" Augie shoved his hand through his red hair, causing his cowlick to spring up.

Brady didn't say anything, but his mouth tightened.

I looked at my longtime friend. "There's no truth to that, is there?"

Brady rubbed his face. "God, I hate gossip." He sighed. "It's too early for any arrests, Ted. I'm still waiting to hear back from Frank. Meanwhile, we're investigating all possibilities."

"Well, here's another possibility for you," I said. "Apparently Stephen Morris was not at all broken up about his father's untimely death."

Brady's eyes sparked with interest. "Is that right?"

"In fact," I continued, "he seemed glad that dear old dad was now out of the picture so his mother could enjoy her remaining years in peace without the threat of continued embarrassment and humiliation from her husband."

"Good to know. Thanks."

"So, are you going to talk to Stephen? He seems a much more likely candidate to have offed Lester than me or Sophie, don't you think?"

"Sophie's no murderer," Augie said, leaping to her defense. "She couldn't kill anyone."

Brady frowned at his young deputy. "As I said, we're investigating *all* possibilities. That's our job. We don't let our personal feelings interfere with carrying out our duties, right?"

Augie flushed and looked down at the floor. "Right, Sheriff."

"And now, if you'll excuse us, Ted, Augie and I have a lot of work to do. Thanks for the cookies and the tip." Brady ushered me to the front door, but before he could open it, Patsy and Stephen Morris barreled their way inside.

"*There* she is, Stephen!" Patsy said, clutching her son's arm possessively. "Teddie St. John, the woman who killed your poor father." Her eyes darted wildly around the office. "But where's Sophie Miller, Sheriff? I know the two of them were in cahoots."

Chapter Eight

I sank onto the barstool and laid my head down on the butcher-block kitchen island. "Got a margarita for your old friend?" I asked my fellow Musketeer.

"At nine o'clock in the morning?" Sharon bustled around the blue-and-white Lake House kitchen in a navy sundress and floral apron, preparing breakfast for her guests. "It's a bit early." She plated frittata and sausages on Blue Willow china and set the plates on a serving tray alongside crystal dessert bowls heaped with glistening fruit. "The best I can offer is a mimosa." Sharon jerked her head to the large fridge behind her. "Or you can make yourself a bloody mary. Back in a few." She backed through the swinging door into the dining room, breakfast tray in hand.

Sharon and Jim had bought the Lake House Victorian for a song fifteen years ago after the descendants of the original owners of the 1880 house died and the estate's executors wanted to unload the family home fast. They'd converted the five-bedroom, three-and-a-half-bath residence that had seen better days into a beautiful bed-and-breakfast with three guest rooms and attached baths. My friends spruced up the foyer and living room, with their arched doorways and beautiful woodwork. A generous dining room, kitchen, large porch, and private family quarters, which included two of the original bedrooms and a bath for twins Josh and Jessica, along with a master suite Jim added on, completed the B and B.

Updating the old Victorian while retaining its vintage, classic features had been a labor of love for Sharon and Jim, and it showed. They'd deep-cleaned and painted all the rooms, redone all the electrical to bring it up to code, ripped out the ratty old carpet, stripped and refinished the original hardwood floors until they gleamed, added an extra bathroom complete with a vintage claw-foot tub and pedestal sink, repaired the sagging porch, and expanded and remodeled the kitchen. Jim had surprised Sharon with the oversized kitchen island he'd built himself using reclaimed wood from an old barn outside of town that was being demolished.

As I looked around the picture-perfect kitchen with its granite countertops, farmhouse sink, large refrigerator with a pullout freezer drawer at the bottom that I'd kill for, and crisp white beadboard walls dotted with Sharon's collection of blue-and-white china, I felt a moment's envy as I compared it to my cluttered, vintage-fifties kitchen with its original tile and ancient appliances. But only a moment. Perfect is overrated. My small kitchen is colorful and kitschy. Like me. I grabbed some champagne and orange juice from the fridge, made myself a mimosa, and drank it down.

"What's up, buttercup?" Sharon set the empty serving tray on the end of the island. "Tell mama what happened." As the only one of our Musketeers trio with kids, Sharon has adopted the role of mother in our friendship threesome.

"Nothing much. Other than Patsy Morris is convinced Sophie and I hatched an evil plot to do away with her sainted husband." I told my gal pal about running into Patsy and Stephen as I was leaving Brady's office and Patsy's insistence that Brady arrest Sophie and me on the spot.

"Hasn't she heard of something called proof? Or evidence?" Sharon made herself a mimosa and poured me another.

I sipped this one. "The evidence is my bloody rolling pin and Sophie's coconut-cream pie. She says I hit Lester over the head and then Sophie suffocated him in her pie."

Sharon's eyes widened. "Wait, doesn't the book you're currently writing have *suffocated* in the title?"

I finished my second mimosa. "Yes. *Suffocating in Soufflé*. But a soufflé is totally different than a pie."

"What's the difference?"

"Pies are hearty all-American comfort food. Soufflés are delicate, French, and temperamental. The slightest thing will set them off and make them deflate. Shut the oven door too hard and bam! Your soufflé falls."

"Like Lester fell in Sophie's pie?" she teased, batting her blue eyes at me.

I pulled the basket of cookies to my flat chest. "Keep that up and I won't leave you any sinkers for milk-and-cookie time."

Although Sharon's a great cook—her breakfasts are legendary—I'm a better baker. Especially when it comes to cookies. That's why, early on when Jim and Sharon opened the Lake House, I offered to bake cookies as an occasional nighttime treat for their guests. Initially I did it once a week as a favor for my friend. The cookies proved to be such a hit, however, that Sharon begged me to make it a permanent—paid—arrangement. Now three times a week I supply the Lake House with my homemade cookies for what has become a nightly signature feature at Lake Potawatomi's only B and B.

"My bad. So how did Stephen Morris react when his mom was going off on you?"

"Oh, he calmed her down—even mouthed an apology to me over her head when she was holding on to him for dear life—and told her to let the sheriff do his job." I shook my head. "Talk about a clingy mother. When I was leaving, though, Patsy said, 'Don't think you're going to get away with murder, young lady. I've got your number. Sophie's too.' " I sighed and nibbled on a sinker.

"Sorry, my friend. What can I do? Want me to talk to Patsy?"

"No." I sighed again. "That will probably only rile her up more. Thanks, though." And then I remembered something. "Hey, you and Jim are members of the chamber of commerce, right?"

Sharon nodded.

"Is there any woman in the chamber—or for that matter, any woman in town you can think of—that Les might have been seeing on the sly?"

She scrunched up her nose. "Seriously? Who would want to be with him?"

"I can't even begin to imagine, but it takes all kinds. Sophie heard something when she stopped by the tent late that night.

It could have been Lester's murderer, but there's also the possibility Les might have been getting hot and heavy with someone in the bushes by the gazebo. Why else would he have been in the park so late?"

"Most of the women in the chamber are married, though," Sharon said.

"So? Les is married, and that didn't stop him from cheating on Patsy. Not all married couples are true-blue like you and Jim."

Speaking of the devil, Jim pushed through the swinging door from the dining room, an empty glass pitcher in his hand, and headed straight to the fridge. "Babe, we're out of OJ." He removed a carton from the refrigerator. Then he turned and saw me. "Teddie!" He set the pitcher and carton on the island to envelop me in a bear hug. "Are you okay?"

"I'm fine."

Jim raked his hand through his salt-and-pepper hair. "Jeez, can you even believe this? Only yesterday I was saying I could smash a pie in Les's face, and now someone's gone and done it." He released a nervous chuckle. "Hope Brady doesn't cuff me and throw me in the slammer."

"He won't." I handed him a sinker. "Not if Patsy has anything to say about it. She's already decided who the killer is. Or rather, killers," I said dryly.

"Seriously? Who?"

I pointed my thumb to my chest. "You're looking at her."

"You've gotta be kidding me. Not again."

While we were talking, Sharon had refilled the pitcher. "I'll take this into the dining room," she said. "You stay and talk to Teddie, hon. She has some questions about the chamber you might be able to answer better than me."

"Thanks, babe." Jim filled two mugs with coffee, pushed one over to me, and sat on the barstool beside me. "What gives?"

I brought him up to speed on the latest, including Patsy's wild accusations, and asked if he knew of any woman in the chamber Les might have been fooling around with. "I know from firsthand experience that he was a pig and a grabber stuck in the Dark Ages with all his creepy comments and come-ons," I said, "but I never heard about him cheating on Patsy, did you?"

Jim snorted. "Plenty of times. Les was a real player. For years. In addition to rating every woman who walked by and his usual locker-room talk, he'd regale some of the old-timers with details of his latest conquest."

"I can't believe any self-respecting woman would choose to be with that creep."

"Bingo." Jim dunked his sinker into his coffee. "That's the key right there. Remember Bobbi Turner?"

"Of Bobbi's Beauty Shoppe?"

He nodded, his mouth full of cookie.

I recalled the larger-than-life former beautician who had set up shop in town years ago. The platinum-blonde, big-haired, big-bodied Bobbi, who had a cousin in nearby Kenosha, blew into Lake Potawatomi from a small town in Texas more than a decade ago. Her cousin had told her about the recently vacated Sally's Salon on Main Street, and Bobbi, who was looking for a fresh start (for reasons we wouldn't discover until later), swooped in and leased the salon from chamber of commerce president Les Morris.

The Texas stylist, who had an affinity for pink, purple, and all things sparkly, promptly painted the inside of the salon lavender with pink glittery accents. She added pink twinkle lights and Lake Potawatomi's first manicure station stocked with vivid nail polish, including several metallic and glittery options and every shade of pink and red imaginable. She renamed the place Bobbi's Beauty Shoppe and immediately charmed everyone with her big hair, big personality, and southern accent. Bobbi celebrated her size and would bat her big brown eyes at her clients and say, "Ah'm not fat, honey, ah'm fluffy; there's just more of me to love," or "Ah'm a big woman, sweetie, and ah believe in livin' life large." It didn't take long, however, for folks to realize that our transplanted living-large Texan had some problems—with booze and the truth.

Six months after Bobbi arrived and was doing a booming business, she got falling-down drunk at a tavern in Kenosha one night. The news spread quickly through town. She told her clients it was her son's birthday and she was feeling melancholy because she couldn't spend it with him. A few weeks after that, Bobbi missed her first appointment of the day because she was passed out in her apartment after a night of binge drinking. She apologized and admitted she was an alcoholic who had fallen off the wagon but said she was back on the straight and narrow again.

A month after that, Bobbi showed up to work bleary-eyed and stumbling around, crashing into furniture and product, clearly drunk. Several bottles of nail polish fell to the floor and shattered, leaving sticky patches of scarlet and crimson on the white tile that looked like blood. Yet the hairdresser continued to approach her client in this inebriated state, scissors in hand, still intending to cut the woman's hair. That client was my mother. Mom promptly switched to a high-end salon in Racine and told her friends why. Word spread.

The stylist's self-destructive behavior continued off and on for more than a year. Bobbi would go for months without touching a drop of alcohol, then get sloppy drunk in public, come to work a mess, slack off on cleaning and sterilizing her tools and the shop, and fall behind on her bills and rent. She would apologize profusely, saying that her ex-husband had turned her children against her and so, to ease her heartache, she self-medicated with Johnnie Walker Red. Her clients felt sorry for her and forgave the brassy blonde Texan—until the shop started going downhill and money began disappearing from their purses after they'd been to the salon. Bobbi lost more and more clients, got further behind on her bills, and began drinking daily. The final straw came when she gave a French manicure to the mayor's wife, who got a bad fungal infection from the unsterilized nail tools and threatened to sue.

Before the woman could make good on her threat, Bobbi slipped out of town in the middle of the night, taking her pink twinkle lights with her. Later we found out that this was her MO and that her husband, whom she frequently badmouthed, had gotten full custody of the kids after one too many of Bobbi's drunken binges and a case of petty theft in Texas.

Returning to the present, I looked at Jim. "Bobbi and Lester had an affair?"

"Yep," he said. "After she skipped town, I overheard Les bragging to one of his buddies about sleeping with Bobbi. Apparently it was short-lived, though. Bobbi wised up and ended it after only a couple weeks. Sven Torkilsen teased Lester about the beauty shop owner dumping him." Jim dunked a sinker into his coffee and inhaled it. "And Les didn't like that one bit. He said something about Bobbi getting too clingy and acted like he was the one who dumped her. Jerry Larsen over at Larsen's Tavern looked him straight in the eye and said, 'Was that before or after you raised that poor girl's rent sky-high?' "

"What a pig," I said. "So she dumps him, and he raises her rent in revenge?"

"Sounds like it," Jim said. "That was basically the beginning of the end for Bobbi in Lake Potawatomi. She couldn't make her rent or keep up with her bills and kept getting farther and farther behind, so she drank more and more and started spiraling down until her life was in shambles."

All of a sudden, those mimosas I'd drunk didn't taste so good anymore. I took a gulp of coffee and crammed a sinker in my mouth to soak up the champagne and coffee acid. "I wonder if Lester did that to anyone else. Raised their rent as retaliation for spurned advances." I gave Jim a questioning look. "Have you heard of any of Lester's tenants having problems paying the rent?"

Sharon returned with a stack of dirty plates in her hands and caught the tail end of my question. "What'd I miss?" she asked.

We filled her in. Mostly. Even at forty-four, my Pollyanna friend retains a sweet sense of naïveté, so we try to shield her from the seamier sides of life.

"Belinda said business has been bad at the creamery these past few months and she's had a tough time making the rent," Sharon said as she loaded the plates in the dishwasher, "so she had to arrange for an extension with Les."

"Belinda Cullen, the coroner's wife?" Jim asked. "Hmm."

"Hmm what?" Sharon said.

We told her the rest of the story.

"Poor Bobbi," Sharon said. "I always liked her and felt bad the way things wound up for her. I had no idea of the part Les played in her downfall." She glowered. "I know it's wrong to speak ill of the dead, and it probably makes me a bad person for saying this, but Lester got what he deserved."

"I agree," I said. "The question is, *who* gave him what he deserved? And who was he meeting that night in the park—if, in fact, he was meeting someone?"

"No idea," Jim said, "but I did notice Les and Colleen Murphy laughing and really yukking it up at the chamber mixer last month."

"Colleen who owns the yarn shop?" Sharon asked.

"Yep."

"Fiftysomething Colleen with the big boobs and the tight shirts?" I added.

"That's the one," Jim said. "Not that I noticed," he added hastily, glancing at his wife.

"Sure you noticed, honey. You're married, not dead." Sharon winked at her husband. "Now if you did more than notice, that would be a whole other story." She gave him a peck on the lips. "Love you."

"Love you too," Jim put his arms around his wife's waist and stared deeply into her eyes.

"That's my cue to go." I slid off the barstool. "Thanks for the mimosas and the conversation, guys." I set three packages of sinkers on the island. "I think I'll stop by the yarn shop and pay Colleen a visit." I took my basket and skipped out the back door as I continued on my Little Red Riding Hood way. I'd gone only half a block when I spotted Sophie and her best friend Lauren Cullen—Belinda and Frank's daughter—in the alley next to Cullen's Creamery.

Half-hidden by the tall green waste can, Sophie's turquoise-striped head was angled toward Lauren's coal-black pixie cut. The girls were so deep in intense conversation they didn't notice me. As I passed, I heard Lauren say, "You can't say anything, Soph. To *any*one. Things are bad enough with my folks already. It'll only make things worse. Please," she pleaded.

Can't say anything about what? I wondered. And then a terrible thought struck me. *Is it possible that Lester did something to Lauren? And that Sophie and Lauren joined forces to knock off Lester together?*

Chapter Nine

I arrived at Colleen's Twisted Yarns to discover that the yarn-and-knitting boutique didn't open until ten. I checked my phone. Fourteen minutes from now. I sat down on a nearby bench beneath a crape myrtle with spent blooms and started tapping notes about what I'd learned so far.

Lester Morris was more than a run-of-the-mill beyond-baby-boomer grabber stuck in the past. Although Jim hadn't heard the president of the chamber of commerce bragging about sleeping with Colleen Murphy (yet), could it be that Colleen, like Bobbi before her, was more than a tenant of Lester's? And what about Lauren Cullen? What was it that Lauren didn't want Sophie telling anyone? Something about her and Les? Or maybe her mom, Belinda?

Maybe I should pay Belinda a visit as well. I thought about what Brady had said earlier to Augie about not letting his personal feelings get in the way of his duty, and I knew that even though Brady was my dear friend, as the sheriff, it was his job to investigate who had killed Lester Morris. The fact that the killer had used my rolling pin to put an end to Lester's lousy life made things trickier, and once again made me a murder suspect.

Sophie, too. Although I knew in my heart that my sweet young neighbor couldn't be a killer, I had a sense that Sophie was holding something back and hadn't revealed everything when Brady questioned her in the tent. Maybe—

"Chewie!" a voice yelled, startling me from my conjecturing.

As I lifted my head from my phone, I saw what looked like a huge black bear hurtling straight for me. I tossed my phone in my purse right before the hundred-and-thirty-pound Newfoundland bounded up and began slobbering all over me.

"Hi, Chewie." I ruffled the massive dog's fur as he slathered me with kisses, turning my face to the side to avoid the drool. "How are you, boy?"

The sound of running feet approached. "Chewie!" yelled four-year-old Noah, his light-brown hair wet with sweat and sticking to his forehead. "Bad dog!" The pint-sized boy shook his finger at the enormous dog as he picked up the end of the dangling red leash. "Sit," he commanded.

The friendly Newfie sat down in front of me, leaving a string of slobber in his wake, some of which clung to the bottom of my dress. I tried to shake it off, but the Swifties force was not with me today.

"Sorry, Teddie," an out-of-breath Amy Lewis said as she joined us. "Noah wanted to hold Chewie's leash, but as I was handing it off to him, Chewie spotted you and took off. I think he was hoping to see Gracie."

The Newfoundland gave a happy woof at the sound of my Eskie's name.

"Sorry, boy," I said, patting Chewie's back. "Gracie's not with me today. She's home catching some z's."

Noah tilted his head at me. "Z's? What's that?"

"That means Gracie's taking a nap," I explained to the newly adopted son of the Lewises. Amy and her husband Mark, pastor of Lake Potawatomi's First Baptist Church, had been trying to have kids for years but after several miscarriages had decided to adopt instead. When the frail, delicate Noah, born to a drug-addicted mom in Milwaukee who'd been in and out of foster homes since birth, was placed in their care last year, Mark and Amy knew instantly that they had met their son. They then took the myriad steps to make it official.

"I catch z's too," Noah said, stroking his dog's thick coat. "every day when I take my nap." He looked up at his mother. " 'Cept Saturdays, right, Mom?"

"That's right, Noah," Amy tousled her son's fine hair. Then she noticed the drool on my dress. "Oh my goodness. I'm so sorry, Teddie, I'll get that dry-cleaned for you."

"Don't worry about it." I scrubbed at the doggy drool with a tissue, leaving white polka dots clinging to my red dress. "I'll throw it in the laundry when I get home. It'll be fine."

Amy pulled a water bottle and baby wipe out of her oversized tote bag and extended both to me. "Here. This will help."

I squirted water on the hem of my dress and wiped off both the drool and tissue dots. "There we go, good as new." I handed back the water bottle. "Thanks."

Chewie panted loudly. Amy reached in her tote and pulled out a collapsible dog bowl, which she set on the ground beside the bench along with the opened water bottle. "Noah, Chewie's thirsty. Can you give him some water while I talk to Teddie for a minute, please?"

"Sure." He looked up at her with enormous brown eyes that brought to mind those big-eyed paintings of plaintive children from the sixties. "I firsty too."

Amy pulled a juice box out of her bag and set it on the bench beside Noah. "Here you go, buddy. You can have this after you take care of Chewie."

The Newfoundland's tail thumped up and down.

"Thanks, Mom." Noah squatted down and began filling his eager dog's water bowl.

With her son otherwise occupied, Amy motioned me a few feet away. "I heard about Lester," she whispered, keeping an eye on Noah. "I'm so sorry. That must have been awful, finding him like that."

I matched her quiet tone. "Not an experience I care to repeat."

"If you ask me," Amy said, tucking a strand of butterscotch-blonde hair behind her ear, "I'll bet it was an angry dad or husband who'd had enough and snapped and killed him."

"Really? You think so?"

She gave an emphatic nod. "I think Lester finally went too far with his unwanted attentions and grabby hands and some furious father or husband confronted him and lashed out instinctively in the heat of the moment while trying to protect his daughter or wife from that dirty old man." Her face flushed.

"Anyone particular you have in mind?" I thought of the dads in town with daughters. "Frank Cullen, maybe? Bud

Olson?" And although I hated to even give voice to the treacherous thought, I had to acknowledge that my Musketeer pal's husband—and my longtime friend—would do whatever was necessary to protect his beloved daughter Jessica from harm. "Jim Hansen?"

A bead of perspiration trickled down the slender neck of the pastor's wife and Bible-study teacher and dripped into the modest cleavage of her yellow cotton sundress. Amy shook her head. "I'm sure there are plenty." She glanced at her watch and then her son. "Hey, bud, you ready to go? We need to pick up Daddy's snacks from the bakery."

"I ready, Mom," Noah sang out. "I wanna bakery snack too."

Amy returned to her son's side. She picked up the mostly empty water bowl, flicked the remaining drops of water to the ground, and stuffed it back in her tote. Then she grabbed Chewie's leash. "Sorry, Teddie," she said, focusing all her attention on the black Newfoundland and not meeting my eyes, "we really have to get going. See you later." She took hold of Noah's hand. "Come on buddy, let's go." They scurried down the street.

" 'Bye, Teddie," Noah called over his shoulder. "Tell Gracie Chewie wants to come over and play soon." He waved.

I waved back. " 'Bye, Noah. 'Bye, Chewie. 'Bye, Amy."

Amy jerked her head in farewell but kept on going. I stared after her retreating form. *Was she trying to tell me something? Did Amy Lewis just hint that her gentle, squeaky-clean preacher husband and pillar of the community might have snapped and killed Lester in an attempt to protect her honor?*

No way. I could easily see Les ogling the pretty, thirty-something Amy and saying something crude to her, maybe even *accidentally* brushing up against her as he passed by or pinching her bottom the way he'd done to me, but Mark certainly wouldn't kill the town lech for that. He'd call Lester out on it and maybe file a complaint, but murder? Not in his DNA. Besides, the big guy upstairs Mark reported to wouldn't like it and had even issued a directive against it: *Thou shalt not kill.* But then, why had Amy said what she did? Why even bring up the prospect of an angry husband? It didn't make sense. I rubbed my forehead.

A familiar voice startled me from my ruminations. "Hiya, Teddie, how's it going?" Astrid Nilsen plopped down beside me in her loose tie-dyed T-shirt, worn khaki shorts hiked up over her wrinkly knees, and black Teva hiking sandals.

"Astrid!" I hugged the wildlife artist whom I've known since childhood. "I haven't seen you in ages. Where have you been?"

"Camping up north. I needed to make some new sketches and had a hankering to do some fishing, so I took my kayak and spent the last month on some of the islands."

Although Astrid had to be in her early to mid-eighties by now (she refuses to reveal her age; says it's nobody's business except hers and her doctor's), she's one of the most active, independent women I know. Astrid is an award-winning artist whose wildlife paintings hang in our state capitol and the governor's mansion and have been featured in prestigious galleries around the country. She still hikes, camps, kayaks, cycles, does tae kwon do, and is an avid angler.

"Did you go up to Chippewa Flowage?"

"Does a bear do his business in the woods? Sure, I went to Chippewa. Best muskie fishing in the state." Astrid grinned. "And believe it or not, I saw a black bear crap in the woods, although I won't be painting that. The bear, yes; the pile of crap, no. There's enough crappy paintings in the world already."

Astrid always tells it like it is. When my Grandma Florence was alive, the earthy artist was one of her best friends. They met at a Daughters of Norway event when Astrid was a teen and Grandma was the mother of a toddler (my dad) and became fast friends. Astrid used to babysit my dad on the odd occasion when Grandma and Grandpa went out. Astrid and Grandma both loved to fish, and they imparted that love to my father. In fact, the two women and my dad took me on my first camping-and-fishing trip to Wisconsin's largest, wildest lake when I was seven. (Mom stayed home—she doesn't do camping.) This wilderness flowage—what Northern Wisconsinites call a reservoir—has more than 140 islands, many accessible only by kayak or canoe; primitive campgrounds; and tons of wildlife, including bears, bobcats, bald eagles, deer, and the occasional wolf.

For a tomboy like me, it was paradise.

I still remember the excitement of catching my first fish—a bluegill, which Dad cleaned and gutted and panfried for dinner that night along with a few of the walleyes the grown-ups had caught. Over the years, Grandma and Astrid kept up a friendly rivalry as to which one would catch the most fish. That long weekend, Grandma won.

"Did you catch a lot of fish?" I asked Astrid.

"Yah, you betcha. I got my daily limit of perch and walleye and also hooked a big ol' muskie." She puffed out her chest. "That sucker must have weighed over forty pounds."

"Wow. And how did he taste?"

"Pretty damn good."

"Did you see any otters?" The playful mammals are one of my favorite creatures. I saw my first otters—popping their heads out of the water and rubbing their faces with their paws—as a kid on that initial camping trip to Chippewa and fell in love.

"Yep." Astrid ran her hand through her cropped white hair. "Beavers, too, and some snapping turtles. Lots of fish and the usual suspects—deer, raccoons, and loons. Couple bald eagles as well. I was able to get a lot of sketches done."

"Sounds like it was a productive getaway."

"Yah." She leaned back and clasped her hands behind her head. "So, what's new around here? Anything exciting? Since I just got back, I'm out of the loop."

Depends on what you consider exciting. I sighed. Time to repeat the pie-in-the-dead-Lester-face story all over again. I knew Astrid was no fan of Lester Morris—she'd slashed him down to size on more than one occasion in front of God and everyone when she saw him being his usual slimy self with one of the young targets of his unwanted affections. "Well, we did have an incident in the baking tent yesterday," I began.

"That's right. I forgot it's the annual baking contest this week," Astrid said. "What happened? Did somebody's cookies burn?" she teased.

Although the ardent angler can fillet and panfry some killer fish over a rustic campfire in the great outdoors, she's the first to admit she has no interest in the domestic arts. Astrid employs a weekly housekeeper to keep her cabin-style home habitable and eats most of her meals out.

"Unfortunately, it's more serious than that," I continued. "You see, Lester Morris was found—"

"Dead as a doornail, facedown in Sophie Miller's coconut-cream pie," Astrid finished. Her eyes crinkled as she chuckled. "Sorry, couldn't resist. I heard all about it as soon as I got back from at least three different neighbors. Matter of fact, I was unpacking my Jeep when Wilma Sorensen raced over to tell me the *dreadful* news," Astrid said, mimicking Wilma's gossipy voice. She snorted. "All I can say is, it couldn't have happened to a nicer fella. Good riddance to bad rubbish." She brushed imaginary dirt off her palms in a dismissive motion.

"What else did Wilma tell you?"

"You mean the part about your rolling pin being found with Lester's blood all over it? Or the part where Patsy Morris accused you and young Sophie of being in cahoots and planning and executing the dirty deed together?" Astrid asked with a wicked gleam in her eye.

"That's our Wilma." I made a face. "Always happy to spread good news."

"Don't pay attention to her. Nobody does." She laid her rough, age-spotted hand on my arm. "I'd like to help you clear your name, honey. I'm guessing the sheriff confiscated your rolling pin as evidence?"

I nodded, trying to unsee the beloved heirloom covered in blood.

"We need to get you your grandma's rolling pin back," Astrid said. "And to do that, we need to prove you didn't bash Lester in the head with it." She got a far-off look in her faded blue eyes. "Florence loved that fancy rolling pin," she said with a fond smile. "I was lucky enough to eat boatloads of cookies your grandma made with that rolling pin over the years. I especially loved her great Christmas cutouts with buttercream icing."

"Grandma made the best cookies," I agreed.

"And you're doing Florence proud carrying on the family tradition." She patted my knee. "Your cookies are definitely as tasty as hers. In fact, I'll betcha your grandma would be mighty impressed with some of your new creations."

"Thanks, Astrid. That's high praise indeed." I pulled out a package of sinkers from my basket and handed it to her. "Here you go. I hope you like these."

She smacked her aged lips. "I'm sure I will, honey. My sweet tooth thanks you." She pocketed the cookies in her khakis. "But back to the matter at hand. How are we going to prove to your good friend the sheriff, and the rest of this whole damn town, that you didn't kill Les?" Astrid pulled a face. "You've already got one strike against you since you spent time in jail as a murder suspect."

"You're kidding, right?" I stared at my elderly Norwegian friend. "The only reason I spent exactly *one* night in jail is because the real murderer lied and accused me of trying to strangle her."

"I know, but people are always fuzzy on the details. 'Specially when you've got women like Wilma running around town whispering behind your back and fanning the flames of suspicion. Particularly among folks that don't know you like the rest of us. All they'll remember is that not long ago you stumbled upon the dead body of a woman strangled with one of your scarves." Astrid flicked the ends of my red-white-and-black swirled scarf. "And now, a few months later, you go on and stumble upon *another* body—Les Morris, the president of the chamber of commerce, killed with your grandma's fancy rolling pin."

"Wilma didn't spare any details, did she?" A huge sigh whooshed out of me like a spent balloon. "When you put it like that, it sure sounds like I'm guilty."

Astrid patted my arm. "Now don't you fret, honey. We both know you didn't kill Lester. We simply need to put on our mystery-solving hats and figure out who did." Her lined face, weathered by years of exposure to the elements, broke into a wide grin. "I've always liked that Jessica Fletcher on TV. I wouldn't mind being her. Although"—her wrinkled lips puckered into a pout—"since you're the one who writes the murder mysteries, I guess that makes you Jessica."

"Not at all. You can be Jessica." I almost added, *You're the right age*, but caught myself in time. "I'll be Jane Tenni-son." I've always loved the British mystery series *Prime Suspect* with Helen Mirren as a fortysomething police detective. Who wouldn't want to be Helen Mirren—then or now?

Slow down, Sparky. What are you getting yourself into? Are you seriously going to join forces with Astrid and play private detective? Remember how Brady warned you against doing that the last time and told you to leave the investigation to law enforcement?

I know, I answered my practical self. *But half the town's already convinced I killed Lester. I need to prove I didn't and restore my good name.*

Good name . . . That reminded me. My publisher, Baker Street Press, had not been happy when I became the prime suspect in the first two murders to hit Lake Potawatomi, especially after an online blogger's libelous statements about me being the killer went viral. Baker Street invoked the morality clause, and overnight I was at risk of having my contract canceled. My publisher said the burden of proof was on me to refute the libelous comments, which I did. The online speculation created such a furor, however, that the resulting publicity wound up shooting my sales through the roof, and my latest book, *A Dash of Death,* hit the best-seller list.

Baker Street did not cancel my contract. *Note to self: Inform editor of latest murder.*

My inner voice of reason brought me back to the present. *Subtlety is not Astrid's strong suit. Can you really see her getting information from people without their catching on?*

You're right. Astrid is blunt and doesn't suffer fools gladly, but she's also lived here more than eighty years. She knows all the old-timers better than you and probably knows where all the skeletons are buried as well.

"Teddie?" The object of my inner argument waved her hand in front of my face. "Where'd you go?"

"Sorry. I was thinking."

"About our plan of action," Astrid said eagerly. "What do you think we should do first? Who should we question?"

I considered. "How well do you know Patsy and her son?"

"Well enough. Patsy and I have never been close, but I babysat Stephen a few times when he was a tyke—when his overly possessive mother could stand to let him out of her sight, that is." Astrid shook her head. "Patsy was always like a mama bear protecting her cub if anyone got too close to Stephen."

"I've noticed. I wonder if that's why Stephen's never gotten married or had a long-term relationship," I said thoughtfully. "Mama Bear always scares them off."

"You hit that nail right on the head."

"Tell you what," I said, "why don't you use that old babysitting connection to see what you can find out from Stephen about his dad? Lester's business dealings, any enemies he might have had . . ." Then I remembered. "Wait, wasn't Les a fisherman too?"

Astrid snorted. "If you can call it that. He was always so busy yakkin' and drinkin' beer with his buddies when they went out on the lake, he scared away all the fish."

"Who were Lester's fishing buddies?"

"Bud Olson, Sven Torkilsen, and Jerry Larsen. Sometimes Al Gibson if he could get away from the garage."

All members of the chamber of commerce. Bud owned the aforementioned Bud's Hardware, Sven was the proprietor of Torkilsen's Funeral Home, Jerry owned Larsen's, the local watering hole, and Al Gibson was the mechanic who'd done car repairs for me since I first started driving. Al kept trying to talk me into buying a new car, but I loved my thirteen-year-old yellow Beetle with its darling bud vase and wasn't going to give it up until I absolutely had to.

"How about you see what you can find out from them?" I suggested. "Maybe one of the guys knows who Lester might have been seeing lately."

"You mean, get the name of the latest little sumpin' sumpin' Lester had on the side?" Astrid grimaced. "I can't see the attraction myself. Les Morris was sure no George Clooney."

"You got that right." I repeated her grimace. "It takes all kinds."

"Why Patsy put up with Lester's philandering all these years is beyond me," she said. "I'd have drop-kicked his sorry ass out the first time he strayed. Did that with my ex. Smartest thing I ever did."

"Grandma told me about that—how long had you been married when that happened?"

"Not quite a year," Astrid said. "I came home early from visiting my aunt up in La Crosse and caught the dirty dog in bed with some bottle-blonde floozy. I grabbed the shotgun and blasted a hole in the wall above their heads. Then I told 'em both to get the hell out of my house and never come back." She barked out a laugh. "You've never seen anybody run so fast. Pretty funny too, since they were naked as jaybirds."

"Remind me never to get on your bad side."

"Aw, honey, you couldn't do that if you tried." She flung her arm around my shoulder and gave me an affectionate side hug. "Tell you what, I'll go over to Larsen's before supper tonight. I usually drop by after my trips to shoot the breeze with Jerry and tell him about the fishing." Astrid shot me a sly wink. "It'll give me a chance to brag about my muskie. Plus, Bud and Sven always stop by for a drink after work, so I can kill three birds with one stone."

"Be careful," I warned. "Try not to let them know you're fishing for information."

Astrid slapped her thigh. "That's a good one. Fishing for information." She gave me a high five. "No problem—I'll buy 'em some beers and say, 'Let's all raise a glass to Lester.' Then I'll buy a few more rounds to loosen their lips. Bud babbles like a brook after a few brewskis, and Sven has never been the soul of discretion—drunk or sober." She rolled her faded blue eyes. "The stories he's told about some of the dead folks in this town would curl your toes. I'll get those two to spillin' their guts or my name isn't Astrid Ingeborg Nilsen. And don't worry, Astrid Nilsen can hold her liquor with the best of them."

"I know you can. Grandma once told me you can drink most men in Lake Potawatomi under the table."

"That's right." Astrid beamed. "Florence always said I had a hollow leg." She glanced around to make sure no one was near and said in a loud whisper, "And what are *you* going to do, Jane Tennison, while I'm busy playing Jessica Fletcher?"

"I've got a few leads of my own to follow." While the wildlife artist and I had been talking, I'd noticed Colleen Murphy arrive and open up Colleen's Twisted Yarns. Time to pay a visit to the knitting lady and see what kind of a twisted yarn she might spin.

Chapter Ten

Five minutes later I pushed open the door of the yarn shop only to discover Barbara Christensen standing at the counter, her sleeveless-chambray-shirted back to me, paying Colleen Murphy for some skeins of yarn.

Colleen, wearing a low-cut white tank top and tight jeans, conveyed a practiced retailer's smile my way. "I'll be right with you."

"No hurry. I'm just looking around."

At the sound of my voice, Barbara turned from the counter. "Teddie!" My fellow baking contestant beamed at me. "Nice to see you, dear. I didn't know you knitted as well."

"I don't, but I've been thinking about taking it up. Either that or crocheting—depending on what's easiest." I gave a small laugh and crossed to the spinner rack of how-to craft books at the other end of the counter, where I plucked one at random.

"I do both," Barbara said, "but I think knitting's easier to get the hang of in the beginning." She turned back to the shop owner. "Don't you?"

"Depends on the person," Colleen said, "but in general, I'd agree. Knitting is a bit easier, since you only use two stitches—" All at once, she grabbed and lifted her sleek brunette blowout off the back of her neck and turned to face the air-conditioning vent. As she did, I caught sight of a tiny blue butterfly tattoo peeking out of her cleavage. "Gotta love those hot flashes," Colleen said as she fanned her face. "The joys of menopause."

"One of the benefits of being old." Barbara smirked. "Those days are long behind me."

"I wish I could say the same," I said, but now was not the time to compare menopause stories. I returned my attention to Colleen. "What were you saying about the stitches?"

"Knitting only uses two stitches—knit and purl," she explained as she splashed water from her stainless-steel water bottle onto her neck and chest. Colleen grabbed a nearby red bandanna, wet it, and pressed it to the back of her neck. "Once you master knitting and purling and have made a few things—scarves, afghans, whatever—you can always pick up a hook and learn to crochet."

"Sounds like a good plan."

Barbara began talking about some of her crochet projects. *What wasn't part of my plan was getting into an in-depth conversation with my fellow contestant, as much as I adore her.* I moved over to a section of vivid red and purple yarns, affecting an absorbed interest in choosing some skeins.

"Those bold colors are right up your alley, Teddie," Barbara said approvingly. "You always wear the most fun colors. What are you planning to make?"

"Absolutely no idea. I thought I might pick Colleen's brain and see what she suggests, since she's the expert."

The older woman deflated. "That's a good idea. She really knows her stuff," she said brightly. "Well, I'll leave you two ladies to it." She picked up her bag and headed for the door.

I hurried over to her. "Barbara, wait. Maybe you could give me a lesson sometime, if you don't mind? Textile arts are a whole new world to me, and I am utterly clueless. Cooking and baking are much more in my wheelhouse. Besides, we still need to swap recipes. I'm dying to make your yummy snickerdoodles."

A warm smile spread across Barbara's face. "Of course, dear. I'd be happy to." She kissed me on the cheek. "Why don't I call you later and we can set up a time?"

"That sounds great." I hugged her good-bye.

As the door closed behind Barbara, I turned back to Colleen Murphy, readying my opening line. She cut me off at the pass.

"Okay, Teddie St. John, what are you really here for?" She dropped the red bandanna on the counter. "Let's cut to the chase."

"Excuse me?"

"Don't play dumb with me." Colleen crossed her ripped arms and regarded me with a steady gaze. "I know you like to play girl detective, Nancy Drew. I've been in this town nearly two years now, and you've never once set foot in my shop before today. But bam, the head of the chamber of commerce buys it in a baking tent, and you beat a path to my door."

"Okay, you got me." I held up my hands in defeat and looked straight into the yarn shop owner's striking emerald-green eyes. "I'll come right out with it. Were you sleeping with Lester Morris?"

Colleen burst out laughing. Then she laughed some more.

I take it that's a no.

She continued to laugh. Hard. So hard, eventually the laughter turned to snorts as she bent over in mirth. At last Colleen straightened up and swiped at her streaming eyes. "That is the funniest thing I've ever heard." She grabbed a tissue and blotted the mascara from beneath her eyes. Then she moved out from behind the front counter to stand in front of me. The incredibly fit middle-aged woman ran her hands down the sides of her slim-hipped, tiny-waisted, big-bosomed body that reminded me of a brunette Dolly Parton. "Do you seriously think *this* would ever go to bed with a wrinkled old goober like Les Morris with that bad rug that looked like a dead rat on his head?"

Well, when you put it like that . . . "Guess not."

"Honey, I'll be the first to admit I'm a flirt," Colleen said. "And yeah, I wear tight clothes and show off my cleavage, but there's nothing wrong with a woman playing up her assets and using them to her advantage."

Actually, there is, my feminist self disagreed, but this was not the time for a lecture.

"But," Colleen continued, "I don't give away the goods to anyone unless they're someone I have the hots for. And trust me"—she made a face—"Lester Morris was not anyone I had the hots for." She shrugged. "Sure, every now and then I'd lean forward and let him catch a peek of the girls, especially if I needed a favor from the chamber, but that's as far as it went."

She ran her hand through her glossy, shoulder-length brown hair. "That randy old man might have *seen* my blue butterfly, but he certainly never touched it, and not for lack of trying. That guy was all over me like a cheap suit. A polyester suit." She scrunched up her nose at the word *polyester*.

Colleen returned to her place behind the counter and took a long drink of water from her water bottle. "And no, I didn't kill the old geezer. Why would I?" She delivered a steady look. "Correct me if I'm wrong, but wasn't it *your* rolling pin covered in Lester's blood?"

"Yes, but I didn't kill him."

"Actually, I never thought you did, contrary to town gossip. You're still dating that rich, gorgeous Englishman, right?"

"Yes, I am." My lips turned up at the thought of Tavish. Now Colleen wasn't the only one with a butterfly. Mine was in my stomach, though, not on my chest. Multiple, not singular. And fluttering like crazy.

"That guy is quite a catch. Why would you want to mess that up by killing Les Morris? Especially for a pinch on the butt? Talk about stupid," she said. "You already put the old grabber in his place in front of half the town; no need to do anything else."

"Exactly." Now it was my turn to be hit by a hot flash. A wave of heat engulfed me and spread like a flash fire from my midsection to the top of my head. I yanked the scarf from around my neck and tied my thick, unruly curls into a high ponytail. Then I grabbed the water bottle from my basket and squirted the top of my head, allowing the cool water to drip through my hair and down my neck to extinguish the raging fire. "Ahhh . . ." I closed my eyes and puffed out a sigh of relief as the hot flash subsided.

When I opened my eyes, Colleen was regarding me with a curious look. "Aren't you a little young to be going through menopause?"

"Not thanks to chemotherapy. Thanks to the miracle of chemo and its side effects, I hit that lovely midlife milestone before I turned forty."

She stared hard at my flat chest. "I've always been scared to death of getting breast cancer," she said, glancing down at her deep cleavage. "I can't imagine not having boobs. What's it like?"

"Very freeing, actually. I never have to wear a bra, and I don't have to worry about tripping over my sagging breasts when I'm an old lady."

Colleen snickered. "Well, you sure have a great attitude about it, I'll say that for you." She tilted her head. "How come you didn't get reconstruction?"

I repeated what I'd told Sophie the other night. Hopefully, now that we'd bonded over boobs and hot flashes, Colleen might be more inclined to provide me with some Lester information. "Are there any other women in the chamber that Les may have been seeing?" I asked casually.

She snorted. "I doubt it. Everyone knew he was a creep and a player. Most women wouldn't give him the time of day. Besides, there's not that many chicks in the chamber," she said. "It's still pretty much a good-old-boys club." Colleen held up her hand and began counting on her fingers. "There's me, Joanie Olson from the hardware store, Cindy Torkilsen,

Bea Andersen, Belinda Cullen, Joanne LaPoint—no, wait." She stopped herself. "Joanne and Ed ended their membership when they retired a few months ago." Then she continued, "The last two women are your pals Sharon Hansen and Char Jorgensen over at the bookstore."

I did an internal head slap. Why hadn't I thought of that? As a small business owner, Char would naturally be a member of the chamber of commerce. And better than that, she would know the inside scoop and reveal all to her BFF. *Time to pay my bestie a visit.*

Chapter Eleven

After taking my leave of Colleen Murphy—and buying a few skeins of yarn for taking up her time—I booked it over to the Corner Bookstore. There I discovered my best friend deep in conversation with Margaret Miller about the latest literary fiction. Char, the brainiac of our Musketeers trio, loves her literary fiction—all that thoughtful, leisurely, Pulitzer Prize–winning stuff that I never understand. Margaret, Sophie's grandmother, loves it as well, so the two of them are always comparing notes.

Don't get me wrong; the writing is sublime in literary fiction. I marvel over the gorgeousness of the language the authors use and find myself highlighting entire sections in the books Char gives me. When I come upon a perfect sentence, I stop and revel in the beauty of the author's words. Occasionally I even retype the sentence, print it out—with full author attribution—and stick it on the bulletin board in my home office as inspiration for my own writing. But that doesn't mean I "get" the book. There's usually some profound, inscrutable meaning that I fail to comprehend. And that's okay. I never claimed to be deep.

For me, a good book is all about the story, not the hidden meaning I have to dig to uncover. I did that in my college English lit class. My instructor was big on theme and symbolism and made us dissect every single book we read so we would understand what the author "really meant" or was trying to "teach" us.

I'll never forget the time an illustrious, award-winning author came to campus for a lecture. During the Q&A afterward, my professor fawned over the acclaimed author and posed a question about the significance of a certain incident in the hero's journey in the author's latest novel—after pontificating at length about the symbolism of the event and what the chapter meant. The renowned author replied, "Several folks have asked me that, including a couple book reviewers. But honestly? I was simply trying to get my hero from point A to point B and I thought that particular occurrence would make a fun scene for the reader." He chuckled.

My kind of author. As a storyteller, I love making readers laugh and giving them an escape from reality for a few hours. I enjoy telling and reading stories—especially mysteries. My love of mysteries began in grade school when I discovered the Boxcar Children, Nancy Drew, and Trixie Belden. I used to dream of writing mysteries myself someday, and now I am. Thank you, cancer, for pushing me to follow my dreams.

While Char was otherwise engaged with Margaret, I headed to the mystery section and began browsing the shelves. Too many mysteries, too little time. I picked up another copy of *The Beekeeper's Apprentice* to replace the first Mary Russell/ Sherlock Holmes title I'd loaned to a friend and never gotten back. Then I rounded the end of the aisle to see if the latest Maisie Dobbs had arrived—and stumbled over Sophie Miller sitting cross-legged on the floor, nose deep in a book. I lost my balance but caught myself before I fell.

"Oh my gosh, Teddie," Sophie scrambled to her feet, face aflame, clutching her book. "I'm so sorry. Are you all right?"

"I'm fine. I should have been watching where I was going."

"It was my fault. I shouldn't have been sitting on the floor blocking the aisle. I was so caught up in a favorite childhood book, I was in another world."

"No problem. Been there, done that." I squinted at the black-and-red cover over my readers. "What book is that?"

Sophie held up the paperback. "*The Bad Beginning*, from Lemony Snicket's A Series of Unfortunate Events."

"I've heard about that series for years. Kids love them, don't they?"

"Yup. Lauren and I swapped them all the time. They're not only for kids, though—as evidenced by my current immersion," Sophie added wryly.

"I'll be sure and add them to my TBR list." My mind wasn't on the popular children's books, however. Since Sophie had brought up her best friend, this was the perfect opportunity to question her about Lauren and what I'd overheard her say. Nonchalantly, naturally.

"You and Lauren remind me of our Three Musketeers when we were growing up. Sharon, Char, and I used to swap all the Baby-Sitters Club books."

"I read those too. They turned a few of them into cool graphic novels."

We chatted about our favorite characters in the series, Sophie saying she related most to bookworm Mary Anne but that Lauren was a combo of style-savvy Stacey and artist Claudia.

"Lauren's pretty talented." I glanced at the turquoise streak in Sophie's blonde head. "She did a great job on your hair."

"Thanks. She wants to try purple next time, but I want green."

Lauren is a stylist at the lone salon in town—formerly Bobbi's Beauty Shoppe. After Bobbi Turner fled town years ago, the shop sat empty for a long time until one day Cindy Torkilsen at the funeral home informed her husband, Sven, that she wanted to buy it. The women of Lake Potawatomi needed their own salon, she said, rather than having to always drive to Racine to get their hair cut and colored, so she opened Cindy's Hair and Nails five years ago. Although Cindy Torkilsen had years of experience doing hair and makeup for dead people, she soon discovered that live, breathing women were not the same thing. She hired a stylist and a manicurist and added Lauren—who appeals more to the forty-and-under crowd—as a second stylist last year.

Sophie glanced at my dark mop of unruly curls, which I'd released from my ponytail after the hot flash receded. "Lauren could color your hair if you want. Maybe add some temporary streaks? Hot pink or orange would look great."

"Thanks, but I think I'll stick with my boring brown and leave the bright colors for my clothes." I flapped my red-white-and black-scarf at her.

She giggled.

"It's good to hear you laugh, Sophie. I know the last couple days have been really hard for you. Me too."

She shivered and hugged her Lemony Snicket to her chest. "I still can't believe someone killed Lester with your rolling pin and smashed his face down in my pie." Tears pricked her eyes. "Why would they do that? What did we ever do to them?'

Good question. I'd like to know the answer to that myself.

Sophie continued, "And that anyone could think you and I were murderers and plotted the whole thing together like a modern-day Thelma and Louise is cray-cray. All because Lester pinched your butt and said something sexually inappropriate to me? Talk about crazy. We already dealt with him when it happened."

"Yes, we did. And you're right, it is pretty crazy that some people are branding us the new Thelma and Louise. Tell you what," I said, "I'll be Susan Sarandon; you can be Geena Davis."

Sophie giggled again.

I guess I shouldn't have been surprised that at her age Sophie knew who two actresses popular during the eighties and nineties were. Many young women have discovered the landmark feminist film in recent years. "Did you and Lauren watch *Thelma and Louise* together?"

"Yup. We loved it. I couldn't believe when I saw Brad Pitt though—he was so young and hot." Sophie blushed. "Such a great movie. As Lauren said, those women were badasses."

Yes, they were. "You and Lauren have been friends for a long time, haven't you?"

She smiled and nodded. "Ever since Miss Vopelensky's second-grade class."

"Char, Sharon, and I met in grade school too," I said. "Longtime friendships are the best, aren't they? You can really trust each other and know you'll always have each other's back."

She nodded again but regarded me with a wary look.

"Sophie," I said quietly, "I have the feeling you didn't tell the sheriff everything about your return to the park the night Lester died. Is there anything you left out? About you and Lauren, maybe? Anything you'd like to tell me?"

Her brown eyes grew enormous. She shook her head. "No, nothing." But she wouldn't meet my eyes.

I stepped closer, keeping my voice down. "I heard you, Sophie, earlier today when you and Lauren were in the alley next to Cullen's. Lauren said, 'You can't say anything to anyone.' What was she talking about? Was it about Lester?" I asked gently. "Had he done something to Lauren? And as a result, did the two of you decide to do something to him?"

"No!" She stared at me in shock and burst into tears.

A customer poked his long-haired head over the bookcase—Jeffrey Hollenbeck, the hippieish gluten-free baker from the contest. "Everything okay here?" he asked.

"Yes, thanks," I said, as I ushered the crying Sophie toward the restroom. "Girl stuff. Sorry about that."

"No prob. Let me know if there's anything I can do to help."

"Thanks." Once the door closed behind us, I turned to Sophie and apologized. "I'm sorry. I didn't mean to upset you. That's the last thing I wanted to do. I'm just trying to figure out what happened to Lester to get us off the hook as suspects." *And trust me, I don't want you and Lauren taking our place.* I plucked a tissue from the top of the antique wooden vanity and handed it to the weeping twenty-year-old. "I mean, sure, the Thelma-and-Louise brush they're painting us with is kind of funny, but it's also totally Looney Tunes. Patsy Morris, in her grief, unfortunately, is peddling that crazy theory all around town." I shook my head. "The woman is like a dog with a bone. She won't let it go. That's why I'm trying to come up with alternate scenarios to figure out who the real killer is."

"Well, it's not Lauren! And it's not me!" Sophie said, her voice trembling. "How could you even *think* that?" She lifted her red, tear-streaked face to meet mine, her brown eyes full of hurt and reproach. "I thought we were friends."

Ouch.

"We are friends, Sophie," I said gently. "That's why I'm trying to help. But I can't help if I don't know the truth of what really happened that night in the park. You're not telling me everything, are you?"

She shook her head. "I promised I wouldn't." Sophie lifted her chin. "But I won't have you thinking my best friend's a murderer. And worse, suggesting that to your good friend the sheriff." Sophie exhaled a heavy sigh and leaned against the restroom wall. "Lauren was meeting her boyfriend that night, and I was covering for her. Her parents don't like him because he's a tattoo artist and has a lot of tats. He's also ten years older than Lauren and has a kid. Her folks don't want her to 'get tied down so young with someone like that,' " she said, making air quotes around the Cullens' comment. "They'd have a fit if they knew she was still seeing Justin. He lives in Racine, where he has a tattoo parlor. That's where they met," Sophie explained, "when Lauren got her hummingbird tattoo last year. Anyway, we told her folks Lauren was spending the night with me, and I went over to her house to pick her up. Then we went to the park, where Lauren met Justin. They split, and I put my cooler with my pie in it under the table." She lifted her chin and fixed me with a steady look. "I'd told Gram that's why I had to run out so late, and I don't lie to my grandmother."

"I wouldn't expect anything less from you." I gave Sophie a warm smile to try to ease the tension between us. "Thank you for telling me. It makes sense. I totally understand covering for a friend. I've been in that position myself, and my girlfriends have covered for me on more than one occasion." I tilted my head at her. "But isn't Lauren your age? She's an adult. She can do whatever she wants."

"You don't know Lauren's parents." Sophie rolled her eyes. "They're really strict. Besides, Lauren's only nineteen and still lives at home. She can't afford her own place, and her folks say as long as she lives under their roof, she must abide by their rules. And one of those rules is to not see Justin." She shoved a strand of sticky hair off her face. "He has a six-year-old kid and shares custody with his ex," she added. "Justin and Lauren are saving up to get a place together with enough room for Tyler, but until then, they're keeping things on the down low."

Sophie turned on the tap in the vanity that Char had repurposed from an old oak dresser and splashed water on her face. After blotting off the water with a paper towel, she turned back to me. "Plus, Lauren's mom and dad have been fighting a lot lately, and she didn't want to make things worse."

Now that's an interesting tidbit of information. What could Frank and Belinda Cullen be fighting about? Anything to do with Lester and the arrangement he made with Belinda on the rent for the creamery? I scratched my neck. "Any idea what Lauren's folks have been fighting about?" I asked.

Before she could answer, Char poked her head around the restroom door. "Hey, Sophie, you in here?" When she saw me and my young neighbor's still-red face, Char's head swiveled between me and Sophie. "What's going on?" Behind my BFF, Sophie shook her head and put her finger to her lips.

"Nothing," I said. "Sophie and I were talking baking stuff. She's going to give me the recipe for her great granola clusters. Right, Sophie?"

"Yup. As long as you give me your sinkers recipe."

"You got it." I reached in my basket and pulled out one of the remaining bags of cookies. "Here's some for you and Margaret."

"Speaking of Margaret," Char said, "your grandma's looking for you, Sophie. She's ready to leave."

"Thanks." Sophie followed Char out of the restroom, but not before turning and mouthing *thank you* to me.

I followed the two women to the front of the store, where we found my elderly neighbor sitting on her padded walker seat, reading her book while she waited.

"Sorry, Gram," Sophie said as we approached. "Teddie and I got to talking, and then I had to use the restroom."

"That's okay, dear. I'm reading Ann Patchett's latest so am quite content."

"Hi, Margaret." I bent over to kiss her crepey cheek. "How are you?" As I straightened back up, Wilma Sorensen entered the bookstore with Beverly Price, the Milwaukee native who'd fled inside Bud's Hardware earlier today after I'd snarkily offered her some coconut-cream pie. Upon seeing Sophie and me together, Wilma gave me the stink eye and whispered in Beverly's ear.

"I'm fine, Teddie," Margaret said in answer to my question. "I'd be even better if some people would stop spreading malicious gossip and unfounded rumors." She snapped her book shut and fixed Wilma with a penetrating gaze, speaking loudly and deliberately. "As Mark Twain said, 'He gossips habitually; he lacks the common wisdom to keep still that deadly enemy of man, his own tongue.' "

"That's a good one." I winked at my literary neighbor. "I'll have to remember that."

Char high-fived her kindred reading spirit and spoke up. "I also like what George Eliot said in *Daniel Deronda*: 'Gossip is a sort of smoke that comes from the dirty tobacco-pipes of those who diffuse it; it proves nothing but the bad taste of the smoker.' " She regarded the notorious town gossip with a steady look.

"Well I never!" Wilma said. "How rude!" She linked her arm with Beverly's. "We don't have to stay here and listen to this. I don't know about you, Beverly, but this is the last time I'll set foot in this store." Wilma stomped off, gray perm quivering, dragging alongside her the Milwaukee transplant, who at least had the grace to look abashed.

"Whoa. You ladies certainly know how to clear a room," Jeffrey Hollenbeck teased as he approached the front counter in his Birkenstocks and loose tan linen pants, carrying a stack of books against his chest.

"What can I say?" Char said. "It's an art." She smirked at the attractive ponytailed senior as she moved behind the counter to the cash register.

"I'm all about art," said the founding owner of Lake Potawatomi's new arts collective. Jeffrey set his books down on the counter—mostly art and nature books, I noticed—revealing his Bob Dylan/Joan Baez concert T-shirt in the process. "Whatever form it takes."

Margaret shot him an interested look. "What kind of art do you do, Jeffrey?" she asked.

"A little of this, a little of that. Some painting, some stained-glass work, but sculpting is my first love."

Demi Moore, Patrick Swayze, and that famous clay-sculpting scene popped into my head, along with the earworm of *Unchained Melody. Down, girl*, I told myself. Tavish's hazel eyes and delicious English accent filled my mind, and the ghostly trio dissolved into movie memory, although I could still hear the faint strains of the Righteous Brothers.

"I also love baking," Jeffrey was saying as Char rang up his books. "I think it's an underappreciated domestic art."

"Hear, hear," Sophie and I said in unison.

Margaret gave the sixtysomething artist an approving look as they all left together. "Jeffrey, you're what I call a Renaissance man."

The moment the door closed behind her three customers and we were alone, Char turned to me and said, "Now what was going on with you and Sophie in the bathroom?"

"Sorry, I can't tell you." I stuck out my lower lip in a pretend pout. "I promised Sophie. It's not a big deal, though; trust me, it has nothing whatsoever to do with Lester." Although I wouldn't share what Sophie had told me in confidence, I did think it would be a good idea for her to tell Brady what she'd told me so the sheriff would have a complete picture of what had transpired that night in the park—at least as far as Sophie knew. I made a mental note to text her later to suggest that.

I filled Char in on what I'd learned earlier from Amy Lewis and Colleen Murphy. When I told her how I'd asked Colleen point-blank if she'd been having an affair with Lester, Char burst out laughing too, the same way the yarn shop owner had.

"Les Morris and Colleen Murphy? You've gotta be kidding me. Why would a smart, attractive woman like Colleen have anything to do with Lester?"

"I don't know," I said, with a trace of annoyance. "I don't know Colleen. Apart from saying hi when we pass each other on the street, this is the first time we've ever really talked. I'm simply trying to cover all the bases to try and figure out if maybe Lester was messing around with someone in the bushes the night he was killed, and if he was, who that someone might have been. Whoever it was could very likely be his murderer."

"I know. But Colleen? She's not desperate. She could have any guy she wants."

"Right. I realize that now," I said. "And I suppose the rustling Sophie heard the night Les was murdered could have been the killer lying in wait."

"Ya think?" Char lifted a box of books from behind the counter and headed over to the self-help section, motioning for me to follow. "Help me shelve these while we talk." She set the box on the ground and lifted a few paperbacks out. I grabbed some other titles and inserted them alphabetically on the shelves.

"I actually like Colleen," Char said, "even if she does flaunt her boobs a bit much for my taste. She's cool and she's doing a good job at the yarn shop."

"Really? I didn't know yarn was that popular, especially in a small town like ours."

"That's because your head is only full of books and baking, writer girl. Textiles and fabrics have never been your thing"—Char sent me a mischievous glance—"ever since your traumatic experience in our Family and Consumer Sciences class, aka Home Economics."

"And rightly so," I said. "The sound of Sharon's screams as I stitched her finger to the blanket we were making for the homeless is something I'll never forget."

Char chortled. "Blondie could easily tie with Jamie Lee Curtis for best scream queen."

"There's a reason I haven't gone near a sewing machine since."

"There's no machines in knitting—only a pair of needles," Char said. "Knitting is really therapeutic and a great stress reliever. Lots of people knit."

"Apparently so, if Colleen's Twisted Yarns is doing so well." But I was tired of talking about knitting. "So is Colleen divorced, or what?"

Char shook her head. "Nope. She's never been married, but she's had a few longtime relationships. Her last one was with some guy in Michigan. They had a candle shop together in"—she paused and scrunched up her face the way she does when she's trying to remember something—"Ann Arbor, maybe? When they broke up, she went online looking for business opportunities in nearby states. Colleen said she's loved knitting all her life, so when she saw that Lila Hetland was selling her yarn shop in Lake Potawatomi, she came here to check it out and bought the shop on the spot, including all of Lila's stock."

"Yeah, I kind of remember hearing something about that at the time but didn't pay a lot of attention."

"That's because you're the bookish baker girl, not the knitting girl."

"Okay, okay," I said. "You made your point. Is there anyone else in the chamber Les might have been having a fling with? Colleen gave me the names of all the female members, and I wondered if you might have seen anything suspicious with Lester and any of the women at one of the chamber meetings or get-togethers."

Char stopped shelving books for a moment to consider. "No, not really. Lester was always saying stupid things to women, but nobody paid him any mind—probably because they're all mostly older, from the generation that thinks 'boys will be boys.' " She made a moue of distaste. "He knew better than to mess with me and Sharon."

"Okay, then what about anyone Lester might have gotten in a fight with or had problems with on the chamber?"

"He and Stephen got into it a few times."

"Stephen?" I tilted my head. "Stephen who?"

"Stephen Morris," Char said, slowly enunciating her words. "You know? Lester and Patsy's son? The fruit of their loins? The love of Patsy's life?"

I stuck out my tongue at my snarky friend. "I didn't know Stephen was a member of the chamber as well. Is he still in the insurance business?" I shelved some Marie Kondo. "He handled my dad's life insurance policy." Then I realized what I'd said. I turned to stare at Char, still clutching a copy of *The Life-Changing Magic of Tidying Up*. "Oh. My. God. I hadn't even thought about life insurance. Do you think Stephen sold his father a policy?"

"Probably," Char said, intent on transferring books to the shelves. "The Morrises tend to keep things in the family. That's why Les was miffed all those years ago when Stephen quit the accounting firm he started to go off on his own and sell insurance."

I leaned against the shelf. "Do you realize what this might mean? I wish I could find out who the beneficiary of Lester's policy is."

"Probably Patsy and Stephen. They're Lester's only living relatives."

Just like in my family. I never knew my mother's parents—they died when I was a baby—or Mom's only sibling, her older brother Carl, who lived in Phoenix and passed away years ago. On my dad's side, his father, Henry, died when Dad was a teenager, leaving his wife, my Grandma Florence, a widow at thirty-nine with a thirteen-year-old son to raise. After my parents got married and had me, my grandma watched me after school while my folks worked. Grandma Florence is the one who taught me to bake at an early age. As her only grandchild, I had a close, special relationship with her. She always told me I could be whatever I wanted to be: writer, baker, president of the United States. Sadly, Grandma Florence died of breast cancer two months after I graduated from college. I'm forever grateful that she lived long enough to see me graduate.

I'm also grateful that my dad lived long enough to see my first book published. When he died at seventy of a sudden heart attack three and a half years ago, his life insurance went to Mom and me in a seventy/thirty split. Dad's policy wasn't huge, but coupled with his pension, it would keep Mom comfortable for the rest of her life. My portion enabled me to pay off my mortgage and sock a small amount away in savings. Dad had always told us he would make sure "his girls" were taken care of, and he had. I blinked back sudden tears.

"You okay?" Char asked.

"Yeah. Thinking of my dad. I miss him."

"I know you do." She squeezed my shoulder. "Your dad was one of the good ones. You two had a great relationship."

"Unlike Stephen and his father." I glanced at my bestie. "I wonder how big a life insurance policy Lester had," I mused. "If it's a huge one, that would be a great motive for murder."

"You betcha," she said, using the common Midwest vernacular handed down through our Scandinavian and Germanic generations. "Didn't you tell me back when you first started writing your cozies and researching reasons for murder that the three most common motives are money, passion, and revenge?"

"Yeah, although recently that seems to have changed. Money and passion are still two of the top three, but the pursuit of power seems to have overtaken revenge."

"Hmm," Char said, reflectively. "If you take money and add it to the pursuit of power, Stephen definitely bears looking into. He's been treasurer at the chamber the past couple years and has been making less-than-subtle noises for a while now that we need new leadership at the top—someone a bit more evolved and not stuck in the sixties." She picked up the now-empty box and returned to the counter. "Tell you what, I'll talk to Stevie-boy and see what I can discreetly find out about the insurance and whatever other tidbits he might drop about his dad."

"Great! With you talking to Stephen Morris and Astrid talking to Les's fishing buddies tonight, we'll soon have a much more comprehensive picture of Lester and his life, including who or what he's been involved with."

She quirked an eyebrow. "Astrid Nilsen?"

Oops. Now, I'm in for it. Thinking fast, I grabbed the last bag of sinkers from my basket and tossed it to her. "Look, I brought you a treat. Cookies."

Char began to pant. "You sure know the way to your best friend's heart." She ripped open the bag and wolfed down a cookie. "Yum." Then she scarfed down another one. "Now what's all this about Astrid?"

I took a deep breath and told my partner in crime about Astrid Nilsen wanting to play Jessica Fletcher and help solve Les's murder.

"Actually, I think that's a good idea," Char surprised me by saying. "Astrid can hold her liquor and not have a headache the next morning like you and I would. She's no lightweight.

I'll bet she'll get those old guys to give it up about Les and his dirty deeds before the night is over." Char munched on another cookie and fastened her eyes on mine. "I don't mind Astrid Nilsen playing Jessica Fletcher, but if she dares step on my Miss Marple toes, all bets are off. You hear what I'm sayin'?"

"Loud and clear."

Chapter Twelve

That night Mom was out late again. Most likely with her mystery man. I tried waiting up so I could ever-so-nonchalantly quiz her about her evening, but at eleven thirty when I kept nodding off to Jean and Lionel in my favorite Britcom, *As Time Goes By*, I finally gave up and went to bed.

I awakened out of a deep sleep to Gracie's furious barking and the doorbell ringing. I looked at my phone: eleven fifty-five. Who in the world could it be at this hour? Gracie shot past me while I was still pulling on my robe and raced down the hall toward the living room, barking the entire way.

"Okay, Gracie-girl, I'm coming. Shh." I hurried after my canine daughter. When I reached the front door and looked through the peephole, there stood Astrid Nilsen on my porch. An unsteady Astrid wearing the same outfit I'd seen her in this morning. As my grandma's elderly friend leaned forward to ring the doorbell again, she staggered.

I yanked the door open. "Astrid, what's going on?"

She straightened up, gave me a loopy grin, and saluted. "Jessica Fletcher, reporting for duty, ma'am!" she said in a stage whisper. Then she staggered again and nearly fell.

I grabbed hold of her and led her into the living room, where she sank down heavily onto the shabby-chic couch cushions. Gracie jumped up beside her, tail wagging madly, and licked the wildlife artist's hand.

Hey, you done with my picture yet? Can I see it, can I see it?

In addition to painting animals in the wild, Astrid paints the occasional pet picture—"for friends only." Years ago, after my beloved spaniel mix Atticus died, Astrid showed up at my house to present me with a watercolor of my first dog, happy and frolicking in the park. It now hangs in my bedroom, where I get to see Atticus every morning when I wake up. A couple months ago, on Gracie's birthday, I commissioned Astrid to do a similar painting of my frisky Eskie as well.

"Hello, beauty!" Astrid said, nuzzling Gracie's neck. "Sorry I forgot your picture, but it's all ready and waitin' for your mom to pick up."

Gracie gave a happy yip.

I sat down on the other side of my dog and ruffled her fur. "Astrid," I said gently, gazing across the back of the American Eskimo between us into my friend's faded blue eyes, "I know you didn't come here at this time of night to tell me about Gracie's picture. Is everything okay?"

"Yah, is better than okay," she said, her Norwegian accent increasing with every boozy breath she expelled. "I come right over after Lester's buddies finally left Larsen's to give you da scoop." She shook her white head. "*Uff da*! Those guys kept poundin' back brewskis, but I matched 'em drink for drink with my brandy old-fashioneds," she said proudly. "I really got 'em nice and shnockered."

Only them? "Have you been at Larsen's all night?"

"Yah, sure. I had to loosen their tongues, didn't I?"

"Did you eat anything?"

"Oh, yah. I had some peanuts an' a li'l beef jerky." Astrid's stomach growled.

I stood up. "You stay here with Gracie and relax. I'll be back in a minute with something to eat."

"*Mange takk*."

Grandma Florence had taught me the Norwegian for "thank you" when I was young, along with a few other common Norwegian expressions, like *uff da* and *god morgen*. "*Tula*," she explained to me, "iss gute to know the language of your ancestors." Grandma, whose mother was Norwegian and her father Danish, often flip-flopped between *Tula* and *Yenta Mi* when addressing me, both of which mean "little girl" in Norwegian and Danish, respectively.

I made my late-night Norwegian visitor a turkey sandwich and a cup of Lady Grey decaf tea and hurried back to the living room, hoping Astrid hadn't passed out in my absence. I needn't have worried. The elderly artist was stroking my dog's tummy and cooing sweet nothings to her.

"Yah, Gracie, you such a pretty girl. Your mama needs to bring you camping again with me. You can chase da rats and mice."

I repressed a shudder. A couple summers ago Gracie and I had gone up north camping with Astrid in a primitive but gorgeous lakeside wilderness area teeming with wildlife. Astrid and I fished together in the mornings, and in the afternoons I wrote on my yellow-lined notepad and she sketched the myriad animals. We were having a great time until two rats ran through our campsite and Gracie chased after them into the underbrush. The sound of frenzied thrashing ensued, and then my sweet Eskie emerged, victorious, with one of the biggest, ugliest rats I've ever seen in her mouth.

"Drop it, Gracie, drop it," I screamed, shaking.

How come? Aren't you proud of me for catching it?

I trembled and backed away. Gracie finally dropped the dead rat and trotted over to me. She tilted her head and gazed up at me with her dark, expressive eyes.

What's wrong, Mom?

"It's okay, Gracie." I attempted a soothing tone while trying to calm my uncontrollable shaking. "Mommy just hates rats." *Mommy has a rat phobia.*

Astrid strode over to dispose of the dead rodent. Only it wasn't dead. The dirty rat limped away into the underbrush.

We haven't been camping since.

I returned my attention to my grandma's friend, who had wolfed down her sandwich and was now drinking her Lady Grey. "So, how did it go at Larsen's?"

"Great!" Her eyes lit up. "I got 'em all to talking and found out plenty." She set her mug down on the coffee table. "Did you know Bud and Joanie Olson separated a coupla years ago?"

"Really? I never heard that he moved out."

"He didn't. Bud let it slip that he slept on a cot in the back of the hardware store for six months, till they patched things up."

"Did it have anything to do with Les?" I asked, leaning forward in anticipation. "Was Joanie involved with him?"

"Nah. Joanie and Bud were just scrappin' about Bud's spending habits. He kept ordering stuff off QVC and running up their credit cards, but as he said tonight, 'the wife' soon put a stop to that." Astrid got a gleeful gleam in her eye. "But speakin' a money, the boys mentioned there'd been some *irregularities* in the chamber's budget lately—includin' the petty cash fund not addin' up. Steve and Les Morris got into it a few times over the money issues." A satisfied smirk lifted the corners of her mouth. "Stephen is the treasurer of the chamber of commerce, ya know."

Now we're finally getting somewhere. "So, did Stephen catch Lester skimming money from the chamber?"

"Not Lester," she said smugly. "Stephen."

"You're kidding. What happened?"

"Les accused Stephen of embezzlement," she said. "I guess since Stephen became treasurer a coupla years ago, he's been putting everything on the computer on those spreadsheet thingamabobs, and Les didn't like it. Said the system he had in place for years using the trusty office typewriter worked fine. Told his son there were no money problems until he went and started computerizing everything."

It looked like the tea and sandwich were helping to ease the effects of the brandy old-fashioneds—Wisconsin's unofficial state drink—Astrid had consumed. Her Norwegian accent was no longer as pronounced, and she seemed more like her usual stalwart self again.

Astrid continued. "Then a coupla weeks ago, Jerry and Bud overheard Les and Stephen going at it tooth and nail back in

Lester's office when they were comin' out of the men's room. Stephen called Les a dinosaur who needed to retire and let someone younger move the chamber into the twenty-first century. Lester yelled, 'Like you? You've been gunning for my job awhile now, boy. The only way you'll become president is over my dead body,' " she recounted with relish. "Accordin' to Jerry, Stephen said, 'Okay, boomer.' " Astrid sent me a puzzled look. "I'm not sure what he meant by that, since Lester's not a baby boomer—he's from my generation—the silent one. Not that I'm silent," she cackled, " 'cept when I'm fishin'."

I explained that "Okay, boomer," is a sarcastic phrase younger people—mainly millennials (although Stephen's a Gen Xer like me)—use to indicate that someone older than them (true baby boomer or not) is stuck in the past, unwilling to adapt and embrace the world as it is now with its changing cultural and social norms and technological advancements.

Astrid's face cleared. "Guess you could say that about me, then. I'm terrible with technology. Heck, I don't even own a computer."

"Sometimes I wish I didn't," I murmured, thinking of how easy it was for me to fall down the Facebook rabbit hole.

The wannabe Jessica Fletcher plowed on. "From what Bud and Jerry said, it kinda sounds like our boy Stephen may have knocked off his old man, don't ya think?" she asked.

"Could be. It definitely bears further investigation." And it would be a good idea if I put a bug in Brady's ear about Stephen's possible embezzlement of chamber funds. Talk about motive. Although not a slam dunk. "Did you learn anything about Les and any possible romantic involvements?" I asked.

"Yah." Astrid's lined face split in a wide grin. She raised a vigorous thumbs-up. "Sven said Les used to see a lady in Kenosha. Sven and Cindy ran into the two of them in the bar of a bowling alley when their morticians' bowling league, the Dead Pins Society, was playing in a tournament there. Les tried to play it off like the woman was a business client, but they knew he was up to something."

Although I was glad to hear we might have at last found Lester's inamorata, I couldn't repress a giggle at the thought of a morticians' bowling league. *They're probably all dying for a strike*, I thought. *I wonder if they go bowling for bodies together. They could set 'em up and knock 'em down.*

Spare me, gutter girl.

Why? Am I bowling you over? my inner punster countered.

I got off the pun train and returned my attention to Astrid. "Do we have a name for this Kenosha woman?" I asked.

"Nope, but that don't make no nevermind. Les told his chamber buddies he broke it off last year 'cause his bowling alley babe was gettin' too clingy." Astrid smirked. "But big-mouth Bud babbled that Lester got himself a new squeeze recently. A bartender who's also an exotic dancer."

"An exotic dancer? Did you get her name?" I asked. "Maybe we can go pay her a visit and ask her some questions."

Or give Brady her name and let him do the questioning, my inner law-and-order self suggested.

"Jerry said her name is Angel. She's from somewhere out past Racine. He was startin' to share more details when old Fred Matson came sniffin' round me again and interrupted. I didn't hear the rest of what Jerry was sayin'."

"Fred Matson?"

"Yah." Astrid puffed out a sigh. "He and I used to go together years ago. Fred keeps tryin' to resurrect our relationship, but I'm not interested. I've told him the past is the past and he needs to move on—that dog don't hunt. But he can't take a hint."

I stared at her. "You and Fred used to see each other?" I asked, unable to wrap my head around this startling new information. "When was this?"

She waved her hand in a dismissive motion. "Years ago." Astrid squinted, trying to recall. "Close to forty years ago now, I think. You were just a little bitty thing when we lived together."

"You *lived* with Fred?" I wondered if I looked as dumbfounded as I felt.

"Yep." Astrid chuckled. "In *sin*." She waggled her eyebrows at me. "Fred kept his shoes and his fishing tackle under my bed for over a decade."

I tried to process this revelation. I'd never have put Astrid and Fred together as a couple. Talk about strange bedfellows. Goes to show you that everyone's got their secrets. "If you and Fred lived together that many years," I said gently, "you must have been in love."

Astrid's face softened. "Yah, sure. But that was a long time ago. Another lifetime."

"What happened?"

"He wanted to get married and I didn't. Simple as that," she said matter-of-factly. "I told Fred I'd already been married once and it hadn't turned out well and I didn't plan on makin' the same mistake again." Astrid sighed. "I told him that when we first got together, and again when he moved in. I couldn't have made it any plainer." She scratched Gracie behind the ears. "And Fred said, 'Fine, darlin', as long as we're livin' in the same house together, that's all that matters." Astrid looked off in the distance, remembering. "And for the first seven or eight years, it was all that mattered. Things were goin' great, but then a couple years later, Fred started pesterin' me about wantin' to make it legal." She shrugged. "And that was never gonna happen. So, after goin' round and round about it for a few months and having a coupla knock-down, drag-out fights, I told him it was best that he moved out and we both move on."

She gave herself a brisk shake. "But that's ancient history, honey. We need to focus on the here and now, and that means finding Lester's killer. Tell you what, I can go back to Larsen's tomorrow and get the rest of this Angel's particulars so you and I can pay her a visit and grill her to find out if she's the killer."

Do I really want Astrid going with me to confront Lester's girlfriend, though? This was a situation that called for finesse, tact, and diplomacy—qualities the blunt, plainspoken Astrid lacked. In this instance, Char would make a much better wingman. But how to tell Astrid that without hurting her feelings? *Maybe I can put her off for a while.*

"Finding Angel's details from Jerry would be great," I said, "but let's hold off on confronting her for the moment. We still need you to use your babysitter connection with Stephen to talk to him, remember? That's even more important now that you found out about the money problems at the chamber and Lester and Stephen's recent fight."

"Yah, you're right. I forgot." Astrid sighed and leaned back against the couch, eyelids drooping. "Sorry, honey, I am plumb tuckered out. I haven't had that much to drink in a while, and I swear I could fall asleep right here on this couch. Could I bother you for a ride home?"

"Why don't you spend the night? You can stay in the guest room."

"Oh no, I couldn't do that. I gotta get home to my animals. They'll be missin' me," Astrid said, " 'specially since I just got back. My neighbor took care of 'em while I was gone, but it always takes 'em a coupla days to get back to normal and stop bein' mad at me for leavin' 'em. They need all my TLC right now."

I glanced at Gracie, who gave me her *I adore you, Mom* look. "I understand completely."

Astrid's house is a zoo. The longtime animal lover and wildlife artist has a menagerie of four or five dogs, three birds, too many cats to count, chickens, bunnies, turtles, a couple guinea pigs, and an aquarium full of tropical fish. She's forever taking in strays and can't turn away any animal in need—a fact that doesn't endear her to some of her neighbors, especially when the animals escape from her yard.

I fixed Astrid a goody bag of the rest of a quiche lorraine, a couple cinnamon rolls, and the last two pieces of my cherry pie left over from the contest that wasn't. Then I drove her home to her rustic cabin-style house on the outskirts of town and made sure she was safely settled in. I promised her I'd stop by the studio tomorrow to collect my painting of Gracie, and then I headed home.

By the time I tumbled into bed, it was nearly two o'clock in the morning. "Gracie, sweetheart," I said with a huge yawn, "you need to let Mommy sleep in tomorrow."

Chapter Thirteen

"God Save the Queen" blared in my bedroom the next morning, startling me from a sound sleep. Gracie released a happy woof at Tavish's ring tone.

I fumbled for the phone on my nightstand. "Hello?"

"I can't leave you alone for two minutes, can I?" Tavish teased in his plummy English accent.

"Why, whatever can you mean?" I adopted my own—bad—English accent in an effort to hide from Tavish that he'd woken me up.

"You should probably stick with your Wisconsin voice."

"Yah, you betcha."

Tavish chuckled. "I hope I'm not ringing too early," he said. "I know you usually start writing between seven and seven thirty, and I didn't want to disturb you once you were in the zone."

"In the zone?" I snickered. "You should probably stick with your English expressions."

"Right, then. What the bloody hell is going on there, anyway? You found another dead body?"

"That I did. I'm thinking of starting up a new company—Bodies 'R Us," I teased.

"Sorry?"

"Never mind. It's an Americanism that doesn't translate well."

"My darling girl, I'm so sorry you're having to go through this again," Tavish said. "My only consolation is that this time I'm not the cause of it. Sharon texted that you discovered the dead judge inside the baking tent. Thankfully, it wasn't Paul Hollywood," he said dryly. "That would cause an international incident." He paused, and I knew he was taking a sip of his tea. Tavish loves his tea—Yorkshire Gold with milk and one sugar. "I believe Sharon said your dead judge's name was Lester?"

I sighed. "Yes. Lester Morris. Lester-the-molester we nicknamed him in high school." I gave Tavish an abbreviated description of the town lecher and told him how Lester's distraught widow blamed me for his murder.

"You must be joking."

"I wish I was." I told him about my run-in with Les on the first day of the contest and how the distinctive rolling pin I'd smacked him with was discovered on the ground beside the dead judge covered in his blood.

"It sounds like someone's trying to frame you," Tavish said. "I do hope Brady realizes that."

"I hope so too, but as you well know from past experience, he has to be objective and investigate all possibilities."

"Right. And I imagine you're investigating some of those possibilities as well?" he teased. "My gorgeous Miss Marple."

"Jane Tennison," I corrected him. "Char's Miss Marple." I filled Tavish in on our plan to learn more about Lester and his possible paramour as well as his son, his finances, and who the beneficiaries of his life insurance policy were. "But enough about me and Lake Potawatomi's latest murder," I said. "How's the new book coming along?"

"It's a bit slow going at the moment, but I'm plugging along and quite enjoying the change, actually."

Tavish had written several action-packed suspense novels in a *New York Times* best-selling series, each featuring the word *blood* in the title, including his latest, *Her Blood Weeps*. His legions of fans loved these novels and couldn't wait for the next one in the series to come out—often urging him to write more than one book a year so they didn't have to wait so long between them. Tavish always demurred, saying he needed a full year to do the research, plotting and outlining, and actual writing. Currently, however, after initially receiving pushback from both his agent and his publisher, who didn't want Tavish to mess with his popular "brand" and confuse his readers, he was writing a more measured, stand-alone psychological suspense novel with a female heroine as the lead.

When Tavish first told me he had an idea that had been nagging at him for some time—a book completely unlike those he'd written so far, but one he couldn't get out of his mind—I'd encouraged him to break out of his usual genre and the narrow, albeit wildly successful, box his agent and publisher had placed him in. "You need to write what's in your heart," I urged him. "You need to write your passion—the story that won't leave you alone until you get it down on paper." This encouragement had not endeared me to Tavish's publisher or his agent, but once their best-selling celebrity author agreed to write his new stand-alone novel under a pseudonym and still continue with the next title in the Blood suspense series, they were mollified. That meant, however, that Tavish had two books to write in a year rather than his usual one, which was why he was hunkered down at home in England for the duration.

After discussing our mutual writing projects, we chatted for a while about friends and family and my upcoming visit to the UK. In less than two months—only six more weeks!—I would be winging my way to England to reunite with Tavish and spend a month in the Cotswolds researching my next book, *Deadly Tea and Scones.*

I. Can't. Wait. As a rabid anglophile who adores Jane Austen, James Herriot, and all things English, I'd visited the UK once before on vacation, after recovering from surgery and chemotherapy. That's when I fell head over heels for Great Britain. The scenery. The history. The small towns and villages with thatched-roof cottages and ancient stone churches. Fish and chips. Tea and scones. And those accents. Oh my, those accents. And soon I'd be hearing my favorite English accent in person again from my favorite Brit.

"You will be careful, won't you, darling?" I heard Tavish say. "I don't want anything happening to my girl."

The first time Tavish called me darling, I was taken aback. *Darling* harkened back to old black-and-white movies from the thirties and forties I'd watched with my dad, or Mrs. Howell on that old TV show *Gilligan's Island*. No one says *darling* in

America anymore. Apparently, though, it's a popular expression in England today.

My heart swelled at hearing Tavish say *darling* and *my girl.* It had been a long time since any man—besides my dad—spoke such sweet terms of endearment to me. Here's the thing: I've never dated much. As a tall Amazon type, I tower over most men. I also tell it like it is and don't play the flirty dating games. Not my style. I'd rather play Scrabble. Besides, the single-men pickings are slim in Lake Potawatomi, particularly for women over forty. Add in my flat, breastless state, and men walk on by.

Until Tavish.

"I'll be careful," I promised my dreamy English boyfriend. "I don't want anything happening to me either. I'm really looking forward to meeting your family and to your introducing me to the Cotswolds. I long to return to . . . *this blessed plot, this earth, this realm, this England . . .*"

"You know the way to this Englishman's heart," Tavish said. "That's one of my favorite Shakespearean quotes. That and Henry the Fifth's rousing Saint Crispin's Day speech: *This story shall the good man teach his son; And Crispin Crispian shall ne'er go by, From this day to the ending of the world, But we in it shall be rememberèd—We few, we happy few, we band of brothers . . .*"

I swooned. *Is there anything better than an Englishman quoting Shakespeare?*

An Englishman quoting Jane Austen, my inner Janeite answered.

I stopped swooning to focus on what Tavish was saying.

"My mother and sister are both chuffed to meet you," he said. "Mum is quite pleased that I've 'finally given up blonde bimbos in favor of a woman of substance,' as she put it." He chuckled.

"Are you sure she knows how much substance she's getting?" I asked, getting out of bed in my white cotton nightgown to regard my sturdy six-foot body in the full-length mirror and thinking of my blunt, tell-it-like-it-is nature. "I can tend to overwhelm people."

"You definitely overwhelmed me," Tavish said in a husky voice. "In fact, I wish you were here right now so we could overwhelm each other," he added seductively.

I returned to bed to snuggle under the covers and exchange sweet nothings with my British beau. After several minutes of romantic back-and-forth, I said, "I hope I can live up to your mother's expectations."

"Never fear. She's going to love you."

Gracie jumped onto the bed, urging me out of it.

"Mum's looking forward to introducing you to an English tea with both cucumber and watercress sandwiches and 'proper' scones with jam and cream. 'Not those huge dreadful dry ones they have in American coffeehouses,' " he said, mimicking her. "My mother's a Cornish girl, so we grew up having our scones the right way, with jam first, topped by cream."

"Isn't that how it's always done?" I asked as I got out of bed and followed my impatient canine daughter to the kitchen.

"Oh no. In Devon, they put the cream first and then the jam."

"Barbarians," I said as Gracie scratched at the kitchen door, eager to go outside. As I was about to open the door to let her out, a flicker of movement at Mom's house caught my eye and stayed my hand. High heels clutched in one hand and her designer purse in the other, my mother swiftly tiptoed across the walkway from her car and slipped inside her mother-in-law cottage, closing the front door softly behind her.

I could hear Tavish saying something, but it didn't register. I couldn't believe what my eyes were telling me. Gracie yipped and nosed at my bare legs. *C'mon, Mom, I really gotta go.*

Dumbly I opened the door, and she shot into the backyard. My eyes flicked to the digital clock on the microwave: 6:57. The last time my mother had gotten up this early was when she took me to the Milwaukee airport for an early-morning flight. Mom had grumbled the entire time about having to get up at the crack of dawn, saying I should have booked a flight at a normal hour when most decent people were awake.

And now here she was, up at the crack of dawn. Or to be accurate, returning home at the crack of dawn after being out all night. All. Night. Which meant, if her stealthy return was anything to go by, that my mother—a faithful, devoted wife to my father for fifty years—had spent the night with someone. A man. Had to be. If she'd stayed over at one of her girlfriends', after drinking too much wine and not wanting to drive home—an unlikely event that had happened exactly once in her life a month after my dad died—she would have called me so as not to worry me. She also wouldn't have sneaked into the house upon her return home.

Tavish's voice came over the phone. "Teddie, are you there? Are you all right, darling?"

"I'm here," I said on autopilot as I tried to process what I'd seen.

"You sound a bit off. Did something happen?"

"No. I mean yes." In a daze, I continued staring at my mother's front door. "Actually, Tavish, something unexpected has come up that I need to deal with. I have to go. Sorry."

Very unexpected, I thought as I hung up the phone. *How am I supposed to handle this situation?* I was tempted to storm over to my mother's house right now and confront her. I imagined myself saying, "And where have you been all night, young lady?" in a tone of righteous indignation when she answered the door. Knowing my mom, however, that would be the absolute wrong tack to take. She'd tell me off again and say it was none of my business.

Maybe I can go over and knock on the door and when she answers—likely in her robe and nightgown, feigning sleep—say that I woke up after hearing a car pull in at the crack of dawn and I came over to make sure everything was okay. "You're not sick or anything, are you, Mom?" I'd ask, showing concern.

I *was* concerned. Concerned about my mother's love life and more determined than ever to discover the identity of her mystery man.

Gracie scampered back into the kitchen. *I'm ready for breakfast now, Mom.*

Absently, I reached into her treats jar and pulled out her morning peanut-butter biscuit and marrow bone as I continued to ponder the best course of action to take. *Maybe coffee would help.* I pulled out my French roast from the canister on my tiled counter top and poured some into the coffee grinder.

As the beans were grinding, all at once Gracie began a frantic barking. I turned off the grinder and heard a car door slam, followed by running feet and a pounding at my back door. Gracie barked even louder and stared intently at the door, nose quivering. Above the barking I heard a familiar voice yell.

"Teddie, you okay?"

I yanked open the back door to discover my best friend, wearing a sleep shirt and slippers and carrying a bat. I pulled her inside. "Shh, you'll wake the whole neighborhood."

Char's long red hair was sticking up all over in a serious case of bedhead above her Ruth Bader Ginsburg sleep shirt, which proclaimed, *Never underestimate the power of a girl with a book.* She looked around wildly, clutching the bat in a death grip. "Is someone in the house?" she asked in a stage whisper.

"No." I stared at her. "Just you, me, and Gracie. What's going on? What are you doing here?"

"Tavish called me all freaked out and said something was wrong. He said you two were talking and all of a sudden you started acting strange, told him something unexpected had come up and had to hang up," she said. "Since there's an unknown killer on the loose again, Tavish was afraid the mystery killer might have somehow gotten in your house."

"Are you kidding me? That's crazy."

Char lowered the bat and sank down on a kitchen chair, bleary-eyed. "No, that's love, my friend."

Love? But we haven't said the L-word yet. Could it be true? Does Tavish really love me?

My best friend, who lives down the street from me, interrupted my romantic wondering. "So, what was the unexpected thing that made you hang up on your gorgeous English author so abruptly and freak the poor guy out?"

I told her about my mother's staying out all night and sneaking into her house, heels in hand, thinking no one had seen her. "*I* saw her, though, and Mrs. Claire St. John has got some 'splainin' to do, I can tell you that," I said. "But I need to figure out the best way to broach the subject."

Char gave a thumbs-up. "Good for Claire. There's life in the old girl yet."

I frowned at my friend. "You're supposed to be on my side."

Gracie barked again as the back door opened and that "old girl," looking anything but old, entered the kitchen in her icy-blue kimono and satin slippers, stifling a yawn. "Teddie, what is all the ruckus about so early in the morning? It woke me up." Mom yawned again.

Did it? Really? Is that how you're going to play it? Continue lying to your daughter? Well, we'll see about that. I started to respond, but my best friend, seeing my face, cut me off.

"Sorry, Claire," Char said. "It's my fault. Brady and I had a terrible fight this morning, and I needed to see Teddie right away to talk about it."

My mother glanced at the baseball bat Char was holding between her bare legs. Her eyes—still sporting her nighttime mascara, I noticed—widened. "Charlotte Jorgensen! Don't tell me you hit Brady with that bat!"

"Oh no, I—"

The back door flung open, cutting Char off in midsentence, and Brady barreled through in his sheriff's uniform, shirt untucked and metal baton in hand. "Everything okay here?" His law-enforcement eyes scanned the room, checking every inch of space. "I got a ca—"

Char leapt up, dropping the baseball bat in the process, and launched herself at Brady. She flung her arms about his neck and locked her long, slim legs around his waist. "I'm so sorry we fought, babe, and that I said those awful things. Can you forgive me?" She grabbed her bewildered boyfriend and gave him a long, lingering kiss.

My mother's collagen-enhanced lips curved in a satisfied smile. "Well, I think I'll leave them to it and go back to bed now." She aimed a reproachful eye at me. "*With* my earplugs in to block out all the noise. I realize you're a morning person, Theodora," she said, "but not everyone shares your early-bird proclivities." Mom slipped past the passionate couple, who were still lip-locked, completely oblivious to everything else. She shut the door quietly behind her, the same as she'd done at her own house not ten minutes ago.

I stared after her, shaking my head. My mother never ceases to amaze me. Claire St. John has an uncanny ability to deflect attention from her misdeeds to focus on mine and paint me the culprit, even when she's clearly in the wrong. She'd been doing it my whole life. And I wasn't going to take it anymore. First things first, though.

"Okay, you two," I said to Char and Brady, "you can come up for air now. She's gone." No response. "Oh my gosh, get a room, would you?" Still nothing. I picked up the fallen bat and thumped it on the floor with a loud whack.

My friends sprang apart, Brady clutching his law-and-order baton, poised to strike.

"At ease, Sheriff," I said. "The danger has passed."

Apparently the word had not made it out to peripheral parties yet, however, as Augie chose that moment to crash through the back door, his cop baton extended in a tight grip. "I got your back, Brady," he yelled.

I raised my hands in a stop motion. "Stand down, Deputy," I told my best friend's younger brother. "It was all a misunderstanding. Everything's okay." I moved to the counter top and grabbed three mugs. "Anyone want some coffee?"

Augie had obviously dressed in a hurry, as his uniform shirt was unbuttoned, revealing a Spider-Man T-shirt underneath. Seeing Spidey reminded me . . . I glanced down and noticed my own state of undress—still in my transparent white cotton nightgown, with nothing underneath. "Excuse me," I said. "Be right back." I raced to my bedroom, swiftly pulled on a pair of panties, and exchanged my see-through white nightgown for a colorful cotton caftan. Then I ducked into the bathroom and brushed my teeth—nothing worse than stale morning breath.

When I returned to the kitchen, my would-be rescuers were seated around the table with its crazy-quilt tablecloth, Char discreetly filling her two lawmen in on the mix-up, being deliberately vague so as not to reveal my mother's sleepover with her mystery man. I pulled on my Jane Austen apron with its *Pride and Prejudice* quote: *Do not consider me now as an elegant female intending to plague you, but as a rational creature speaking the truth from her heart.* As I poured coffee, a light knock sounded at the still-open back door.

"Everything okay?" a tentative Sophie Miller asked. My young neighbor was wearing a Minnie Mouse T-shirt and cotton sleep pants, her blonde hair mussed from sleep. "Gram and I heard a lot of noise and saw all the cars in the driveway, including the sheriff's, and we wanted to make sure Teddie was all right."

"I'm fine, Sophie," I said. "I'm sorry to have caused such a commotion and worried you and Margaret. It was all a big misunderstanding." I raised the coffeepot. "Why don't you come in and have some coffee? In fact, why don't I make breakfast for everyone?"

"That's okay," Sophie said, her eyes zeroing in on Augie and his Spider-Man T-shirt. She blushed. "I don't want to interrupt."

"You're not interrupting anything. Really," I said. "It's the least I can do. Please go get your grandmother and come for breakfast. Tell Margaret I'm making my killer scrambled eggs especially for her."

Sophie blushed again. "Okay, thanks." She tucked her silky blonde hair behind her ears. "We'll be over in a few minutes."

Char cast a mischievous glance at her baby brother, whose longing eyes were locked on the back of my departing, diminutive neighbor. She reached up her hand to smooth down her still-sticking-up red hair. "I wish I looked that good in the morning," she said. "Even with bedhead, Sophie still looks adorable, don't you think, Augs?"

His face flushed. "Sophie always looks good."

Char scraped back her chair and stood up, her sleep shirt skimming her thighs. "Teddie, mind if I use your hairbrush and borrow something to wear? I don't want to offend Margaret's delicate sensibilities with my scantily clad self."

"As I recall, Margaret is a huge RBG fan," I said. "She'd love your shirt, but you're right—it does barely cover your butt." I waved my hand toward my bedroom at the end of the hall. "Be my guest. You know where everything is."

As Char left to make herself presentable, I pulled sausage, eggs, cheese, cream cheese, and green onions from the fridge. I dumped the sausage links in the frying pan and turned the burner on low. As I sliced the green onions, I said casually over my shoulder to Brady, "Any new leads yet on who might have whacked Lester, or am I still the prime suspect?"

He sighed. "Ted, you know I can't tell you that."

"Aw, c'mon. Can't you even give me a little hint?" I started whisking the eggs. "Have you talked to Stephen Morris yet? I think he's a pretty likely candidate. Does he have an alibi for the night his father was killed?"

"As a matter of fact, he does. Stephen was over at his folks' house knitting baby blankets with Patsy for First Baptist Church's fall blanket drive for the hospital," Brady said.

"Stephen Morris knits?" I could hear the incredulity in my voice.

Sexist much?

"I know, right?" Brady said, sending me a bemused smile. "Who'd have thought?"

"Knitting's dope," Augie piped up. "I knit. It's relaxing. You should try it sometime."

"Augie, you're a man of many talents," the sheriff said.

His deputy's face reddened. "Colleen at the yarn shop had a class last year, so since I didn't have anything going on Thursday nights, I took it and learned to knit."

Brady shot him a curious look. "Were you the only guy in the class?"

"Nope. There were three of us: Sven Torkilsen, Stephen Morris, and me. Stephen's really good. He made a cool Doctor Who scarf."

Char returned, her hair pulled back in its usual ponytail, wearing one of my boho cotton dresses that was way too long on her. She'd cinched it with a belt so it didn't drag on the floor. "What'd I miss?" she asked, reclaiming her seat next to Brady.

I telegraphed her a discreet warning look, hoping she wouldn't mention our sleuthing plans to her boyfriend. "I was asking Brady about Stephen Morris as a possible suspect in his father's murder, but apparently he was home knitting with his mother the night Lester was killed."

"Is that right?" she said. "Augie knits too. We knit all the time at home, don't we, Augs?" Char gave her baby brother an affectionate punch on the arm.

"Yup. If you need a winter hat, scarf, or mittens, come over to the Jorgensens' and we'll fix you right up," Augie said. He sent me a broad wink. "It'll cost you, though."

Char turned her attention to Brady. "Was Lester at home during this Morris knitting marathon?"

"No. Patsy and Stephen said he was in Racine at a meeting of chamber presidents. They didn't expect him back until much later that night. Little did they know," he added sotto voce.

Except maybe Stephen did know, I thought. He could easily have slipped over to the park after his mom went to bed and killed dear old dad.

Nah. My money's on Angel, my inner self argued. *She's from somewhere in the Racine vicinity, remember? Les probably didn't even have a meeting. Or if he did, he might have slipped out early to meet his new girlfriend.*

I made a mental note to tell Brady about the mysterious Angel later. I cut the cream cheese into pinto-bean-sized pieces and added them to the eggs. "Does Stephen live at home with his parents?"

"No," Char said. "He's got a little house over on Durand. A fixer-upper he's been renovating."

Brady glanced at his girlfriend. "And you know this how?"

"Because the guy buys home-improvement books and magazines from the bookstore, and we got to talking about it," she said. "We were both big fans of *Fixer Upper*. Stephen loves shiplap."

Brady's eyes glazed over. He turned to me as I poured the egg mixture into the frying pan. "Ted, aren't you forgetting something?" he asked.

"What?"

"Tavish. After all, he's the reason we all jumped out of bed and raced over here."

"Oh my gosh, you're right." I wiped my hands on my apron. "I need to call him."

"No you don't." Brady set his phone on the table and selected a number from his contacts. Then he hit speakerphone.

Tavish's concerned voice came over the line. "Brady, is Teddie all right?"

"Ask her yourself. She's right here."

"I'm fine, Tavish," I said as I used a spatula to scramble the eggs under the interested eyes of Brady and the two Jorgensen siblings, who were listening to my every word. "I'm so sorry I made you worry and caused all this fuss."

"So, what's going on?" he asked.

Brady tilted his head my way with a look of expectation.

"I can't really talk about that right now," I said, "but it's nothing serious. I got distracted by something when we were talking earlier. Can I ring you back in a bit?" I yearned to add a comma and the word *love* to the end of that sentence, but not in front of Brady and Augie. My term of endearment for Tavish was still too new to share with the rest of the world. "Sorry, I'm making breakfast right now. I'll ring you after everyone leaves."

"Everyone?"

Sophie's voice rang out from the back door. "I'm baaaack, and we brought kringle."

Chapter Fourteen

Ah, kringle. The official state pastry and Southern Wisconsin's preferred breakfast treat. Kringle and coffee are a staple in Lake Potawatomi. Thirty-six (or more) layers of buttery flaky crust, reminiscent of a croissant, compressed into an oval shape wrapped around fresh fruit, nuts, or other specialty fillings and topped with a glaze of white icing. Although pecan is traditionally the most popular bakery flavor, my favorites are cherry-cheese and raspberry. Grandma Florence taught me how to make this delicate Danish pastry years ago, but it was a painstaking, three-day process, so once was enough for this baker. Now whenever I want kringle, I simply run up the road to Racine—unofficial kringle capital of the world—and buy a few. Luckily, it freezes well.

After the breakfast club left, I rang Tavish back, apologizing profusely, and revealed why I'd had to hang up so suddenly earlier.

"That must have been a shock, seeing your mum coming home at that hour and realizing she'd stayed out all night," he said sympathetically.

"You got that right. I was gobsmacked."

"Listen to you, using British slang."

"It's a great expression. In fact, I'm adding it to my list of favorite words. I'll be slipping it into conversation as often as I can."

We chatted for another half an hour, and this time when we talked, I gave Tavish my full, undivided attention. After we hung up, I started making a list and a plan for the day.

I'm a big list girl. I've always made lists, but after going through cancer and chemotherapy, I discovered I needed them even more when I developed "chemo-brain." My memory sucked with chemo-brain. I walked around in a mental fog for nearly a year. I couldn't concentrate or remember things and even had trouble spelling common words, a grievous affront to this Lake Potawatomi spelling bee champ. The mental fog frightened me at first because I thought I might have gotten early Alzheimer's, but my doctor assured me that chemo-brain was a common, temporary condition that would eventually go away. And it did, but until then, lists became my lifeline. They still are.

On my yellow-lined notebook, with my favorite gel pen, I wrote, *To do:*

1. *Follow Mom to figure out who her mystery man is*
2. *Decide when/where to confront Mom about last night's sleepover*
3. *Go to Cullen's Creamery—talk to Belinda and Lauren*
4. *Check in with Char on Stephen conversation*
5. *Pick up Gracie's painting*
6. *Reconnect with Astrid on Angel's details from Jerry*

I changed into my summery pink-and-white-striped maxi dress with the large pockets, put on my white walking sandals, and stuck the folded to-do list in my pocket. Then I clipped on Gracie's leash to set off on a long walk. She needed the exercise, and so did I.

As we walked, I smiled, thinking about the cute interactions between Augie and Sophie at breakfast. Sophie, who'd caught sight of Augie's T-shirt underneath his uniform shirt when she first arrived, shyly asked him which movie Spider-Man was his favorite. And they were off. As the two twentysomethings animatedly debated the relative merits of the Spider-Mans and the best version of love interest Mary Jane, Margaret caught my eye and winked.

Doesn't look like Char and I will have to do any matchmaking after all.

I took Gracie to the park, where she enjoyed sniffing to her Eskie heart's content. Then we made our way over to the gazebo to check out the place where Sophie had heard the rustling the night Lester was killed.

The dense shrubbery provided great camouflage from prying eyes. Planted close together years ago, the boxwood bushes had grown into a hedge over time, adding an extra layer of concealment for illicit deeds. As I circled the gazebo, I noticed the three-foot gap between its outer edge and the thick shrubbery. Plenty of room to get down and dirty if a person was so inclined. I slipped into the gap with Gracie and walked slowly around the perimeter of the gazebo, closely examining the area and searching for any evidence of Lester's possible late-night encounter, but the hard-packed earth didn't yield any clues. Not surprising, since Brady had sent his deputy over to these same bushes to poke around and see what he could find. Unfortunately, Augie had found nada. Zip. Zilch.

Me either. I released a sigh. "Okay, girl," I said to Gracie, "let's head on home now. Nothing to see here."

But my Eskie wasn't quite ready to leave yet. She was too busy nosing around beneath the bushes. Something had definitely grabbed her interest.

Oh no, what if it's a rat? I tugged on her leash. "Come on, Gracie-girl, let's go."

She gave an excited yip and scrabbled deeper beneath the bushes.

Oh. My. God. I know it's a rat. A big, ugly, disease-carrying rodent with a long, slimy tail that will dart out and run across my foot. I broke into a sweat and started trembling as my rat phobia kicked into high gear. I yanked on the leash. "Gracie, I said come," I commanded in my stern voice that brooked no refusal. "Now!"

She slunk out of the bushes; her ears flattened as her face took on a hangdog expression.

I'm sorry, Mom. Don't be mad. Gracie crept toward me, guiltily, minus her usual happy-go-lucky bounce.

As she drew near, I noticed something sticking out of her mouth. Something skinny and dark. Like a tail. *Oh. My. God. She's got a rat in her mouth.* I shrank back, my heart pounding.

Settle down, Sherlock, my sensible, nonphobic self said. *If it were a rat, you'd see the whole body. Besides, rat tails are light, not dark. Take a closer look.*

Gracie sat down before me, ears still pressed back, looking up at me with a mournful expression in her big, dark eyes and, I was relieved to see, a scrap of fabric hanging from her mouth.

I'm sorry for not listening, Mom. I'll be good.

"What have you got there, girl? Show Mommy."

Gracie panted, and as she did, the piece of fabric fell from her mouth to the ground.

"Good girl." I squatted down and patted her head. "That's a good girl, Gracie. Mommy's sorry she scolded you." Gracie's ears perked up, and she wagged her tail and licked my hand.

From my still-squatting position, I plucked the scrap of fabric from the ground. As I examined it, I saw that it was a small strip of shiny black satin, about two inches long. Slinky satin that looked like it might have come from a teddy or camisole, perhaps—something I might have worn back in the day when I still had breasts. Something sexy a woman would wear for a late-night assignation, perhaps?

Augie had somehow missed this tiny slip of fabric during his search. I didn't fault him, though. If it hadn't been for Gracie, I'd never have found it either. I'd told Brady before that he needed a K-9.

Gracie lay down at my feet to take a snooze as I pondered the implications of the black satin. Could it be from Lester's new girlfriend, Angel? Had they been messing around in the bushes and her teddy gotten torn?

Or was it even from the night of Lester's murder? Someone could have been walking past and snagged their clothing on the bushes, unknowingly leaving this scrap behind.

Why do you always have to bring logic into everything? I asked my inner voice as I stuck the scrap in my pocket. But the voice had a point. I have a tendency to gravitate to the farfetched when I'm trying to solve a mystery. I do that in my cozy novels as well. Thankfully, my logical side usually intervenes before I go too far down an implausible path. And when it doesn't, Jane, my editor, does.

As I straightened up behind the tall hedge, I heard voices. A man and a woman. Someone was approaching the gazebo. A familiar scent wafted my way. I'd recognize that Chanel No. 5 anywhere. I've always had a strong sense of smell, and since I went into menopause my smelling sense has become even more acute. My mom's worn the classic perfume since her wedding day when my dad splurged on a bottle of the expensive scent as a gift to his new bride. Every year after that, Dad gave Mom Chanel No. 5 on their anniversary. When he passed away, I carried on the tradition.

The voices drew near, and instinctively I crouched back down. *Could this be Mom and her mystery man?* I tried to peek through the shrubbery to get a good look at the guy who had kept my mother out all night, but the boxwood hedge was too thick to see much. I caught a glimpse of a slender, bare female leg in a leopard-print flat. Definitely my mother. The male legs next to hers were covered in gray suit pants above expensive Italian leather loafers. Mom's favorite.

She'd bought my father a pair of similar loafers on his sixty-fifth birthday to replace his ubiquitous Hush Puppies. When she'd proudly presented Dad his gift, Mom had also schooled the two of us fashion Philistines on the uniqueness and superior quality of Italian leather. "Handcrafted, not mass-produced in factories; the patina has a weathered sheen to it," she explained, "and the smell . . . ah, the smell." She held up Dad's expensive new shoes to her nose, closed her eyes, and took a deep, appreciative sniff. "Real Italian leather has a distinctive and unmistakable smell."

I caught a whiff of that distinctive smell as the duo stopped beside the gazebo on the other side of the hedge from where I was hiding.

"Thank you for meeting me here, rather than coming to the house," I heard my mother say. "I don't want my daughter knowing about this."

I did an inner fist pump. *Definitely the mystery man.*

He replied in a low voice that I couldn't make out. Eager to hear what Mystery Man was saying and also to get a better look at him, I moved deeper into the shrubbery. As I did, I inadvertently stepped on my snoozing dog's paw.

Gracie yelped.

Oh Gracie-girl, I'm sorry. Mommy's sorry. I scooped up my canine daughter and hugged her to my chest, stifling the usual soothing noises I'd make. Gracie snuggled against me and laid her creamy head on my shoulder.

"Who's there?" Mom said. "Show yourself. You'd better come out, whoever you are. I have pepper spray and I'm not afraid to use it."

Like mother, like daughter. I'd used pepper spray to effectively halt a threatening suspect in the last Lake Potawatomi murder earlier this year. In an attempt to shush the now-squirming Gracie, I put my finger to my lips and mouthed

Shh, but to no avail. Gracie barked and jumped out of my arms. She made a beeline through the shrubbery to my mother, emitting excited yips.

I sighed and stood up sheepishly to my full height to find myself looking straight into the striking cobalt-blue eyes of a drop-dead gorgeous guy. A guy who didn't look much older than me. Those cobalt-blue eyes, framed by impossibly long lashes, were set in the chiseled face of a fortysomething man with great cheekbones and jet-black curly hair.

The breath whooshed out of me. *It's worse than I thought. My mother has a boy toy.*

"Theodora!" Mom exclaimed, staring at me, her waxed eyebrows lifting slightly—very slightly—on her smooth, Botoxed forehead. If it hadn't been for her raised voice, I wouldn't even have known she was surprised. "What in the world? What are you doing hiding in the bushes?"

"I wasn't hiding."

Liar.

"Gracie and I were taking a walk, and she, uh, ran after a squirrel"—I rushed out the words—"so I followed her and got tangled up in her leash in the bushes."

My mother's mystery man, who was wearing a pinstriped gray suit and cobalt-blue silk tie—which perfectly matched his eyes, I noticed—cast me an amused look.

You think this is funny, do you, Mister Man? It won't be so funny when I'm done with you.

I lifted my chin and pinned my mother with a penetrating gaze. "The question is, what are *you* doing, Mom? And *who*, may I ask, is this?" I regarded the good-looking guy in the fancy suit, perfectly tailored to accentuate his broad-shouldered, slim-hipped body.

Gracie, who was standing next to my mom, focused her dark eyes on me.

What's wrong, Mom? How come you're still in the bushes?

My mother leaned in close to the man in the spendy suit and murmured something in his ear. He nodded and said, "I'll call you later." He delivered a small smile to me, spun on his heel, and strode away.

"Was it something I said?" I called after his fast-departing form as I stepped out from behind the boxwood hedge.

He raised his left hand in a brief wave. That's when I saw it. His wedding ring.

Numbly, I picked up Gracie's leash and faced my mother in her sleeveless black linen column dress, topped by a gold rope necklace, matching earrings, and her favorite leopard-print flats. "Mom, what are you doing with that guy?" I asked.

"What do you mean, what am I doing?" She picked a piece of invisible lint from her dress and dropped it to the ground with a studied casualness. "We had a business appointment."

"What kind of business?

"That's none of your affair." She cast me a steely glance.

You can't ask for a better opening than that. Go for it.

I took a deep breath and blew it out. "Speaking of affair . . . are you having an affair with that guy?"

"What?" Mom stared at me, openmouthed. Her nostrils flared, and she started to say something, but then a voice startled me from behind.

"Why hello there, Claire, Teddie. Isn't it a beautiful day?" said Wilma Sorensen. Her syrupy-sweet voice punctured the charged air between Mom and me. "Are you two taking your morning constitutional as well?" She stretched her thin lips in an approximation of a smile. "It's always nice to see a mother and daughter spending time together."

Dear God. Did she overhear me? Please let her not have heard.

She tilted her gray head to the side and adopted a quizzical expression. "Although, come to think of it, I don't believe I've ever seen the two of you strolling in the park together before." Wilma tinkled out a laugh. "I guess there's a first time for everything, isn't there?"

Gracie growled.

"Oh goodness." She took a step back. "I hope you keep that dog on a tight leash, Teddie. She looks vicious."

"Gracie doesn't have a vicious bone in her body," I said. "Unlike some."

"She's simply protecting her person," my mother interjected. "That's what dogs do, Wilma. They're fiercely loyal and protective of their owners. When they perceive a threat, dogs will do whatever is necessary to neutralize that threat."

Whoa. Is this the same "I'm not a dog person" woman who never let me have a dog growing up because they shed and are too messy?

"Yes, well . . ." Wilma clutched at the ancient fanny pack around her waist. "I need to keep moving to get in my daily number of steps." Spotting another gray-haired woman off in the distance, she brightened and called out, "Yoo-hoo, Olive, wait up. Do I ever have something juicy to tell you!" She shot a malicious glance at Mom and me and scuttled away.

I felt sick to my stomach. Thanks to me and my big mouth, by tonight it would be all over town that my mother was having an affair. "I'm sorry, Mom," I said.

"For what?" She adjusted her necklace and locked her eyes on mine. "Are you sorry that the town rumormonger overheard you and will be dragging my name through the mud, or are you sorry that you asked me what you did?"

Talk about screwing up big time. The sick feeling in my gut intensified. "I'm sorry Wilma overheard our conversation. I should have waited and talked to you privately at home."

"Yes, you should have, rather than spying on me in the park." Mom shook her head. "I can't believe you were hiding in the bushes. Was that all to catch me out and confront me about this supposed affair you think I'm having?"

My hand closed around the scrap of black satin in my pocket. "No. I was actually checking out something to do with Lester's murder—it had nothing to do with you."

Only because you hadn't gotten around to that item on your to-do list yet.

"It's only that when I heard you say, 'I don't want my daughter to know about this,' it made me wonder," I continued. "Especially after you stayed out all night last night and sneaked home early this morning so I wouldn't know."

She lifted surprised eyes to mine. Surprise quickly replaced by guilt. Mom looked away.

"Yes, I saw you tiptoeing in with your heels in hand earlier," I said. "Who is that guy, anyway? Where did you meet him?" The words tumbled out before I could stop myself. "I grant that he's gorgeous and a sharp dresser. I can see how you'd be attracted to him. But he's married," I said quietly. "Plus, he must be a good thirty years younger than you."

Did I really say that aloud?

I braced myself for the fireworks to come. But what happened next was worse than any explosion.

My mother sank down heavily on a nearby bench, unconsciously pushing up the strap of her leopard-print purse that had slipped off her shoulder. "I know we have our issues, Teddie," she said quietly. "We've never been close like you and your father. We've never had much in common." She gave a short little laugh. "Well, anything, really, except your father." Mom looked down at her hands and twisted her wedding ring. "You were daddy's little girl, since the day you were born. You two shared a special bond. We didn't." She looked up at me, sadly, her eyes bright with unshed tears. "But I never thought I'd see the day when my child—my only child—would think so little of me as to imagine I would have an affair with a married man." Mom plucked her sunglasses from her purse with a shaking hand and put them on her face as she stood up. Then she turned and walked away.

Chapter Fifteen

"Mom, wait!" I jumped up to hurry after her, but as I did, Gracie and I collided with Barbara Christensen, who was passing by with a small dog, and I went down in a tangle of leashes and yapping, barking dogs.

"Oh my goodness, Teddie, are you okay?" Barbara asked. She reached down a hand to help me up.

Other than the fact that I just annihilated my mother, I'm great. I tried to extricate myself from the twisted jumble, but the tiny caramel-colored dog kept running to and fro, gamboling with Gracie and twisting the leash even more, tightening it around my legs. Gracie wasn't much better, delighting in her new pal, who kept taking playful nips at her heels and legs.

"I'm sorry, Teddie," Barbara said. "She's still a puppy. She hasn't been trained yet."

"That's okay. I remember those days." My adult dog *had* been trained, however. I adopted my command voice. "Gracie, sit."

She did so, promptly.

"Stay."

Okay, Mom, whatever you say.

I unclipped her leash and disentangled it from that of the other dog, who continued to scamper around Gracie. Although it was clear Gracie wanted to continue playing with the frisky pup, she stayed still.

"Good girl." I scratched my Eskie behind the ears and clipped her leash back on.

Barbara squatted down and picked up the fluffy little dog as I simultaneously turned around in a circle to unwind myself from its leash. Once free, I extended the back of my hand for the playful puppy to sniff and looked into its big dark eyes surrounded by curly, fluffy fur the color of a caramel apple. "And who are you, cutie pie?"

The puppy licked my hand and wagged its tail.

"This is Taffy," Barbara said proudly, "my mini goldendoodle. Isn't she the most adorable thing you've ever seen?" she cooed, scratching her fur baby under the chin.

"She's pretty darned cute. Where did you get her?"

"From my friend Shirley's daughter in Sturtevant. She got a new job in Chicago, and the place she's moving to doesn't allow pets." Barbara ruffled the little dog's fur. "Shirley knows how lonely I've been since I lost Robert and Duke last year, and she thought Taffy and I might make a nice family." She planted a kiss on top of the puppy's head. "Isn't that right, baby girl?"

Taffy gazed up at her new mom adoringly and licked her on the nose.

"I think your friend Shirley was right," I said. "You two are a perfect match. Taffy's lucky to have found you."

"I'm the lucky one," Barbara said. "This little girl has made my empty house a home again." She hugged her new pup. Taffy gave a happy yip and laid her head on Barbara's shoulder. Then she squirmed, jumped out of Barbara's arms, and scampered straight back to Gracie.

My canine daughter gave me a pleading look. *Please, Mom, can I play with my new friend?*

I nodded at Gracie, who splayed out on her back and batted her paws at Taffy as the puppy nipped and frolicked on top of and around her. I sat down on the bench. "Might as well take a seat, Barbara, and let our pooches enjoy their playdate."

While the two dogs played happily together under Barbara's watchful eye, I excused myself to text my mother.

Me: *I'm sorry I hurt you, Mom. I got waylaid at the park, but I'll be home in a few minutes. Can we talk?*

Her text response was curt and to the point.

Mom: *Need a break. Gone away for a couple days. BY MYSELF!*

Great.

Nice job, Theodora. What are you going to do for your second act?

I puffed out a sigh, lifting up my bangs, and group-texted my fellow Musketeers.

Me: *Guess who totally blew it with her mother this morning? I am a terrible, horrible, person. I need some girl time so you can tell me that I'm not the worst daughter on the planet. Drinks tonight? My place?*

Char: *I'm always up for a drink, worst daughter ☺ Looking forward to hearing the latest with Claire.*

Sharon: *You're NOT a horrible person! You and your mom are just oil and water.*

My friends have listened to my litany of complaints about my mom since my preteen days. We always joked that I must have been switched at birth, since I don't resemble Claire St. John in any way—physically, temperamentally, and definitely not stylistically.

Me: 😐 *Our personalities have never mixed. We're from different planets. You know that old book* Men Are From Mars, Women Are From Venus? *That's my mother and me, except we're more like Mercury and Pluto.*

Char: *Pluto's no longer a planet.*

Me: *I rest my case.*

Sharon: *Why don't you come to the Lake House tonight instead? I've got leftover enchiladas and I'll make margaritas.*

Me: *You're on.*

Char: *Sounds like a plan, man. I'll bring the guac and chips.*

Me: *I'll bring dessert.*

Sharon: *See you at seven.*

I looked up to check on the two dogs, but they were in doggy heaven, and so was Barbara, watching her new pup's antics with total adoration. I pulled out my to-do list from my pocket. With a twinge I drew a line through the first two items, which I hadn't expected to accomplish quite so fast:

1. *Follow Mom to figure out who her mystery man is*
2. *Decide when/where to confront Mom about last night's sleepover*

I focused on the next item on the list:

3. *Go to Cullen's Creamery—talk to Belinda and Lauren*

"Okay, Gracie, time to go." We made our farewells to Barbara and Taffy. Since Mom was out of the picture for now, I decided to focus all my energy on Lester's murder instead. *Who knows? Maybe between me and my fellow amateur sleuths as well as Brady and Augie, we'll have discovered Lester's murderer by the time my mother gets back and I can take a bottle of champagne over to her house to celebrate.*

Ha! You mean as a peace offering, don't you?

That too.

Once home, I settled Gracie in the kitchen with a fresh bowl of water and headed to the ice cream shop. After walking only a block, I needed a shower to wash away the stickiness covering me like Saran wrap. I should have known better. Although August temperatures usually never rise above the low eighties, the humidity, especially in the early days of the month, can be a killer. It didn't help that another hot flash assaulted me on the way. I lifted my thick, curly hair off my neck and pulled it up into a ponytail as I walked. *Should've driven my Bug.*

For two blocks?

I know, but it has air conditioning.

Tough it out, Wonder Woman.

As I pushed open the etched glass door to Cullen's Creamery, an icy blast of cold air welcomed me. "Ah, heaven!" Shutting the door behind me, I plucked my dress away from my overheated body and lifted my face to the overhead air conditioning vent.

Bliss.

"Hi, Teddie," Belinda Cullen called from behind the fifties-throwback ice cream counter where she was serving two teens. The owner of Cullen's Creamery is a diehard Coke fan ("never Pepsi"), so she decorated the red-white-and-chrome ice cream shop with vintage-reproduction Coke signs, a classic jukebox from the fifties, and tons of Coca-Cola memorabilia. The strawberry-blonde Belinda smiled at me. "Take a seat, and we'll get you some water. You look great, by the way. Love the dress. Reminds me of peppermint-stick ice cream."

"Thanks. It's nice and cool." I flapped my hands in the oversize pockets and slipped into the retro red front booth near the AC vent. I leaned my head back and relaxed, but the image of my mother's tears and the hurt in her eyes intruded. Hurt that I'd caused. Obviously, I'd jumped to conclusions about my mom and the man in the Italian leather loafers.

Ya think, Sherlock?

Lauren Cullen set a glass of ice water down in front of me. "Here you go, Teddie. How's it goin'?" The spiky-black-banged nineteen-year-old gave me an anxious look from her kohl-rimmed brown eyes.

Sophie must have told her about our conversation, and she was clearly worried I might say something about her meeting her boyfriend in the park. I smiled reassuringly. "Hi, Lauren, nice to see you. Are you back working here again? What about the salon?"

"I didn't have any appointments today, so I'm helping out my folks," she said. "Their last server quit, and Mom's been running herself ragged trying to do it all."

"That's nice of you to help out."

What a good daughter. Not like others I could name.

Oh, stuff it, I told my guilty conscience.

I took a drink of water. "I love your hair—you remind me of Liza Minnelli in *Cabaret*."

"Who?"

"Sorry. Way before your time," I said wryly. "Before my time too, but I'm a sucker for old movie musicals."

Lauren shot a quick glance over her shoulder. When she saw her mother engaged in conversation with another customer, she turned back to me and said quietly, "Sophie said she told you about me and Justin. Please don't say anything to my folks," she pleaded. "They'd lose it. They hate Justin," she said bitterly, "just because he has tattoos and is older with a kid."

"Don't worry. Your secret's safe with me," I told the modern-day Juliet with the pixie cut, keeping my voice down so Belinda wouldn't hear. "I wanted to ask you, though—that night at the park, did you see anything? Like Lester and a lady, perhaps?"

She shook her dark head. "We weren't there very long. I met up with Justin and then we left—Tyler was asleep in the back seat and we had to get him home."

"Get who home?" Belinda appeared noiselessly behind her daughter in her soft-soled Skechers, red capris that hugged her curvy figure, and white polo shirt with *Cullen's Creamery* embroidered in red on the breast pocket. "Who are you two talking about?"

Lauren shot me a pleading look before turning to face her mother.

I thought fast. "I was telling Lauren about one of Astrid Nilsen's dogs getting loose and how I had to take him back home to her. You know how her neighbors are always on Astrid about her animals escaping from her yard."

Her daughter released a nervous laugh. "Yeah. Remember that time, Mom, when we found one of her guinea pigs in the road and almost ran over it? And then her bunny startled us when he hopped by?"

"Oh yeah, I nearly had a heart attack," Belinda said. "Astrid really needs to get a new fence. The one she has is falling down around her."

We nodded our agreement.

Lauren poised her pen over the old-school order pad. "What would you like today, Teddie?"

"Honey"—Belinda laid her hand on her daughter's arm—"why don't you go take care of those folks at the counter that just came in, and I'll take Teddie's order. The two of us haven't talked in ages and need to catch up. I want to hear the latest on her books."

"Okay, sure. See ya, Teddie." As the nineteen-year-old walked away, she put her hands together in prayerful supplication behind her mother's back and mouthed the word *please.*

"See ya, Lauren." I couldn't acknowledge the teen's plea with her mother right there, but I hoped Lauren realized I had meant what I said—her romantic secret was safe with me. I focused my attention on Belinda, trying to figure out the best way to bring up Lester and the whole rent thing. "So, what's new with you?"

"Not much. Same old, same old. Unlike you, Ms. Best-Selling Author," Belinda said. "Congratulations! That's so exciting *A Dash of Death* made the best-seller list. You must be thrilled." She didn't give me a chance to reply and continued on without a breath. "I loved it! I think it's my favorite Kate and Kallie yet. That dog is such a scream, the way she gets in trouble all the time and makes a mess of everything yet always manages to help Kate solve the mystery and save her in the end."

"Good always triumphs over evil. At least in cozy world."

"When's your new book coming out? What's it called again?"

"*Suffocating in Soufflé*. I'll be turning it in to my editor in a couple weeks. It comes out next September."

"Gosh, a whole year?" Belinda said. "That's such a long time. My girlfriend in Florida wrote her first book a couple months ago, and it got published within a week."

I explained the difference between self-publishing and traditional publishing, and we chatted for a few minutes about books and the ins and outs of the publishing world. Belinda shyly confessed that she'd always wanted to write a book.

Doesn't everyone?

"Besides mysteries, I really love romance novels," she said. "That's what I'd like to write someday if I ever have the time—a historical romance set in the Wild West during the gold rush days. I've already started doing the research on that time period."

"Good for you," I said. "And as far as having the time, if you really want to write, you need to *make* the time," I encouraged her. "Even if it's only an hour a day. When Mary Higgins Clark started writing, she was a young widow with four or five children to support, so she'd steal time in the early mornings before her kids woke up to write."

"Wow, I didn't know that," Belinda said. "I love her books."

"Me too."

"You want your usual?" she asked. "Hot-fudge sundae with a scoop of vanilla, scoop of strawberry, and whipped cream, no nuts?"

"Let's mix it up today. I think I'll take one scoop of cookies-and-cream and one scoop of chocolate instead, with hot fudge and whipped cream."

"Sounds good." Belinda stole a glance at the counter, where Lauren was engrossed in conversation with a young couple, then turned back to me and said quietly, "Word's out on the street that you're going around town asking folks about Lester Morris," she said. "You know I was one of his tenants, right?"

I did an inner fist pump. *Thank you for bringing it up before I had to.* I nodded.

"You need to know I had absolutely nothing to do with Les's death. Yeah, that creep hit on me after he gave me an extension on the rent, thinking I *owed* him, but I told him to shove it and that was that," she said. "He made some suggestive comments to Lauren too, but I told him to knock it off or

I'd stick his ice cream cone where the sun doesn't shine. After that, Les behaved himself. For a while." Belinda frowned and rubbed her eyebrows the way I do when I'm getting a headache. "One day, though, a few months back, he stopped in the salon, thinking Lauren was all alone, and cornered her. He tried to kiss her—and more." Belinda shuddered. "But Frank came out of the restroom when he heard Lauren yell and threw Les up against the wall. He told Lester if he ever came near our daughter again, he'd kill him."

I could feel my eyebrows shoot up.

"Frank didn't kill him, though," Belinda added quickly. "That was just something he said in the heat of the moment. He could never kill anyone. He's the coroner, for God's sake. Frank's more familiar with death than anyone in town. He would never take someone's life. Even that swine Les." She pulled a face. "Unfortunately, though, someone showed up for a haircut exactly when Frank had Lester pinned against the wall and heard what Frank said. Now that Lester's been murdered, they might think my husband is the one who killed him."

Is that what you and Frank have been fighting about lately? I didn't verbalize the question. Some things are private, including couple's squabbles. Besides, I wanted to keep Belinda talking.

"Let me guess," I said. "Was Amy Lewis the person getting her hair cut?"

Her eyes widened. "How did you know?" She scowled. "I guess it would be too much to expect that a pastor's wife wouldn't go around town spreading gossip. I thought the Bible was against that," Belinda said bitterly.

"Actually, Amy never mentioned Frank's name or what happened with Lauren," I said. "Your telling me now is the first I've heard of it. Amy simply remarked she wouldn't be surprised if whoever killed Lester turned out to be a protective father or husband who'd finally had enough of his behavior and unwanted attentions to someone they loved and lashed out in the heat of the moment." I gave Belinda a gentle look. "I could certainly understand that, couldn't you? In fact, as far as we know, Lester's death may not have been murder at all. Maybe it was manslaughter or even self-defense."

Self-defense? Are you cray-cray? The back of Lester's skull was bashed in. How could that even remotely be self-defense? My inner logician rejected the idea.

"Excuse me, Teddie." Belinda's voice broke into my thoughts. "I need to take care of my other customers. I'll bring your sundae over in a minute."

"Sounds good." As she left, I pulled out my to-do list to see what I still had to accomplish today. Then I texted Char.

Me: *Hey, have you talked to Stephen M. yet?*
Char: *Yep. He came in to get the latest DIY magazine.*
Me: *And?*
Char: *Definite motive. Sorry, can't talk now—customers. Will tell all tonight.*

I sighed and set my phone down. Patience is not my strong suit. But I still had a couple other things to do before girls' night, including checking in with Astrid. She doesn't text, though, so that would have to be an in-person visit. Once I finished my sundae, I'd stop by the artists' warehouse and get the scoop (no pun intended) on Angel, Lester's lover. Astrid had said last night she'd be at the studio most of the day today, so that would be the best place to find her. I could pick up the painting of Gracie at the same time. Two birds, one stone, and the last item on my list crossed off.

"Boy, it's sure humid out there today," I heard a familiar voice say. I looked up to see Margaret with her walker entering the ice cream parlor as Sophie held open the door for her. Margaret raised her lined face to the AC vent in a repeat of my overheated arrival. "God bless the person who invented air conditioners," she said.

I waved to my neighbors. "Hi, Sophie, hi, Margaret. Come join me."

Margaret made her laborious way over to the booth with her walker, Sophie at her side patiently accompanying her. By the time the two Miller women joined me, Lauren had delivered my sundae and had two glasses of ice water on the table waiting for them.

"Thank you, dear," Margaret said. "You're a sweetheart."

Lauren kissed her on the cheek. "Anything for my surrogate grandma."

"Hey, Laur," Sophie said, smiling at her best friend.

"Hey, Soph. How's it goin'?"

"Good, but I'd kill for a root beer float."

"You got it," Lauren said. "Margaret, do you know what you want?"

"Same thing. Root beer float, with extra ice cream, please." She winked at Lauren.

After Lauren left, Margaret said, "My goodness, Teddie, your mom left in a rush this morning. Where was she off to in such a hurry? I saw her come home around nine thirty and go inside, but less than ten minutes later she reappeared, tossed a suitcase in the trunk, and kicked up a cloud of dust as she left. You'd have thought the hounds of hell were after her."

I exhaled a long sigh. "That was my fault. We had a fight. Words were exchanged, and afterwards Mom felt the need to get away for a bit." I lifted my shoulders. "To tell you the truth, I'm not even sure where she went—I'm trying to give her some space."

Margaret reached across the Formica tabletop and patted my hand. "Space is a good thing." She shared a look with her granddaughter. "We know all about mothers and daughters, don't we, Sophie?"

"Oh yeah," Sophie said, throwing me a sympathetic glance.

From the corner of my eye I noticed a man approaching. Stephen Morris, Lester's son. Clad in chinos and a muted gray-and-white Hawaiian shirt—Tommy Bahama. Although designer duds are not my thing, I recognized the tropical shirt as the type Mom had bought Dad. My father had loved his Hawaiian shirts in summer; Mom, not so much. However, if her husband insisted on wearing tropical prints, she insisted they be high quality and not so in-your-face.

"Excuse me for interrupting, ladies," Stephen said. "I was hoping I could chat with you for a minute. Do you mind if I join you?"

Sophie regarded him with a wary eye.

"Depends on what you have to say." Margaret gave the insurance agent a steely-eyed gaze. "If you've come to accuse my granddaughter and Teddie of killing your father like your mother has been doing all over town, then no, you cannot join us."

"Understood," Stephen said, holding up his hands in a gesture of peace. "Actually, I came over to apologize for my mother. As you can imagine, my father's death has hit her pretty hard. She's overwrought. That's why she's been throwing out these wild accusations." He inclined his salt-and-pepper head to Sophie. "I don't believe you had anything to do with his death, Sophie." He looked me in the eye. "You either."

I scooted over to my side of the booth. "Have a seat."

He slid in next to me, careful to leave space between us as Lauren arrived with the root beer floats. She set the floats down on the table and telegraphed an inquisitive look to Sophie at the sight of Stephen. Sophie raised her shoulders in a shrug.

"Can I get you something?" Lauren asked politely. I wondered if Stephen recognized the undercurrent of subtle sisterhood solidarity in her voice.

"I'd love a glass of water." He smiled, turning on his salesman charm. "And one of your mom's great hot-fudge brownie sundaes, please."

After Lauren left, Stephen resumed the conversation he'd started. "As I was saying, I don't think either of you are responsible for my father's death. Personally, I think it was a passing thief trying to steal something, and dad caught him in the act and tried to stop him. Either that or it could have been one of those gangs from a big city nearby—I've heard they're starting to infiltrate small towns."

Gangs in Lake Potawatomi? That's a new one. I'd never seen any evidence of gangs here. I stole a glance at Stephen as he answered a question Margaret posed. *No, I think the thief angle is much more likely. Only I don't think it was a passing one.*

Exactly. What's there to steal in the baking tent, anyway? It's not like there would be any chamber of commerce funds lying around to embezzle.

I was now more eager than ever for girls' night tonight to hear what Char had found out about our chamber of commerce treasurer. It was bound to be good. My lips curved up as I ate a spoonful of my hot-fudge sundae.

"Teddie," Stephen said, turning his head to face me. "I hope you don't mind my saying so, but that's a pretty dress. It looks really nice on you."

I nodded my thanks to prevent dripping hot fudge all over that dress.

"I hope you don't think I'm like my father and trying to hit on you or say something inappropriate," he added. "That's the last thing I'd want to do. In fact"—he squirmed in his seat—"I'd like to apologize to both you and Sophie for my father's sexual harassment. It was completely unacceptable, not to mention humiliating to my mother." He shook his head in disgust. "Why she put up with it, and him, all these years is beyond me. I kept telling her to leave him, but she wouldn't. She'd say, 'I made a vow before God, Stephen; for better or worse.' "

At that moment Lauren reappeared with his water and sundae.

"Thanks," Stephen said. He looked embarrassed, as if he suddenly realized he'd said too much. He took a sip of water and excused himself to go to the restroom.

We exchanged looks as he retreated.

"Awkward," Sophie said.

"A bit," her grandmother agreed, "but it took guts for Stephen to say what he did. And it's nice to know he doesn't take after his father, at least as far as women are concerned." Margaret sipped her root beer float. "Although that was fairly evident by his behavior over the years—he's never been crude or coarse like his dad."

"Thank God," I said. "One Lester was more than enough."

My phone buzzed with a text.

Sharon: *Where are you?*
Me: *Cullen's, having a hot fudge sundae.*
Sharon: *Don't move! Stay right there. I'm leaving Bud's now and will be there in a minute with big news.*
Me: *You're pregnant.*
Sharon: *Bite your tongue.*
Me: *Want to give me a hint?*
Sharon: *No. This is best told in person.*
Me: *I'll be waiting with bated breath.*

I continued eating my sundae. Although the cookies-and-cream tasted great with the hot fudge, I found myself missing my usual strawberry.

Moments later, Sharon burst into the creamery and hurried over to our booth. "Oh good, you're here too, Sophie.

That makes it easier." She beamed at us both. "You're never going to guess."

"What?"

Sharon paused for effect, then blurted out, "The baking contest is back on."

"What?" I said. "Are you kidding me?"

She shook her blonde curls. "Patsy Morris called me and Bea Andersen and asked us to come over. When we got to her house, she insisted the contest continue. In fact, her exact words were, 'The baking contest must go on! Les would have wanted it.' "

"Seriously?" a nonplussed Sophie said. Her head swiveled from Sharon to me.

Margaret frowned. "Wouldn't that be too painful for Patsy with all that's happened?"

Sharon shook her head. "We asked her that, and she said baking would be a good distraction for her. Patsy said she and Les looked forward to the contest every year and she needs it to continue this year in her husband's honor. She said that's what he would have wanted."

"But Brady's still in the midst of Lester's murder investigation," I said. "I can't imagine he'd agree to that. Doesn't he need to keep the tent sealed off until the investigation's complete?"

"Bea and I asked that same question," Sharon said, "and Patsy said she talked to both Brady and Frank Cullen and they said they've already processed the evidence from the crime scene, so it's fine to use the tent again."

I texted Brady to double-check. He confirmed what Sharon had said and texted back that Patsy had told him continuing the contest would help her in her grief, so how could he refuse?

"Okay," I said. "I'm game. When does the contest start up again?"

"Day after tomorrow," Sharon said. "Thursday."

Sophie's eyes bugged out. She set down the glass of water she'd raised to her mouth with a trembling hand. "There's no way I can make another coconut-cream pie," she said. "It would be too ooky."

"We agree," Sharon said. "It would be ooky. That's why, as the remaining two judges, Bea and I talked it over and decided to switch to cobbler rather than pie. The grand-finale showstopper will be a fancy, special-occasion cake as always, though."

Good. Because I was going to pull out all the stops with my cake. It was a guaranteed winner. I'd been practicing for weeks now, and it was sure to be a crowd pleaser. Even perennial first-place finisher Patsy wouldn't be able to top it. "So, there will only be two judges now?" I asked.

Sharon shook her head. "No, we need a third in case there's a tie."

"Who's the third judge going to be?" Sophie asked.

"That would be me," Stephen Morris said as he returned to the booth.

Chapter Sixteen

I checked my to-do list as I left the ice cream parlor. Only two items left—picking up Gracie's painting and getting Angel's details from Astrid.

Ten minutes later I pushed open the glass front door of the artists' warehouse with its stunning Mondrian-inspired abstract stained-glass window made up of rectangles, squares, triangles, and other angled shapes in vibrant hues of red, orange, yellow, green, blue, indigo, and deep violet.

Jeffrey Hollenbeck had installed his creation—made in Chicago before he moved to Lake Potawatomi—in the brick three-story formerly abandoned industrial warehouse at the end of Main Street when he opened the collective with a few local artists five months ago. Everyone had oohed and aahed over the artsy stained glass when they first saw it—even my mother, who never oohs and aahs over anything.

"That is simply exquisite," she said, when we stopped by the open house Jeffrey and the other artists held in April to christen the space. "The colors take my breath away."

"Thank you," Jeffrey said as he introduced himself. The good-looking gray-haired artist with warm brown eyes was wearing cotton drawstring pants, Jesus sandals, and a flowered hippie-style shirt that made me think of Woodstock. "Art should always take one's breath away."

"Not all art," my mom sniffed. "Some of it actually makes me want to hold my breath until I pass by."

Jeffrey threw back his ponytailed head and laughed. "You have a point."

Six months ago, the senior-citizen sculptor/painter and glassworks creator had been considering opening an artist's collective in Racine or Milwaukee. Then he discovered that Astrid Nilsen, one of the country's greatest wildlife artists, lived in Lake Potawatomi. When Jeffrey contacted Astrid, she encouraged him to locate the collective here instead. Astrid told him she and a couple other local artists had been discussing banding together to open a gallery in town, but the costs were too prohibitive. A collective, however, would share work space and materials, marketing, and promotion and even do collaborative works together. And thus the Lake Potawatomi Artists Collective, comprising Jeffrey Hollenbeck, Astrid Nilsen, Colleen Murphy, Jim Hansen, and Cheryl Martin, was born.

Cheryl, my mother's book club pal, does mosaics—mirrors, vases, tables, and garden art; Colleen, who owns the yarn shop, specializes in textile arts; and Sharon's husband Jim paints watercolors. Jim's always had an interest in architecture, so his watercolors are mostly of local historic buildings and older houses. For my birthday last year, Jim presented me with a lovely watercolor of my fifties blue bungalow, which proudly hangs in my living room.

To enhance the collective's thin coffers, Jeffrey and Astrid started offering art classes to the public in the former warehouse, which they'd refurbished into an open, light-filled artist's space. My mother even took a couple of the classes—pottery and oil painting.

When I expressed my surprise at her new interest, my mom said, "Theodora, when I met your father, I was studying art in college. I used to love to paint," she added wistfully.

"How come I never knew this?"

"You never asked." Mom waved her hand in a dismissive motion. "I switched my major to fashion design the next semester—you know how much I love clothes."

That was an understatement.

"Then your father and I fell in love and got married," Mom continued. "And not long after that we discovered I was pregnant. We needed health insurance, so I dropped out of school and took a job as a secretary instead."

That part I did know. Sadly, my mother miscarried my older brother or sister and had two more miscarriages after that. And then nothing. No matter how hard they tried. Dad had always wanted a houseful of kids. Mom, not so much. One or two would be enough, she'd said. When I was born seven years later, I was their "miracle" child.

Mom enjoyed her art classes. She followed up pottery and oil painting with sculpture and drip painting with fluid acrylics.

As I walked down the hall now, I passed by one of her contemporary drip paintings—a bold mixture of orange, blue, and yellow drips, a far cry from the monochromatic gray throughout my mother's house. *Who knows? Maybe Mom's finally adding some color to her life.*

Between that painting and Italian-leather-shoe guy, sure looks like it.

Not going there.

I glanced up at a mobile sculpture—a sphere of twisted black-and-bronze metal hanging from the high beam in the vaulted ceiling. "What is *that*?" I squeaked.

"That, my dear," said Astrid as she came to stand beside me in a paint-spattered T-shirt and khakis, "is the work of a young Racine artist named Julian. He's a new member of the collective. He installed that yesterday."

"Very unique," I said. "Not my style, but my mom probably loves it."

"Yah, you betcha," Astrid said. She reached behind me, plucked a painting from an easel, and handed it to me. "Hope *you* love this."

My sweet Gracie-girl stared at me from the canvas with her big soulful eyes.

"Oh my gosh, Astrid. It's gorgeous! Of course I love it." I hugged her. "Was there ever any doubt?"

"Well, ya never know." She grinned and handed me a slip of paper. "Speaking of knowing, here's the details on Angel, Lester's *lady* on the side."

* * *

"Can you believe that the contest is starting up again and Stephen is replacing his father as judge?" Char asked over the top of her margarita glass in the Lake House kitchen that night.

"No. Especially since he made it quite clear he's nothing like his father and Lester embarrassed him." I scooped a tortilla chip through the bowl of guacamole on the butcher-block island we were clustered around. "I feel bad for Stephen, actually."

"Don't feel too bad," Char said. "He may not be a dirty old man like dear old dad, but he's still an embezzler. And maybe something worse," she said in an ominous tone.

"Spill it." I took a long drink of my margarita, enjoying the crunch of salt mixed with tequila. "What'd you find out?"

"Yeah," Sharon said. "Don't keep us in suspense."

Char crammed a tortilla chip full of guacamole into her mouth and followed it with a swig from her margarita. "Stephen came into the bookstore today to get his favorite DIY magazine. He also bought a pricey book on kitchen remodels, so I asked him, 'Oh, you going to do a little remodeling in the kitchen?' and he said"—Char paused dramatically—" 'Not a little. I'm gutting the whole damn thing and starting from scratch.'

"He said instead of doing the work himself this time, he's going to hire a contractor to enlarge the space and turn it into a state-of-the-art chef's kitchen with an open floor plan," Char continued. "Then he listed everything he plans to have in his fancy new kitchen." She ticked off items on her fingers:

"Custom cabinets, two ovens, two sinks, a subzero fridge, walk-in pantry, quartz countertops, custom lighting, and a large marble-topped island."

Sharon released a long whistle. "That's going to cost a pretty penny. Over fifty grand, I'd bet. When Jim planned our kitchen remodel years back, he got a couple bids, and the contractors wanted to charge us twenty-five thousand bucks. Way too rich for our blood," she said. "That's why we wound up doing most of it ourselves, except for the electrical. And we didn't have all the custom features and bells and whistles Stephen's planning. Plus, that was more than fifteen years ago, so you know prices have gone up."

Char nodded. "I read in a renovating magazine a few months ago that the national average—depending on what part of the country you live in—ranges from sixty to seventy thousand bucks for a midrange kitchen remodel," she said. "The upscale ones like Stephen's talking about are a lot higher—more than a hundred grand. On those HGTV shows, I've seen people pay anywhere from a hundred and twenty-five thousand to a hundred and fifty grand for one of those big, fancy chef kitchens. Can you believe it?"

"Yikes. I could buy a house for that," I said. "Why doesn't Stephen buy a new house instead?"

"I asked him that, but he said he loves his home and all he's done to improve it over the years. Except for the kitchen. He told me he's been wanting to redo it forever, and now he'll finally be able to afford to do so. He was positively giddy talking about it," Char said. "I mentioned—casually—that I knew where he was coming from. I told him that when my dad died, I used the insurance money to do some remodeling at my house too."

"What did Stephen say to that?" I asked.

"He clammed right up. I think he realized he'd said too much and changed the subject."

"Interesting." I grabbed some more chips. "But that doesn't prove anything. We still don't know for sure if Stephen's getting a big chunk of his dad's life insurance—we're simply assuming he is because he's planning a pricey kitchen remodel."

"It's more than an assumption," Char said with a smirk. She leaned forward on her barstool. "Do you guys remember my friend Paula who worked part-time at the bookstore a while back?"

"The cute college grad from Carthage who loved books and used to do story time for the kids?" Sharon asked. "Sure. She was a sweetie."

"I remember her," I said. "She only worked for you a year or so, right? Until she got a full-time job"—my eyes widened—"at Stephen Morris's insurance company."

"That's right," Char said smugly. "Paula worked for Stephen for five years until she got married and moved to Madison with her husband. She and I have stayed in touch, though, so I called her to catch up. During the course of our conversation, I happened to mention Lester's death. Paula immediately said, 'Well, Patsy and Stephen Morris will be sitting pretty now.' Apparently she typed up the paperwork for Lester's insurance policy, and the payout was—wait for it . . ." Char paused. "A million dollars. Seventy percent to Patsy and thirty percent to Stephen."

"Wow, so Stephen's portion will be . . ." I scrunched up my nose trying to do the math, never my strong suit.

"Three hundred thousand bucks," Jim said as he entered the kitchen, wearing his ubiquitous Cubs cap. He grabbed a beer from the fridge. "I'd knock off my old man too for that kind of money," he said. He popped off the bottle cap and took a swig of his Miller High Life.

"Honey!" Sharon scolded him. "You would not. You love your dad."

"Yeah, but love doesn't pay college tuition," Jim teased. "I'm sure my dad wouldn't mind kicking the bucket if he knew it would take care of his grandkids' education."

Sharon picked up the hot pad beside the enchilada pan and threw it at him.

"Aw, you know you love me, babe." He held up his beer and nodded to us. "Ladies. If you'll excuse me, I've got a baseball game to get back to."

As he left the kitchen, we resumed our murder-related ruminations.

"For my money, Stephen Morris is now the top suspect in Lester's murder," Char opined.

"Maybe, maybe not," I said. "There's someone else we need to check out as well." My fingers closed around the scrap of black satin in my pocket. "Turns out Lester was seeing someone on the side. A bartender named Angel who works at a nightclub out past Racine and does double duty as an exotic dancer."

"Really?" Sharon said. "Poor Patsy."

"Yep." I pulled out the satin and showed it to my friends. "I found this in the bushes by the gazebo this morning."

Sharon took the slip of fabric from my hand and examined it closely. "Looks like it's from a piece of lingerie. A teddy, maybe?"

"That's what I thought too. I think it belongs to Lester's girlfriend, Angel." I pinned my gaze on my fellow Musketeers as I prepared to drop my bombshell. "I think Angel might have been in the park with Lester on the night he died."

Char's eyes lit up with a Miss Marple gleam. "Maybe she's the one who killed him."

"Exactly what I was thinking."

"That would be great!" Sharon spun around on her barstool with glee. She added hastily, "I mean, not great for Patsy and Stephen, but great for you and Sophie." She straightened her back and adopted her "all for one and one for all" Three Musketeers stance. "Now everyone can stop giving you the stink eye. What did Brady say about this new development?" Sharon asked eagerly.

"I haven't told him yet."

"Why not? You need to let him know so he can go question this Angel." Sharon returned the strip of cloth to me. "And you need to give him this evidence too. It may help prove Lester's lady friend was his murderer and Brady can arrest her. Then Patsy can stop blaming you and Sophie for her husband's death and things can get back to normal again." Sharon finished off the rest of her margarita and slapped the glass down on the island.

"Don't worry," I reassured her. "I am planning to let Brady know. Soon. But before I do, I wondered if maybe we Three Musketeers might want to pay our own undercover visit to Angel on the job before involving our beloved sheriff."

"At some sleazy bar where nearly naked women shimmy up and down a pole in front of a bunch of men?" Sharon scrunched up her nose in distaste. "I don't think so."

"Pole dancing isn't sleazy," Char said. "It's gone mainstream now. Lots of gyms today offer pole fitness classes. It's a great cardio workout and helps build muscle." She patted her thigh. "Who did you have in mind to play the part of J-Lo, Teddie?"

"Not me, obviously." I eyeballed my flat chest. "I'm missing some of the vital equipment. I was hoping one of you could act out the role?"

Sharon snorted. "Not in this universe."

"That's what I figured." I turned to my best friend. "How 'bout it? You've always had mad dancing skills."

"Not that mad."

"I could always take Astrid," I said casually. "She volunteered to go with me."

"Astrid?" Char snorted. "You're kidding, right? She'd stick out like a sore thumb in a place like that."

"Yes, she would. Astrid realized after she made the offer that she would be way too conspicuous and likely blow our cover. In this instance, she said, Jessica Fletcher would humbly defer to Miss Marple."

"Especially since it sounds like our Miss Marple has some pole-*exercising* experience, am I right?" Sharon sent Char a sly glance.

"What can I say? I'm a well-rounded individual." Char expelled a loud sigh. "All right, I'll do it for the team, but Brady can't find out about this. He'd kill me." She turned her stool to face me. "What's the plan, Jane Tennison?"

I told my friends my idea, and we discussed all the ins and outs and potential problems until we were satisfied.

Char emptied her margarita glass with a final gulp. "Okay, Tennison. You and me. Tomorrow night. Let's do this."

Sharon didn't like it, though. "I think this is a bad idea," she fretted. "You have no clue what this Angel is like. If she's Lester's killer, what's to stop her from killing you too if she figures out you're onto her?"

"There's two of us and one of her," I said. "Besides, I'll have my pepper spray with me."

"I still don't like it."

"Tell you what," Char said. "We'll text you when we arrive. We won't stay long—only enough time to talk to Angel and see what she has to say about Les. As soon as we leave, we'll text you again." She looked at me. "How long do you think it'll take us to grill her?"

"I don't know. Depends how busy the club is. And when we get to meet up with her. An hour, maybe? Hour and a half?" I focused my attention on Sharon. "How about this? We'll go around ten. If you haven't heard back from us by eleven thirty tomorrow night, you can send in the cavalry. Sound good?"

Sharon shook her head. "Nope. One of you needs to text me by eleven to let me know everything's okay, then text me again when you leave, and send me a final text when you get home. Got it?"

"Okay, Mom," I said, smiling at our Three Musketeers mother hen. "You got it."

"Speaking of moms, we still haven't talked about the elephant in the room," Sharon said. "Your mother."

"That's right," Char said. "I almost forgot, with everything else going on. What happened with Claire today?"

I recounted the disastrous encounter in the park, filling them in on the hot guy in Italian leather and how, after he left, I'd confronted my mom about having an affair with a married man.

Sharon's eyes grew huge in her cherubic face. "You didn't."

"Yes, I did. I told you I'm a horrible, terrible daughter."

"How did Claire react?" Char asked.

"As if I'd stuck a knife through her heart," I said miserably.

"You made a mistake, Teddie," Sharon said in her wise-mom voice. "You screwed up. But you owned it and you apologized. Right?" She looked at me. "You *did* apologize, didn't you?"

"Yes. Almost immediately, but she wasn't in the mood to listen. She just left."

"Give her some time. She'll come around." Sharon gave me a wry smile. "Mothers always do."

* * *

That night as I was getting ready for bed, I thought about what Sharon had said. Then I thought about how intent I'd been on discovering the identity of my mother's mystery man.

Intent or obsessed?

And right then I decided to stop.

Stop trying to solve the mystery of the man in my mother's life. Stop bugging her about him. Stop judging her. Stop being upset about her having a new man who wasn't my dad. Just stop. And accept it and let Mom live her life. When she was ready to tell me about the mysterious man, she'd tell me. Or not. Her prerogative.

I crawled beneath the crisp sheets and gazed at Astrid's mesmerizing watercolor of my canine daughter on the wall. "Good night, Gracie-girl," I said.

Gracie jumped up on the bed and laid down on the pillow beside my head.

Good night, Mom.

Chapter Seventeen

Char tugged at her short leopard-print pencil skirt as we disembarked from my yellow Bug in front of the nightclub the next evening. "How do I look?" she asked.

I gazed at my best friend. She had on a form-fitting low-cut black crop top that grazed her belly button and highlighted her taut tummy. Below the top, her fitted leopard-print knit skirt hugged her lithe form above bare legs glistening with bronzer and three-inch stiletto heels. Oversized gold hoop earrings flashed against her long red hair, which she'd released from its ubiquitous ponytail and curled into beachy waves. Char had done a full-court-press makeup job complete with foundation, blush, smoky eyes, luxe false eyelashes, eyeliner, and a bright-red lip.

"Hot, baby, hot."

"I don't know how women dress like this every day and wear all this goop," she grumbled. "It's so suffocating. I'm going to need a trowel to scrape off all this makeup when I get home."

Since Mom was out of town, we'd gotten dressed at my house away from prying eyes. We didn't want Brady or Augie seeing Char in her ultrasexy outfit.

For tonight's investigative outing, instead of going for my usual boho-chic vibe, I'd pulled on my best jeans and a snug black tank top. In honor of our club excursion, I'd strapped on a bra, which I'd stuffed with my knitted knockers (fake, lightweight boobs for breast cancer survivors). I'd added a skinny rhinestone belt and chandelier rhinestone earrings that sparkled when the light hit them and finished off my look with black strappy sandals and a red pedicure. The crowning touch was to spritz my unruly coffee-colored curls with a shine spray. When I looked in the mirror, my hair resembled a shorter, darker version of Julia Roberts's cascading tresses in *Pretty Woman* (after she'd removed the ugly platinum Dutch-boy wig).

"Are you ready?" I asked Char.

"Yup. Let's do this."

We texted Sharon we'd arrived and made our way past a phalanx of cars, Harleys, and rusty pickup trucks with gun racks.

"Pretty crowded for a Wednesday night," Char observed.

"Yeah. I wonder why."

We approached the red door set into the long, white wooden building off the highway. Above the door, a large black sign with white lettering identified the venue as The Candy Club. A smaller neon sign below flashed the words *Exotic Dancers*. The faint sound of a thumping bass could be heard.

A tired-looking Mexican restaurant of salmon-colored stucco with the name *Hot Tamales* emblazoned in faded turquoise on the front hugged the left end of the club—the only other structure in sight. A few clusters of men stood at the intersection of the restaurant and the club huddled in a circle, smoking cigarettes and shooting the breeze.

"Do you suppose they eat before or after their visit?" Char asked with a smirk. She answered her own question. "I'd say after. They're probably jonesin' for some nachos after all that dancing." My bestie nudged me to check out the hand-lettered sign in the smoked-glass window next to the club's front door. "Hunters welcome!"

"Well, we *are* hunting for information," I murmured. I adopted my Jane Tennison bravado as I pulled on the door handle and we entered the club's dimly lit foyer. Immediately inside, we were assaulted by pounding rock music and a burly, towering man dressed all in black with enormous biceps and a shaved head.

"Hello, ladies," the doorman said in a deep voice as he gave us a slow once-over. "I haven't seen yous guys in here before. If I had, I would've remembered."

I gave the Incredible Hulk my most dazzling smile. "You're right. It's our first time."

"I hope it won't be the last," he said, his eyes lingering on Char. "I'd really like to see more of you, if you know what I mean."

Still think it was a good idea to come here, Tennison?

"You've got a pretty full parking lot out there," I said, ignoring his innuendo. "Is it always this busy on a Wednesday?"

"Yeah," the burly doorman/bouncer in the tight black T-shirt said. "Wednesday night's our drink-and-dance special. Half off. Brings everyone and their brother out."

"Half off?" I gave him a thumbs-up. "I guess we picked the right night to come."

"Yup. I'll need to see some ID, ladies."

"Thank you for the compliment," Char purred. "It's been a while since someone thought I was under twenty-one." She batted her false eyelashes at him. "Don't worry, we're legal."

"Oh, I can see that you are, Red," he said, giving her a slow smile, "but rules are rules."

"And I suppose you're a man who never bends the rules, are you?" she said in a flirtatious voice. "What's your name anyway, big guy?"

"Vince." He puffed out his chest as his dark eyes homed in on her long legs. "What's yours?"

"You already guessed it." Char ran her hand through her wavy red hair. "Everyone calls me Red."

"Well, Red, there's a ten-buck cover charge," he said. "That'll be twenty bucks for you and your friend here."

Char reached into her purse—but not for money. She removed her lipstick and compact.

I pulled a twenty out of my wallet along with my driver's license and extended both to him. "Here you go, Vince."

He took the cash but was too caught up watching Char reapply her red lipstick that he barely glanced at my ID, to my relief. So far, the plan was working perfectly.

"Is Angel working tonight?" I asked casually. "We were hoping to see her dance. We hear she's really good." I inclined my head to Char. "Red's a dancer too, and she wanted to check out Angel's style."

Char smacked her freshly reddened lips together in the mirror and snapped her compact shut. "There, that's better."

"I shoulda guessed you were a dancer," Vince said as he gave my best friend a seductive smirk.

The door opened behind us with a burst of loud voices and laughter. I turned around to see three young fraternity jocks in jeans and T-shirts sporting Greek letters enter, jostling and high-fiving each other.

"This place is the bomb," one of them announced.

While Vince was busy checking the college boys' IDs, we escaped through the red velvet curtain at the back of the foyer into the crowded club. A long bar off to the right greeted us, where myriad bottles of booze glistened and three male bartenders frenetically mixed drinks and poured beers for the crush of customers. Obviously, Angel wasn't tending bar tonight.

"Thank God for those frat boys," Char murmured. "I think Vince was about to ask me for a dance demonstration."

"So do I. Unfortunately, since he was so besotted with you, though, he never answered my question about Angel."

"What can I say?" Char fluffed her hair. "When you're hot, you're hot."

I linked my arm with hers. "Well, hottie, let's find a table and sit down before some other guy is blinded by your beauty and interrupts our Angel search."

Relieved that Wisconsin now had a no-smoking ordinance, we excused ourselves—"Excuse me," "Excuse me"—as we pushed through the mass of men and a few women to find a table. Finally, we found a middle-aged couple leaving a chrome-and-glass-topped table for two in the center of the club close to the stage, which reminded me of a beauty pageant runway. Only smaller and with a pole in the center. "Is this table free?" I asked the heavyset woman, in a glittery blue top and black pants, supporting the balding, bespectacled man beside her, who was having trouble standing.

"Take it, honey; it's yours," she said. "Time to get birthday boy here home and put him to bed." She sighed. "So much for my fiftieth-birthday surprise. Next year we're going to Outback." She escorted the drunken man toward the exit.

Char and I sat down as Donna Summer's *Bad Girls* blared out and three women of varying ages in skimpy outfits strutted onto the stage and began dancing around the pole. The first dancer looked to be in her early forties. She had long, curly red hair and large, obviously silicone-enhanced breasts (I can always tell—they don't jiggle), a slight pooch, and a tiger tattoo on her thigh. The second dancer was a slightly younger, petite, big-bosomed (also fake) blonde with a black velvet choker around her neck and body glitter on her legs and chest. The final dancer was the youngest, the quintessential fresh-faced girl next door—only with pink hair. All three dancers wore varying colors of open-toed stilettos—black, red, and silver—with three-inch platforms beneath the front of their feet and seven- or eight-inch heels.

I had never seen such obscenely tall shoes in my life. *How do they not fall and break their necks?*

The blonde dancer in the velvet choker faced the pole, grabbed it, and hooked her left leg around it. I watched, mesmerized, as she fell easily into a spin by pulling her right leg around the pole. As the spinning slowed, she began climbing while twisting and moving her body through a series of athletic contortions. The other two dancers continued dancing on either side of the pole to approving catcalls and whistles from the audience.

"Do you suppose one of those women is Angel?" Char leaned over to ask me, raising her voice to be heard over the din.

"I'm guessing so, but which one?"

"My money's on the bodacious blonde," Char said. "She seems like Lester's type."

"I was thinking more the curvy redhead with the tattoo."

At the table next to us, a middle-aged guy, in worn jeans and a wife-beater shirt straining against his paunch, leaned over and said to Char in a slurred voice, "Hey, gorgeous, how 'bout I buy you a drink and we get to know one another?"

"No thank you," Char said, politely, inclining her head to me. "I'm here with my friend."

"Aw, c'mon," he wheedled. "I'll buy her a drink too and the three of us can have ourselves a nice little party. Whaddya say?"

"No thanks," Char repeated.

I was about to put the drunk in his place, but at that moment our server appeared.

"What can I get you ladies?" asked the Britney Spears wannabe in a tight white tank top with *The Candy Club* printed across the chest and a pair of Daisy Duke shorts.

"I'll take a cosmopolitan," Char said, in a sophisticated nod to *Sex and the City*.

"A Sprite for me."

The server raised dark eyebrows up to her blonde bangs.

"I'm driving," I said.

"Hey, Mindy," the drunk in the wife-beater said, "put their drinks on my bill and bring me another Budweiser."

I gave her a discreet shake of the head no.

"Sorry, Pete, but I think you've had enough," she said.

"Whaddya mean?" He stood up stumbling and weaving and knocked his chair over in the process. "You can't cut me off."

Mindy signaled to someone. Within seconds a more compact version of Vince the doorman materialized next to us. Same shaved head. Same black T-shirt stretched across a beefy chest. Same imposing manner. Only a couple inches shorter.

"Okay, Pete," the burly bouncer said to our obnoxious neighbor, "you need to come with me now." He gripped the drunk's shoulder and led him away, Pete protesting all the while, as Mindy left to get our drinks.

"How's that for an exciting start to our evening?" Char asked.

"Let's hope it doesn't get any more exciting than that."

We returned our attention to the stage, where the redhead was now hanging upside down, legs hooked around the top of the metal pole as she arched her back against it and began a series of pull-up-style moves, impressively engaging her core. Talk about strong. Then she reached up between her knees, grabbed the pole with both hands, and extended her legs straight out in either direction in the splits position.

"That's called a Jade Split," Char said.

The tiger-tattooed dancer then straddled the pole and extended both her legs straight out until her body was in a prone position from the waist down and she was holding on to the pole with only her right arm.

"And that's what they call a Superman," Char informed me.

"It should be called a Superwoman," I said. "That's amazing."

While the redhead worked the pole, the girl-next-door dancer with pink hair was doing a sultry dance at the end of the runway for a group of men clustered there. Her admirers tucked tips into her scanty costume, making me feel as if I'd stumbled into a bad R-rated movie.

Embarrassed, I lowered my head, causing my hair to act as a curtain, and pretended to look for something in my purse. I scrabbled around for an Altoid and sent a quick text to Sharon.

Me: *Good thing you didn't come—not your kind of world. (Mine either.)*

"You ladies enjoying yourselves?" a husky-throated female voice asked.

I dropped my phone into my purse and looked up to see a woman with shoulder-length, obviously dyed jet-black hair that belied the extensive network of lines around her mouth and eyes. Her hair said forty, but her face, even with its cover-up makeup excess, said seventysomething. The weathered senior citizen, who smelled of smoke and whiskey, held an amber-colored drink in her hand and wore a black V-necked

T-shirt stretched against her chest that displayed her mottled, sun-damaged cleavage and hugged the double muffin top poking over the top of her skinny jeans.

"Sorry about Pete bothering you," she said in her gravelly voice. "He's one of our regulars and has trouble holding his liquor. I hope he didn't get out of line. I don't stand for that." She pulled over a chair from a nearby table and joined us. "I'm Candy. This is my club. Welcome."

"Hi, Candy," I said. "I'm Teddie, and this is Red. Nice to meet you."

"Don't worry about that guy Pete." Char waved her hand in a dismissive motion. "No big deal. We can handle ourselves."

"Glad to hear it." Candy fastened her aging eyes—bookended with some serious crow's-feet—on Char and looked her over. "Vince tells me you're a dancer. Is that right?"

She nodded. "We were watching your girls. They're good. Is Angel the blonde?"

"Nah, that's Star." Candy nodded to the stage. "Tiger's the redhead, and Angel's the young one with the pink hair."

Should have figured. Although Lester hit on women indiscriminately, when I thought about it, he did tend to gravitate toward the younger ones, which was why we had christened him Lester-the-molester back in high school.

I returned from my Les reflections to hear Char say to the club owner, "I'm looking forward to Angel's dancing. I hear she's really good. How long has she been working for you?" she asked casually.

"About a year and a half. Angel's my newest girl. Star's been with me the longest—twelve years—and Tiger's been here seven." Candy let out a sigh. "Unfortunately, Tiger's leaving me soon. She's getting married next month. Decided she wants to hang up her dancing shoes and do the whole white-picket-fence wife-and-mom thing. More power to her." Candy took a swig of her whiskey. "That was never my bag, but I always tell my girls they gotta do what makes them happy."

"Always the best rule for life," I said, thinking back to my past cubicle job where I wasted too many years pushing a pencil, sitting through mind-numbing meetings, and dealing with the endless bureaucracy of local government. It took cancer to shove me out of my career-comfort-zone nest and pursue my writing dreams.

Candy refocused her attention on Char. "With Tiger leaving, I'll be needing another dancer." She studied my best friend over the top of her whiskey glass. "Who knows? Maybe your coming here tonight was fate." Her eyes locked on Char's hair. "I'd like another redhead. They're popular with the customers, and I always like to keep my customers happy."

"*I* can be a redhead," a female voice announced brightly. Server Mindy appeared next to Candy and set our drinks down on the table. "I'm happy to dye my hair, boss," she said eagerly. "You know how much I've been wanting to become a dancer."

"I know, honey, but you're not ready yet." Candy patted Mindy's hand.

She pouted. "I've been practicing lots with Star, and Angel's been teaching me some of her moves too. Please, boss," Mindy pleaded. "I've gotten so much better since I first auditioned."

"That you have," Candy said. "I've seen you working out with Star, and you're definitely coming along, sweetie, but you're not quite there yet," she said gently. "Give it another few months."

Out of the corner of my eye, I noticed a nearby table of plaid-shirted hunter types ogling us. Unthinkingly, I glanced their way, and one of the plaid shirts leered at me. I quickly returned my attention to the drama at our table.

Mindy shot a jealous look at Char. "But don't you want someone *younger*?" she asked Candy. "I've heard lots of the guys say they like Angel the best 'cause she's the youngest."

Char crossed her bronzed legs and sipped her cosmopolitan, returning the young server's stare without batting a false eyelash.

"Is that right?" Candy said coolly to Mindy. "And exactly how many is *lots*?"

She fidgeted. "I don't know. Seven or eight? Nine or ten?"

Her boss, who it was clear had been around the block a few times, swiveled her overly made-up eyes around the packed club before returning a sharp gaze to her young employee. "And how many men would you say are here tonight, Mindy?"

"I don't know," she said miserably. "Seventy-five or eighty, I guess."

"Our seating capacity is a hundred and fifty," Candy informed her, "and as you can see, we're almost full up, so your mention of 'a lot' constitutes seven to nine percent at the most. Mindy, do you think I should make my hiring decisions based on what less than ten percent of my customers want?"

The server looked down at her drinks tray. "I guess not."

"Okay, then. Thanks for your input, though, honey. I'll be sure to keep it in mind when I decide what's best for my club," Candy said. "Now, why don't you get back to your other customers."

"Yes, boss." Mindy turned to leave, but first threw in a parting shot. She sneered at Char. "Can you even dance? All we have is your say-so." She flounced away in her Daisy Dukes.

Candy exhaled a sigh. "You'll have to excuse Mindy," she said. "That girl's been wanting to get up on the stage ever since I hired her three months ago. She came in to audition as a dancer, but she was pretty bad." Candy chuckled. "I told her I'd start her off as a cocktail server but if she practiced and improved her dancing, I'd give her another shot at the stage. Told her to work with the girls and have them show her the ropes." Candy shook her head. "She's gotten better, but she's just not good enough yet. I'm not sure if she ever will be. Some girls have it and some girls don't. You know what I'm sayin'?"

We nodded.

"I danced, back in the day," Candy said, smiling at the memory. "I was a natural. Best damn dancer on that stage. I made more tips than all the other girls combined." She sighed. "But then I got old and my knees wouldn't take it anymore, so I stopped dancing and bought the club from the original owner. Much easier on these old bones." Candy ended her walk down memory lane and gave Char a probing look. "Tell me, Red, where have you danced?"

I held my breath. Could Char pull it off? I sent up a quick prayer as I took a sip of my Sprite.

"Here and there. A couple clubs out west. I'm from Phoenix originally. That's where I got my start," Char said, lying smoothly and effortlessly. "You ever heard of the Landing Strip or the Admiralty Club?"

Candy shook her head. "Nope. I'm not familiar with any clubs outside of the Midwest—other than the big ones in Vegas."

That's what we'd counted on when we concocted our cover story last night. And should the dance club owner want to check out the validity of Char's story, it didn't matter. No one at the Candy Club knew my bestie's real name, and we would be long gone before they checked her background. Back to wholesome, family-friendly Lake Potawatomi. *After* we talked to Angel about Lester Morris, our mission for the night, which was taking longer than I'd hoped.

Come on, Charlotte, let's move this along.

"I'd be happy to audition for you," Char continued smoothly. "Anytime you like. And when I do, I'll bring my references. Meanwhile, though, would you mind if I talked to one or two of the girls? I'd like to see how they like working here, find out what kind of tips they make—that kind of thing."

"Fine by me," Candy said. "My girls are happy. They have a sweet deal going here and they know it. They make a lot in tips. Why don't you come back tomorrow morning at eleven, and you can audition for me then. Make sure you bring those references."

"Will do. Thanks for the opportunity," Char said. "I really appreciate it."

The club owner then turned her attention to me. "How about you? You a dancer too?"

"Oh no," I laughed. "I've got two left feet and absolutely no rhythm. Red's the dancer, not me."

"Too bad." Candy pushed back her chair and stood up. "Now if you'll excuse me, ladies, I need to do some circulating. Red, I'll send Angel over to talk to you, and I'll see you back here tomorrow at eleven sharp." She tossed back the last of her whiskey. "I hope you dance as good as you look," she said with a wink. "Good night, ladies. Have another drink on me and enjoy the rest of your evening."

"Oh. My. Gosh," I said quietly to Char after Candy had walked away. "I can't believe we pulled that off."

She gulped her cosmopolitan. "Me either."

"This place is beginning to gross me out, though," I whispered, as the catcalls to the dancers grew louder and I could feel the stares from some of the men around us, including the plaid shirts, intensifying. "The second we finish questioning Angel, let's get out of here."

"You got it." Char drained the rest of her cosmopolitan.

On the other side of the stage, I noticed the strip club owner talking to Angel. Candy pointed to our table. The young dancer glanced our way, listened to her boss, and nodded. Then she disappeared backstage.

Oh no, what did Candy say? Did we give ourselves away somehow? Did Angel split? I was leaning over to tell Char I thought we'd better leave when Angel appeared at our table, wearing a sheer black cover-up over her bikini and carrying her phone and a glass of water.

"Hey," she said, sitting down in the chair her boss had recently vacated. "How's it goin'? I'm Angel." She set her phone and water on the table.

Up close Angel looked even more like the girl next door. Big brown eyes. Flawless skin. Dimples in her cheeks. And a fresh, wholesome, innocent look. She reminded me a little of Selena Gomez. Only with pink hair.

Angel turned to Char. "Candy says you're auditioning for her tomorrow and you want the deets on the club? Yeah?"

"If you don't mind," Char said. "How do you like working here?" She lowered her voice. "And how's Candy as a boss?"

"I like it. It's better than a lot of the other places I've danced. Candy's cool, and the other girls are nice." Angel did a furtive sweep of the room. "I can't say the same for Vince, the doorman, though. He's always sniffing around."

"How's the money?" Char asked. "Do you make good tips? Candy said you do."

Angel nodded. "Tips are decent. I usually make about two hundred a night." She took a drink of water. "Fridays and Saturdays, though, I bring home about five hundred a night at least. I always take home more than a grand every weekend."

"Sounds good," said Char, the bookstore owner who can't afford to pay much more than minimum wage to her employees.

"Was Lester Morris a good tipper?" I asked.

A wary look crept into Angel's eyes. "Lester? I don't remember anyone named Lester."

Char described Les to the young dancer. "Scrawny old guy in his seventies with a bad silver rug on his head?" she said. "Always wore polyester. Drove a big gold Cadillac?"

Angel's face cleared. "Oh yeah, now that you describe him, I do remember," she said, releasing a conspiratorial giggle. "That really is a bad rug, huh?"

"Yeah, especially when it's covered in blood. Lester's dead," I said bluntly, watching her face closely for a reaction.

Angel paled beneath her makeup. "Dead? No way. Are you kidding me? What happened?"

"Someone killed him," I said. "Last Saturday night in the baking tent in our town park. Bashed him in the back of the head with a rolling pin."

"Oh my God. Oh my God." The young dancer clutched her cover-up, white-knuckled.

"Angel," I asked gently, "were you with Lester last Saturday in Lake Potawatomi Park?"

"No," she whispered.

"I don't think you're telling us the truth." I removed the scrap of black satin from my purse and slid it across the table to the dancer. "This is yours, isn't it? I found it in the bushes next to the park gazebo."

Her eyes bugged out. Then Angel reached over and picked up her glass of water, casually palming the strip of satin as she did. She leaned back nonchalantly in her chair, her eyes casually scanning the room, and took a drink of water. "Look," she said, pasting on a smile that didn't reach her eyes as she set her water back down. "Chill out. Don't be so intense. They're watching."

"Who?" I asked, stifling the urge to look around.

"Candy and Bruce, the bouncer. They always keep a close eye on us girls." She sent a flirtatious wink to the burly, compact man who'd thrown out our drunken admirer earlier. The bouncer stood at the back of the room looking our way. He returned Angel's wink.

At the same time, I noticed Candy leaning on the bar, chatting to one of the bartenders. Although she was talking and laughing with him, the club owner's eyes continuously circled the room, always returning to our table.

The next time they did, I caught Candy's eye and smiled, lifting my hand in a half wave.

She returned the wave, then turned her back and returned her attention to the bartender.

"Here's the deal," Angel said, rushing out the words after seeing Candy turn away. "Les and I started seeing each other about a month ago. He kept coming to the club and asking me out, and I kept turning him down. But one night he brought me this cool diamond bracelet, so I thought, why not? He took me out to dinner at this fancy, high-end restaurant in Milwaukee and gave me these dope diamond earrings." She pushed back her pink hair so we could admire the sparkling studs in her ears. "We started dating after that, and he always brought me nice presents."

"Where did you usually go on your dates?" I asked.

Her heavily made-up eyes narrowed. "What are you, the cops or something?"

"No," I said. "I'm just curious if Les ever took you to Lake Potawatomi."

"A couple times," she said. "Late at night. Usually we went to a restaurant and hotel in Milwaukee, but our last couple dates he took me to his hometown; said he wanted me to see it."

"Was one of those dates last Saturday night?" I asked. "In the park?"

Angel nodded. "Yeah. The one with the baking tent."

My pulse quickened. "What happened?"

She gave me a wry look. "You want the play-by-play?"

Char made a face. "Please, no."

Angel stole a peek at the bar to make sure Candy wasn't watching. "First off, you need to know that I got sick last Saturday night in the middle of my shift and had to leave work early and go home."

"What was wrong with you?" Char asked.

"Nothing." She made a face. "I just told Candy that so I could see Les. I'd already made four hundred in tips that night and knew I'd only make another hundred at the most, so when he called and said he really wanted to see me and that he'd make it worth my while, how could I refuse?" Angel cast a sly glance our way. "A girl's gotta look out for herself, you know."

"Ain't that the truth," Char said in exotic-dancer solidarity.

"Okay, but what about the baking tent?" I asked. "What happened there?"

"Well, after we fooled around a bit"—she smirked—"we had some wine and a little weed. Lester got high and tipsy. He was laying there on the tent floor in that ugly polyester suit of his, bragging about how he was the head judge and how he was going to make sure two of the bakers didn't win, no matter what. He started getting all worked up, waving his arms and stuff. Then he jumped up and stubbed his toe on something under one of the tables."

"An ice chest?" I said.

"Yeah. He was all like, 'What's this doing here?' I shone my phone at the cooler so he could see better, and when he opened it up, we both saw the pie inside." Angel shook her head. "Les started laughing like crazy, saying, 'I've got her now. She thinks she can humiliate *me* in front of the whole town? Ha! Let's see who's humiliated tomorrow.' " Angel continued, "And he pulled out that pie, sat down at the table, and started *eating* it, right then. Can you believe it?" She shook her head.

"Then what happened?" I asked. "Did you have some pie too?"

"No way. I asked Les to take me home, but he said he was 'otherwise engaged,' " Angel said, gesturing quote marks around the last two words. "The dude was giggling and really high and out of it at that point, so I called an Uber. I left him there in that stupid tent eating that damn coconut-cream pie."

"What time was all this?" I asked. "I mean, what time did you leave the park?"

"Eleven forty-five," she said promptly. "I know, 'cause I checked my phone when the Uber arrived. I had to get back for a date with another guy I've been seeing, and he doesn't like to be kept waiting."

Angel's phone buzzed. "That's my timer. I gotta go. Break's over." She stood up.

"Not so fast, young lady," a familiar voice said.

My head whirled around to see Brady and Augie standing behind our table in full uniform.

Chapter Eighteen

"Brady?" Char squeaked. Her head swiveled from her steel-jawed boyfriend to her beet-red blushing brother, who couldn't meet her eyes. Augie made sure not to look at the young dancer either.

Angel clutched her cover-up and gave me an anxious look. Before anyone could say anything, though, Candy and Bruce the bouncer materialized beside the two lawmen.

"What seems to be the trouble, Officer?" Candy asked. She narrowed her eyes at the frightened young dancer before returning her full attention to the law-enforcement presence in her club. "Is there a problem? Has my dancer done something she shouldn't have?"

I heard the sound of chairs scraping back and noticed, out of the corner of my eye, the plaid hunters and a few other tables of men nearby take their leave as unobtrusively as possible.

Candy noticed her customers' departure as well. Her lined mouth thinned. "As you know, Sheriff, exotic dancing is legal in Wisconsin. And Angel here is twenty-one. She's of age, even though she might not look it." The club owner continued, "I'm happy to show you my licenses—they're all in order and up-to-date," she said. "I comply with the law and run a clean club here. I don't want any trouble."

"Thank you, ma'am." Brady conveyed a brief nod. "I don't have any problems with you, your club, or any of your dancers—as far as I know," he said. "My issue is with these two *ladies* here." He inclined his head to Char and me. A muscle twitched near his left eye, a sure sign that Brady was furious and keeping his anger in check.

We are so busted. I exchanged a look with Char, who was pale but defiant. I could see she was simmering beneath the surface but holding back her anger as she continued to play her part for the club owner's benefit and not throw Angel under the bus in the process.

"What have they done?" Candy asked, the picture of innocence. Her wrinkled eyes tightened to slits when they landed on Char.

"I'd rather not say," Brady said. "They've been on our radar for a while, and we've been keeping a close eye on them. A little birdie told me they might try to pull one of their scams here tonight, so I came over before they caused too much damage."

Crap. I forgot to text Sharon back, so she freaked and called Brady. What time is it, anyway?

"Thank you, Sheriff," Candy said in a simpering tone. "I appreciate that."

Brady peered at Angel—keeping his eyes on her face, I noticed. "What I'm not sure of is whether this young lady here is involved with these two or not."

"I'm not!" Angel burst out. "I only met them fifteen minutes ago." She threw a pleading look to Candy. "Right, boss?"

The club owner gave her dancer a thoughtful gaze. "Well . . . that's what I assumed, but how do I know for sure?"

Angel's mouth dropped open. "But *you* sent me over to their table! That's the only reason I'm talking to them. You said the redhead had questions about working here she wanted answered before her audition tomorrow."

"Audition?" Brady swiveled his head to Char.

Augie's eyes about popped out as he stared at his sister, slack-jawed.

"Yes, audition." Char lifted her chin and gave Brady a bold stare. "I *am* an exotic dancer, after all, and this is an exotic dance club, isn't it?" She tossed her head. "I came here with my friend tonight to check it out and see if the Candy Club might be a place I'd like to work."

Candy snorted. "You can forget that idea right now, sweetheart. I don't want anyone working in my club who's involved in something illegal." She affected a tone of righteous indignation.

Then I wondered how much Sharon had actually told Brady. Did he know the purpose of our undercover visit?

Sharon must *have told him*, my voice of reason said. *She had to have divulged what we were doing here when she called in the cavalry to rescue us.* Not *that we needed rescuing. We were doing fine on our own.*

Yeah, right.

From the stage, Tiger threw us an interested peek as she continued her dance routine.

Brady returned his attention to Angel as he pulled out his notebook. "Did you discuss anything else with these two women besides working here?" he asked. "Were they trying to involve you in some scheme? They have a reputation for that—going around to clubs and latching on to the youngest dancer, trying to steal her away for their own nefarious reasons."

"No, nothing like that." Angel made her eyes wide, playing the innocent card to the hilt. She pointed at Char. "She was asking what it's like to work here, what kind of tips I make, and what the other employees are like." Angel turned to Candy and laid it on thick. "I told her this was a great place to work. We're like a family here and all have each other's backs," she said meaningfully, locking eyes with her boss. "Right?"

Candy nodded. "Right." She draped her arm around Angel's shoulders and gave her a reassuring squeeze. "My girls are like my daughters. We have a great relationship with no secrets. They know they can come to me with any problems—personal or professional—and I'll be there for them. I'm sorry I doubted you, honey." She chucked Angel beneath the chin. "I should have known better." Candy's eyes glittered as she regarded Char and me. "I'm sorry I sent you over to these two. I don't know what kind of game they're playing, but I don't want them playing it in my club and trying to pull my girls into something shady."

Brady continued to press Angel. "Are you sure you've told me everything? These two didn't say anything more specific to you about their plans?"

"Leave her alone, Johnny Law," Char burst out. "The poor kid had nothin' to do with it. You caught us, all right? Happy?

Now get us out of here and I'll tell you what you want to know." She stood up and glared at Brady. Then Char turned her attention to Candy and smirked. "I'll skip that audition tomorrow, if you don't mind," she said sweetly.

Brady telegraphed a look to Augie, who took Char by the arm and said, "Ma'am, if you'll come with me now, please." He led his sister toward the exit.

I stood up and started to follow, but Brady stopped me. "You stay right there. I'll escort you out when I'm finished." He returned his attention to the dancer and her boss. "Thank you for your help. Angel, is it?"

She nodded.

"I'll need your phone number, please, in case I need to ask any more questions."

"No prob." Angel flashed him a girlish smile, showcasing her dimples, and rattled off her number.

Brady entered it into his phone and glanced at Candy. "I'd like your number as well."

"Of course, Officer." Candy reached into her back jeans pocket, pulled out a business card, and extended it to him. "That's got my personal number as well. Feel free to call anytime if I can be of any further assistance."

"Thank you, ma'am. I'm sorry my presence here ran off a few of your customers. Some folks freak out when they see cops of any kind."

"They must have a guilty conscience." Candy smiled at the sheriff. "Maybe they've got some unpaid parking tickets or they're afraid their wives or girlfriends will find out they've been sneaking over here instead of playing poker with the boys."

"Probably," Brady said. "Thanks again for your help." He gripped my arm with his right hand and tipped his hat with his left. "Ladies."

I shrugged my shoulders at Candy as Brady led me to the exit. In the foyer, Augie was waiting for us with Char, and Vince the doorman was ogling my best friend's legs.

Brady's lips tightened. So did his grip on my arm.

"Ow!"

He relaxed his grip but not his lips, which were set in a thin line. "Let's go, Deputy." Brady pushed open the front door and led me out, Augie and Char following close behind.

"Sorry to see you go, Red," Vince called after Char in a seductive tone. "You come back again now, ya hear?"

Outside the club, the smoking gallery watched us with interest.

Brady held out his hand to me. "Car keys, please."

"Wh—" I started to say, but then I realized everyone's eyes were on us, including those of the doorman Vince, whose silhouette I could see through the smoked-glass window. I handed Brady my car keys.

He tossed them to Augie and said curtly, "Take her car and meet me back at the station."

"Yes, sir." Augie hit the fob on my key chain and trotted over to my yellow Bug while Brady ushered my wannabe Jane Tennison and Char's Miss Marple over to the patrol car. He opened the back door.

"Are you kidding?" Char said.

Brady cut his eyes to the club, then back to his girlfriend. "Get in," he said in a clenched voice.

Yah, you betcha. I got into the back seat and slid over to make room for my best friend. She followed, tugging her skirt down as she lifted her legs inside. Brady slammed the door shut behind her and stalked over to the driver's side. He yanked his door open, got inside, fastened his seat belt, slapped the door locks, and gunned the engine. Then he turned on the siren and roared out of the parking lot, tires screeching.

From behind the protective grille that separated the criminals from the cops, I could see Brady's white knuckles as he gripped the steering wheel.

"I'm sorry—" I started to say, but he cut me off.

"Don't say anything," Brady spat out in a clipped tone. "I don't want to hear a single word from either of you."

"I know you're mad, babe," Char said, "but—"

"Not a word!" the sheriff said as he sped down the highway. Brady's warning sounded remarkably like the dad's in *A Christmas Story* when he yelled, "Not a finger!" after his wife *accidentally* broke his beloved leg lamp.

I held back a nervous giggle as I recalled the scene from one of my favorite Christmas movies. A heavy silence, thick with anger and tension, descended upon the car. I sighed. If Brady would only let me explain, I could tell him what we had uncovered about Lester and Angel on the night Les died and he could investigate further.

You go right on ahead, Jane Tennison. Meanwhile, I'll curl up in this dark corner over here and pretend I'm asleep.

After about fifteen miles, Brady pulled into a rest stop, cut the engine, and exploded. He clicked on the dome light and spun around to face us.

"What the hell did you think you were doing?" He released a string of expletives that turned the air blue and his face red. Then he added some more for good measure. Brady slapped his hand on the top back of his driver's seat. "You two have pulled some stupid stunts in your time, but this takes the cake. What were you thinking going to a place like that, especially dressed that way?" His angry blue eyes fastened on his girlfriend's skimpy outfit.

"For the record, *Sheriff*,"—Char's eyes glittered dangerously—"I'll dress however I please. It's none of your business what I wear. I don't have to clear my fashion choices with you. You're not my father. Or my husband. In fact, I like this outfit so much, I may even wear it to church on Sunday."

Thank God for the protective grille between the seats.

Then the two of them really went at it. Char and Brady are fighters. Always have been. In fact, it was a fight back in high school that first brought them together all those years ago. Since then, they've fought and made up more times than I can remember. Their fights are legendary. Char and Brady are both passionate people—that's what attracts them to each other. It also pushes them apart. They've broken up several times over the years, but they've always gotten back together. When they fight, however, I've learned it's best to stay out of their way.

As they continued to argue, I decided to tune out and be productive. Time to take what we'd learned tonight at the Candy Club and put it all together. I started a list in my head.

- Lester's girlfriend Angel had left the club "sick" Saturday night to meet up with Les. He took her to Lake Potawatomi Park for some romance in the baking tent.
- If Angel was telling the truth, that solved one piece of the puzzle. Now we knew Lester was the one who had taken Sophie's pie out of the cooler to enjoy a little midnight snack—and ruin Sophie's entry for day two of the contest.

What a vindictive SOB.

That's the pie mystery solved, but we're still no closer to finding out who killed the head judge.

If *Angel's telling the truth, that is*, my inner cynic interjected. *She lied to her boss about being sick. If she could dupe hard-bitten Candy into believing her, she could lie to you and Char.*

You think Angel killed Lester? What would have been her motive?

Theft? Angel knew Les was rolling in the dough with all the expensive gifts he had given her. Maybe instead of jewelry and trinkets, she now wanted cash. Or . . . maybe when Les refused to drive her home, she got mad and, in the heat of the moment, grabbed the rolling pin and hit him. When she realized she'd killed her sugar daddy, she panicked, called an Uber, and split.

I rubbed my forehead. My head hurt imagining all the possible scenarios. *I need a break from murder.* I checked on Brady and Char, but they were still going at it full bore, so I turned my inner focus to tomorrow's contest instead.

Barbara Christensen had told me she'd be making blueberry cobbler—her husband's favorite. She would be submitting her entry in his honor. Barbara didn't care about winning; she simply loved to bake—a healthy attitude and one I wished Patsy Morris shared. Patsy seemed obsessed with winning. She seemed to live for winning the baking contest every year.

Then it clicked. The throwback-to-the-sixties devoted housewife and mother had held no control over her pig of a husband who had flaunted his coarse come-ons and infidelities for years, but she *could* control her baking—the one thing she excelled at and took pride in, besides her son. Stephen, however, was now a man in his forties. Patsy couldn't control him either—as evidenced by his alleged embezzling. What she *could* control, however, was winning the baking contest every year—at least while her head judge husband was still alive to award her first prize.

I knew Patsy would enter her classic apple cobbler—her go-to for church potlucks and picnics and a town favorite. Sophie was making a cherry cobbler. She had taken Margaret on a trip to Door County recently, and the two had come home with a mass of cherries. When she told me about her contest entry earlier today, Sophie had suddenly stopped and asked if I planned on doing a cherry cobbler. If so, she would bake something different.

"Not at all," I said. "I already made a cherry pie this week; I want to mix it up a bit."

The one wild card was Jeffrey Hollenbeck. I had no idea what kind of cobbler the hippie artist and gluten-free baker planned to bake. No matter what, though, I still planned to make peach cobbler. I love peaches. As I ran through my grandma's recipe in my mind, I decided that for a bit of color

I'd add halved cherries around the edge of the golden cobbler. *Maybe I could—*

"Ted?" Brady's voice punctured my recipe musings.

"Sorry." I lifted my head to regard him, then Char, both of whom seemed to have cooled down. "You two done fighting now?"

"For the moment," Char said. "Tell Brady what we found out from Angel."

I brought the sheriff up to date on everything the young dancer had said—how she'd admitted she and Lester had been in the park Saturday night around eleven and how Lester later found Sophie's pie in the tent and dug in, and how when Angel left the park the head judge was alive and well and gorging himself on coconut-cream pie.

"And you believed her?" Brady asked in a skeptical voice.

"Well . . . yeah. You saw her. She looks so young and innocent."

"Looks can be deceiving." Brady turned and grabbed his digital radio. "Dammit. She's probably hightailing it out of the county right now."

"Not with Candy watching her," I said. "She keeps a close eye on her girls. I'll bet after tonight's episode, she'll be keeping an even closer eye on Angel."

We listened as Brady told someone on the other end of the radio that he had a probable murder suspect at the Candy Club who was a likely flight risk. He gave his contact Angel's particulars and asked them to pick her up before she skipped town.

"Roger that," Brady said as he ended the call.

"Who were you talking to?" I asked.

"Racine PD. They're the closest," he said in a clipped voice. "They can be at the club within five minutes. If I'd known sooner Angel was likely the last person to see Les alive, I'd have picked her up myself."

I tried to tell you about her dalliance with Lester in the park the night he died, but you wouldn't let us speak. I wasn't about to say that aloud to Brady, however. I'm no fool. I slid a sidelong glance to my best friend. Question was, would she?

Char kept her lips firmly pressed together.

Brady picked up his cell and punched in a number. "Candy? Hello, this is Sheriff Brady Wells—I was in your club about twenty minutes ago?" He listened and nodded. "Yep, you got it. I've received some new information, and I'll need to talk to Angel again so she can corroborate it." He listened as Candy said something. "Nah, that's okay. I don't want to interrupt her set. I'll come back and talk to her again once I finish up here. Say, another hour or two? What time does Angel get off work?" Brady nodded again. "Thanks. Okay, I'll see you both then." He ended the call, his lips curving up in a smile.

"Babe," Char said, "don't you think Candy's going to warn Angel to get the hell out of there?"

"Yup. But if I know the Racine PD, they'll be arriving in another five, four, three, two, one . . ." Brady's phone buzzed with a text. He checked his phone and grinned. "Mission accomplished."

Chapter Nineteen

Gracie woke me early the next morning. Too early. She bounded on the bed, bright-eyed and curvy tailed.

"Not yet, Gracie-girl. It's too early," I said groggily. "Mommy needs some more sleep." But that wasn't happening. When a determined canine daughter needs to go, her human mother must get up and go.

Ya got that right, barked the alpha female in the house.

I let Gracie into the backyard, then dragged myself over to the coffeemaker and started a fresh pot. I yawned as I sat down at the kitchen table. It had been a long night.

After Brady dropped Char and me off at my house, he'd immediately headed to the Racine County Jail, where Angel was being detained, and I'd called an anxious Sharon, who had left us multiple texts and messages.

The first words out of our third Musketeer's mouth when she picked up the phone were, "I'm sorry I called Brady and told him where you were, but you didn't call when you were supposed to, and I was worried."

"My bad. I'd set an alarm to call you at eleven as agreed, but the club was so noisy I never heard it go off." Then I filled her in on what had transpired at the Candy Club.

"Does Brady really think this poor Angel girl—only a year older than my Jessica—murdered Lester?" she asked.

"Apparently she's a pretty strong suspect," I said. "Angel was in the park with Les on Saturday night and likely the last person to see him alive. Plus, it fits with the time frame when Frank Cullen estimates Les was killed. Very close, in fact."

Too close. Char and I had realized that after Brady left. Angel had said she'd left the park in an Uber promptly at eleven forty-five, with Les still alive and chowing down on Sophie's pie. For Angel to be telling the truth, someone else had to have been in the park at the same time. Hidden nearby, waiting and watching for Lester's girlfriend to leave. Once Angel's Uber exited the park, this mysterious someone then had to have almost immediately entered the tent, crept up behind Lester while he was devouring Sophie's pie, and hit him in the head with my rolling pin.

After coming up with this unlikely scenario, Char and I looked at each other, shook our heads, and said, "Nah."

Sadly, this meant the not-so-innocent Angel had probably murdered the head judge of our baking contest. Mystery solved. For the young Angel's sake, however, I hoped the charges would turn out to be manslaughter rather than murder. Whatever happened, though, my work was done. It was up to Brady and his law-enforcement pals to take it from here. After he dropped us off at my house last night, we'd expected him to return to Lake Potawatomi within the hour with Angel, but Brady had texted Char that he would be late and not to wait up for him.

I poured coffee into my largest mug—a regal Downton Abbey one Sharon had given me for Christmas a few years ago—and checked the fridge for any leftover kringle. *Yes!* Two small pieces left. I nuked the cherry kringle and spread a little butter on the sides of the flaky croissant-like pastry. I took a bite and moaned. *Perfection.* Nothing beats warm, buttery Danish kringle and a cup of strong coffee in the morning. After finishing off my carb-laden breakfast, I took Gracie on a quick walk around the block. Then I started making my peach cobbler entry for the day's contest.

Unlike the abundance of apples and Door County cherries Wisconsin is known for, locally grown peaches aren't plentiful in the Dairy State the way they are down south. Our cold winters often kill the trees, and a spring freeze will prevent the budding fruit from blooming. That's why I was delighted a few years ago when I discovered a nearby family-run orchard where the owners had planted several hardy varieties of peach trees. Since then, it's become a summer tradition for me to pick peaches at the small orchard every August. Earlier that week, I'd stopped by the family-run orchard and picked a grocery bag full.

I pulled out my largest saucepan and filled it with water, then preheated the oven. While I waited for the water to come to almost a boil, I gathered the ingredients I'd need, including the remaining cherries left over from the pie I had made earlier in the week. I washed, pitted, and quartered the cherries, then set them to one side and filled a bowl with cold water. Gently

I lowered the peaches into the pan of nearly boiling water, one by one so as not to bruise them. Thirty seconds later, I removed the golden-orange fruit from the hot pan, immersed them in the bowl of cold water until they were cool enough to handle, then set the peaches on the cutting board and removed the peels. They slipped off easily thanks to this insider baking trick Grandma Florence had taught me years ago.

In the mood for some music, I pulled up my show-tunes playlist and hit *Les Misérables*—the original recording with the sublime Colm Wilkinson as the first Jean Valjean. As I listened to Eponine sing "On My Own," I sliced peaches and sang along to one of my favorite Broadway songs, thinking about Tavish across the ocean and missing my British boyfriend. My anglophile heart swelled at those two words I'd never expected to say—*British boyfriend.*

He's a peach and a hottie. You hit the jackpot there, my friend.

Don't I know it.

As Eponine wound down her plaintive love song, I placed the sliced peaches in a greased baking dish, sprinkled them with lemon juice and baker's sugar, and dotted the mixture with butter. I slid the dish into the 375-degree oven and started mixing the topping. Once that was finished, I spread the topping over the golden hot peaches and randomly decorated the cobbler with the quartered deep-red cherries.

While the cobbler baked and the *Les Mis* soundtrack clicked over to "Master of the House," I went outside to cut flowers from the backyard. Although my garden can't compare to Margaret Miller's abundance—fifty beautiful rosebushes ring the edge of her yard—over the years, under Margaret's rosarian tutelage, I've planted a selection of hybrid tea roses and floribundas in a variety of colors. In addition to the gorgeous single-colored roses like Mr. Lincoln (rich velvety red), John F. Kennedy (white), Julia Child (yellow), Queen Elizabeth (pink), and Tropicana (coral), I have several multicolored roses I adore. I snipped a few Heart of Golds (two-toned pink and peachy yellow), Voodoo (yellow, orange, and peach), and Peace (cream with pink tips) to take with me to the tent. Then I cut some sprigs of lavender and rosemary for contrast.

"Hi, Teddie, how's it going?" Sophie called as she stepped onto her grandmother's backyard patio.

"Great. I'm getting roses together for my table decoration. How are you?"

"I'm good. My cobbler's in the oven." Sophie walked over to the picket fence that separates our yards. As she approached, I noticed the concerned look on her face.

"Everything okay?"

"Yeah, I guess." She pushed her turquoise-striped hair behind her ear. "But I'm kinda freaked out about the contest today."

"How come?"

"To be back in that tent again is creepy—the last time I was there, I saw Lester's dead face in my pie." Sophie shuddered. "And what if Patsy goes off on us again and accuses us of killing him in front of the whole town?"

"I don't think she'll do that." Especially if Brady told her they had a suspect in custody.

Would he reveal that to Patsy at this stage, though? I wondered. Angel had been picked up only last night. She still needed to be questioned and have her story investigated. Unless she confessed to killing Lester, it wasn't a slam dunk, even though everything pointed to her as the killer. Brady tended to keep things close to the vest in his professional capacity. He'd probably give Patsy Morris a vague update but not share all the details quite yet.

"I've heard there's a couple more likely suspects," I said offhandedly, "so as far as I'm concerned, that puts us in the clear."

Sophie sagged with relief. "That's good to know. Thanks. That helps. Now I need to exorcise the image of Lester and my pie from my mind." She added wryly, "I don't think I'll be making another coconut-cream pie for a long time."

We chatted for a couple minutes, and then I went back inside to finish my contest prep. I gathered the rest of my table decorations together—a creamy Battenberg-lace tablecloth, vase, and my grandmother's square, wedgwood-blue rosemaling box with peaches and vines on the top. The timer dinged, and I pulled the cobbler out of the oven and set it on the counter to cool.

Now it was time to decorate myself. I took out the peachy-salmon calf-length crinkle-cut dress I'd bought on clearance last summer at a nearby open-air market and began riffling through the repurposed coatrack that holds my myriad scarves—also known as camouflage for my slightly concave chest. Since I hate wearing a bra and wear knitted knockers only for special occasions (like last night's undercover investigation), scarves take the place of bras on my breastless chest. If the surgery had left me perfectly flat, I wouldn't have needed the flowing accessories. But my noticeable dent makes some people shift their eyes away in embarrassment or fear. I've discovered it's easier to cover my concave chest with a pretty or whimsical scarf instead. After sifting through the rack of swirling colors, I finally plucked a multihued blue scarf with salmon fringe to complete my contest ensemble.

Once I'd loaded up my car with the decorations and the cobbler as well as an insulated cooler bag with water, whipped cream, and the last of my sinkers cookies, I dropped by the art studio on my way to the baking tent. Astrid had called that morning to get the scoop on Angel, so I'd said I'd come over and tell her in person.

I pushed open the stained-glass door and entered the cavernous warehouse.

"Hi, Teddie." Astrid stuck her head out from behind a large canvas on the left side of the studio. "Give me a minute to finish this damn fish, and then we can talk."

"Mind if I take a peek?"

"Knock yourself out. But don't hold the fish against me," she grumbled.

I moved over to her canvas and stepped behind it, where I beheld a bald eagle in flight, wings spread, talons out, swooping down and grabbing a fish at what I recognized as Astrid's beloved Chippewa Flowage. "That's amazing, Astrid! That eagle looks like he's going to fly right out of that painting. Your wildlife is always so lifelike."

"Except for this darn fish, who's not behaving." The elderly artist tossed down her brush. "I need a break." She stood up and stretched. "Let's have a seat so Jane Tennison can bring Jessica Fletcher up to date," she said with a wicked grin.

We sat down on two clear acrylic chairs opposite Astrid's painting-in-progress. I reached into my cooler bag and pulled out the bag of sinkers and two bottles of water and set them on the small mosaicked table between us.

"You sure know the way to my heart." Astrid took a long drink of water and munched on a cookie. "Okay, spill," she said. "I'm all ears. What happened last night on your undercover mission?"

I glanced around the studio.

"Don't worry. We're the only ones here. Except for Jeffrey, but he's back in the office behind closed doors, working on the books."

I told the wannabe Jessica Fletcher the whole story, complete with Angel's confession about being in the park with Lester on the night he was killed and how she was now in the Racine jail, awaiting questioning.

"You did it, Teddie!" Astrid crowed. "You solved the mystery." She high-fived me. "Way to go."

"Maybe," I said. "I hope this is all over. But"—I raised my finger to my lips—"what I told you doesn't leave this room. I don't think Brady wants it getting out yet until things are more official. I'm not even sure if Angel's been questioned yet, so until we hear more from Brady, this doesn't go any further. You know how the sheriff is."

Astrid made a zipping motion across her mouth. "My lips are sealed," she said as the front door opened.

Colleen Murphy entered with a huge bag in her hands. "Hi, Astrid, hi, Teddie," she said. Her eyes flicked between us. "What's going on?"

Uh-oh. Did she hear Astrid?

"Oh, nothing," the wildlife artist said guiltily. Astrid rushed out the words. "Teddie just stopped by to shoot the breeze for a couple minutes before she heads on over to the park for the contest. Right, Teddie?"

"Right." I stood up nonchalantly to direct Colleen's focus away from Astrid's awkward and obvious lie. "Nice to see you again." I smiled at the middle-aged artist with the great blow-out and inclined my head to the bag in her hand. "What's that? Did you bring me a present?" I teased. "You shouldn't have."

"Maybe next time." Colleen grinned and reached into the bag. She pulled out a massive jumble of vivid fuchsia, turquoise, emerald, and violet yarn. "This is my latest piece—I brought it over to hang up for next week's show and fund raiser." She unfurled the mass of yarn to reveal an exquisite, capacious shawl wrap with multicolored tassels at the bottom.

"That. Is. Absolutely. Gorgeous." I shot Colleen a pleading look. "Are you sure it's not for me? After all, I am the colorful-scarf queen of Lake Potawatomi." I flicked the bottom of my salmon-fringed blue scarf and struck a pose.

Colleen laughed and walked over to me. She laid the heavy shawl/scarf on my shoulders and wrapped it loosely around my neck, twisting the long ends into a casual knot in front. "Tell you what; I can't give this piece to you, but you're welcome to bid on it at the fund raiser." The textile artist and yarn shop owner turned me to face one of Cheryl's mosaicked mirrors on the wall. "What do you think?"

What do I think? I think it's one of the most beautiful scarves I've ever seen. It looks great against my hair. I must be wearing it when I step off the plane at Heathrow into Tavish's waiting arms in October. I stuck out my hand to Colleen. "You've got yourself a deal."

We shook on it.

Jeffrey Hollenbeck emerged from the back office, wearing a paisley cotton shirt and his ubiquitous drawstring linen pants. "Hey, everyone. Why wasn't I invited to the party?" He inclined his gray ponytailed head to me. "Killer shawl. Looks great on you. Fabulous colors."

"Thanks. It's not mine quite yet, but will be after next week's fund raiser," I said. "Isn't Colleen's work amazing?" I fingered the soft, multihued yarn. "A bit hot for August, though." I removed the heavy wrap with regret and handed it back to her.

Jeffrey nodded appreciatively at his fellow artist. "Gorgeous piece, Colleen. I think you'll get lots of bidders for this beauty." He noticed the open bag of sinkers on the table. "What's that?"

"My Everything but the Kitchen Sink cookies," I said, "or as I call them, sinkers. They're not gluten-free, though, so you can't have one."

Jeffrey smirked and filched one. "Yes, I can. I'm not the one with the gluten intolerance; my daughter is. I simply adapted my baking around her." He bit into the cookie, closed his eyes, and released a sigh of bliss. "Mmm, this is incredible, Teddie. Would you share the recipe?"

"I might be persuaded, but only if you give me your gluten-free chocolate-chip cookie recipe."

"Deal." He finished the first cookie and grabbed another.

Colleen glanced down at her trim waistline in her skinny jeans. "I know I really shouldn't, but may I have one too?"

"Of course." I extended the bag to her. Colleen lifted out a sinker.

"You wanna pass that bag this way," Astrid said.

The four of us munched contentedly on cookies and chatted.

I cut my eyes to a bulky, oversized bright-orange metal contraption in the far-right corner of the artists' space that looked like it belonged on an outdoor construction site. "Is that the newest piece of art? What's it called? *Under Construction*?" I teased.

"That's a scissor lift," Jeffrey said. "The forklift's nimbler cousin with an aerial platform. We rented it to install the hanging art pieces for the fund raiser. It has a higher, more stable reach than a ladder, and the platform can easily hold three people."

"Including me." Astrid grinned. "Pretty fun going up and down on that thing."

"You be careful," I said to my elderly Norwegian friend. "Don't you get on that alone—I don't want you falling and killing yourself." What I'd nearly said was "falling and breaking a hip," but I'd corrected myself in time, knowing the geriatric reference would tick off my ultra-independent friend. "Then who would I get to paint another picture of Gracie for me?" I teased.

Astrid released a theatrical sigh. "You only love me for my art."

"It's a cross all we artists must bear," Jeffrey said, winking at Astrid.

"I'd rather be loved for my art than my boobs," Colleen joked, glancing down at the cleavage poking out of her snug white T-shirt.

"Tell me about it," Astrid said. "I had the same problem back in the day. I had to beat them off with a stick." She sent a sly glance to the handsome Jeffrey. "I'm sure you know what I'm talkin' about."

"I never kiss and tell," he said, a twinkle in his brown eyes.

"Jeffrey, are you ready for the contest today?" I asked. "What kind of cobbler did you make?"

"Blackberry-and-huckleberry combo. I wanted to do something different than the standard cherry, blueberry, or peach."

I sent him a wry smile. "Those do seem to be the usual suspects, don't they? Barbara's doing blueberry, Sophie made cherry, and yours truly did peach—with a twist."

"Oops," he said with an abashed grin. "Guess I really put my foot in it, huh?"

"Nah. Don't worry about it."

Astrid chased her third cookie with a drink of water. "Is Patsy doing her apple cobbler?"

"Yep. Patsy likes to stick to the tried and true."

"I was so surprised when I heard the contest was continuing," Colleen said. "Won't that be too hard on Patsy, considering her husband's death in the tent?"

"It was her idea." I shrugged. "She insisted Lester would have wanted it. Patsy wants the contest to continue in Les's honor."

Astrid grunted. "I'd never put the words *Lester Morris* and *honor* in the same sentence."

Nobody would, Astrid. Except Les's wife.

"Well, I sure hope the sheriff catches the murderer soon." Colleen shuddered. "It's scary having a random killer running around loose in our town." She shivered again and rubbed her toned arms. "I mean, any one of us could be the next victim."

"I don't think we need to worry about that," I reassured her. "I think Lester was the only target. Brady's good at his job. I have a feeling it won't be long before we hear of an arrest."

Colleen's vivid green eyes widened. "Do you know some—"

Barbara Christensen walked through the front door with her mini goldendoodle in her oversized tote. "Hi, everyone," she said brightly. "Teddie, I saw your car out front and wanted to ask you something before the contest starts." The squirming puppy jumped out of Barbara's bag and ran to the back of the art studio, yipping and toppling a wastebasket and art supplies in her wake.

"No, Taffy!" Barbara shouted. "Get back here!"

Jeffrey reached down to grab the energetic pup as she raced past, but she eluded his grasp. I chased after her, adopting a coaxing tone. "Come here, Taffy. Come here, sweet girl."

But the excited puppy was too entranced by all the new toys and scents to explore. Taffy scampered behind a four-paneled Japanese plum blossom room divider screen in the far back corner of the studio. I hurried after her before she could do any damage. Behind the screen stood a large object covered by a sheet. Taffy latched on to a corner of the sheet trailing on the ground and started chewing on it.

"No!" yelled Jeffrey, who had followed in the chase. He lunged for the puppy, but Taffy dodged out of his way and raced back to the front of the studio, the sheet still firmly in her mouth. The sheet slipped off, revealing the hidden piece of art in the process—a sculpture of a reclining nude woman.

And not just any nude woman. My mother. Claire St. John.

Chapter Twenty

Oh. My. God. So this is what Mom's been doing on all her late-night mystery dates.

Is that all *she's been doing?*

I glanced from the sculpture of the aging nude to the aging artist.

"It's not finished yet," Jeffrey said. "I'm having trouble with the eyes. It's called *Beauty*," he said simply, quoting, " 'Age cannot wither her, nor custom stale her infinite variety.' "

"Shakespeare?"

"*Antony and Cleopatra*."

"Magnificent sculpture, my friend," Astrid breathed, as she appeared beside us. "I know you've been working on it for a while. I've been champing at the bit to see it."

"Thanks," Jeffrey said. "It's not ready for public consumption yet." He glanced in Colleen and Barbara's direction. The two women had managed to corral Taffy and were chatting as Colleen petted the caramel-colored pup and made cooing sounds to her.

"Understood," Astrid said. She retrieved the fallen sheet from the floor, and together she and Jeffrey covered up my mom. Jeffrey adjusted the privacy screen.

Then the three of us rejoined Colleen and Barbara at the front of the studio.

"I'm so sorry," Barbara said. Two spots of color stained her cheeks. "I hope Taffy didn't do any damage. Please tell me she didn't destroy any of your precious works of art," she pleaded.

"Nah," Astrid said. "All she did was knock over a can of brushes and a wastebasket. No harm, no foul." The animal lover scratched Taffy behind her ears. "That's what puppies do, right? Even pretty puppies like you."

"Jeffrey, I'm so embarrassed," Barbara said. "I don't know what in the world I was thinking, bringing a dog inside an art studio."

"It's cool," he said. "Don't worry about it." He flapped his hand in a laid-back wave. Then he winked. "But maybe wait until she's no longer a puppy?"

Barbara blushed. "Better than that, you have my word that I will never bring a dog in here again. I saw Teddie's car outside, and it reminded me I needed to ask her something, so I blundered in, not knowing my sweet puppy would transform into a bull in a china shop."

"At least no china was broken," Astrid said as she petted Taffy. "Good girl."

"What did you need to ask me, Barbara?" I said.

She puckered her forehead in thought. "You know what? I can't even remember now." Barbara released a self-conscious giggle. "The joys of old age."

"Happens to the best of us," Jeffrey said.

"*All* of us," Astrid added. "I'm always saying, 'What was I going to say? Now why did I come in here again?' "

"I hear you on that," Colleen said with a chuckle.

"Was it something to do with the contest, maybe?" I asked, trying to jog Barbara's memory. "You said you wanted to ask me something before the contest started."

"Oh my goodness, the contest! What time is it?" Barbara placed Taffy back in her tote. "I still have to go decorate my table."

"So do I." I checked my phone. "Yikes. It's later than I thought. The contest starts in twenty minutes. We'd better get going." I grabbed my insulated cooler bag, leaving the rest of the sinkers behind. "Jeffrey, are you coming?"

"I'll be there in a few minutes. I need to grab a couple things."

"Okay. We'll see you in the tent." I nodded to the other artists. " 'Bye, Astrid. 'Bye, Colleen. Hope to see you there."

"I wouldn't miss it." Astrid licked her lips. "I will be the first in line for all your delicious cobbler once the judges announce the winner."

Barbara and I rushed over to the park together, making our way through the crowd of townspeople already gathered around the baking tent and gazebo—lolling on picnic blankets on the grass or sitting in assorted lawn chairs and camp chairs. I spotted the LaPoints, the Torkilsens, and the Lewis family with Noah's legs splayed casually across Chewie. Frank and Belinda Cullen were there too, with their daughter Lauren sitting in the shade next to Margaret Miller, both of them sipping from aluminum water bottles.

"Hey, Teddie-girl, I hope you win," Fred Matson called out as I hurried past.

"Thanks, Fred." I gave him a half wave as I continued on to the baking tent while Barbara handed off the squirming Taffy to her grandkids, who had scored a prime spot near the front of the gazebo.

"*There* you are!" Sharon said when we entered the baking tent. "I was beginning to get worried."

"Sorry," I said. "We got sidetracked at the art studio. Jeffrey will be along in a minute."

Barbara scurried in and began decorating her table as I pulled out my tablecloth and covered my card table.

"You want some help, Teddie?" Sophie asked. With the judges' permission, she had moved her table next to mine rather than leaving it in the location of Lester's demise.

"Thanks. I could sure use it." As we set up my decorations, I saw that Sophie's table had a cute red-and-white polka-dotted cloth across the top, with three small red square boxes of descending size in the upper right corner. Atop the red boxes, one per box, stood ceramic figures of Mickey Mouse, Minnie Mouse, and Pluto, eyeing a bowl of plump cherries beneath them. To complete the whimsical tableau, a tall Spider-Man action figure stood guard over Sophie's cherry cobbler.

"Your table is adorbs, Sophie," I said. "I have a feeling a certain young deputy will especially like it."

Sophie blushed.

Patsy, whose table stood directly opposite ours, had gone the Mom-and-apple-pie patriotic route, I noticed. The multiple-time contest winner had covered her card table with a red-white-and-blue checked oilcloth and topped it with red silk roses and white silk carnations in a blue vase, with two miniature American flags poking out the sides of the vase. Next to her apple cobbler centerpiece, Patsy had placed a red-white-and-blue plastic bowl filled with familiar red wax apples straight from the sixties. (Grandma Florence had the same retro waxed apples on her dining room table for years.)

"Glad you could make it, Teddie," Patsy snarked. "May the best baker win." The elderly baker, in a powder-blue polyester capris set complete with a blouse studded with appliqued red apples, had been cozying up to the three judges, Bea, Sharon, and her son, Stephen, who was sporting a more colorful Tommy Bahama shirt and khakis for today's festive occasion.

Sharon caught my eye and rolled hers.

After I finished setting up and Sophie returned to her table, Bea and Sharon casually approached me. Meanwhile, Patsy continued talking to Stephen, gazing up at her son adoringly and patting him on the arm as he talked.

Char entered the tent just as Bea and Sharon arrived at my table. Her eyes fixed on Patsy and Stephen across the way, who were still deep in conversation. "Hey, bestie," she said, keeping her voice down, "have you heard the latest?"

Has Angel been charged with Les's murder? Already? My pulse quickened. "From Brady? What's going on?"

Char shook her head. "Not Brady. Stephen," she said quietly. "Word's gotten out about him playing fast and loose with the chamber's funds."

"That's what we came to tell you too," Sharon whispered. She glanced around to make sure no one was listening. "Wilma

Sorensen overheard Jerry Larsen and Bud Olson talking about the fight Les and Stephen had where Lester accused Stephen of embezzling money. The whole town is buzzing."

Char's eyes slid to Patsy, who was busy picking a loose thread from her son's Hawaiian shirt. "Yeah, especially when Wilma announced that Les was about to turn Stephen in for siphoning the money but before he could, Lester wound up dead." She mimicked Wilma's sugary maliciousness. "And wasn't *that* a coincidence."

I stole a glance at the remaining Morris family. Stephen was looking down at his phone, but Patsy was staring straight at us and fidgeting nervously. She kept clutching and unclutching the legs of her polyester capris. I pretended not to notice her twitching and allowed my eyes to casually roam the tent, landing on Barbara's Blue Willow–themed tableau that complemented her blueberry cobbler.

"Barbara, your table looks beautiful," I called out.

"So does yours, Teddie. Your roses are gorgeous! I love all the different shades of peach and salmon. So pretty."

I offered my thanks. Then, out of the corner of my eye, I noticed Stephen shove his phone in his back pocket and give his mother a perfunctory kiss on the cheek. He whispered something in her ear and started to stride away, but Patsy grabbed his arm.

"Where are you going, son?" she hissed, loud enough for us to hear. "The contest is about to start, and you're the head judge."

"Sorry," he said curtly. "Something's come up that I need to take care of. I'll be back in a few minutes."

"But Stephen—"

He shook off Patsy's hand impatiently. "Mom, I *said* I'll be back soon. Jeez." Stephen strode out of the vinyl tent, colliding with Jeffrey Hollenbeck in his haste. Jeffrey had sauntered in, cobbler in hand, backpack looped over his shoulders. The glass baking dish holding the artist's blackberry-and-huckleberry cobbler tilted and nearly fell from his hands.

"Hey, man, watch it," Jeffrey said.

"Sorry. Excuse me." Stephen kept right on moving. Clearly a man on a mission.

But what was the mission?

"Where's he going in such a hurry?" Jeffrey asked us. "Isn't he one of the judges?"

"He certainly is," Sharon said, looking down at her watch and shaking her head.

"I'm sure he'll be right back," Bea reassured Jeffrey.

"That's cool. Gives me time to get my stuff set up." He moved over to the last remaining unadorned table and set his cobbler pan on it.

Char leaned over and whispered, "Let's take bets on whether Stephen returns. I say no. I bet he's heard all the chatter and is going to blow this popsicle stand before it all comes crashing down."

"And run out on his mother?" I said quietly. "Especially now that she's a widow? I don't think so. Those two are joined at the hip."

Char shook her head. "You're wrong, my friend. Patsy is, for sure, but I think Stephen's ready—long past ready—to finally cut the apron strings."

I glanced at Patsy, standing alone and forlorn beside her table. She adjusted the American flags in her blue vase with a trembling hand and kept fiddling with the placement of her cobbler, moving it a couple inches one way and then back again. *Had Patsy heard the scuttlebutt about her son? Is that why she's so fidgety and anxious? And what exactly made Stephen rush out of here so fast?*

Face it. Char may be right. At this very moment, Stephen could be getting the heck out of Dodge.

Brady appeared in the doorway of the baking tent. He and Char had obviously patched things up, because he sent her a slow, seductive smile, which Char returned in kind. Brady ambled toward us as Sharon and Bea left to make the rounds of the other contestants, leaving Char and me alone to talk to the sheriff.

Good. Now I can ask Brady what's going on with Angel and if she's confessed. "Brady, what—" I started to ask, but Patsy Morris cut me off midsentence.

She rushed over and clutched desperately at Brady's uniform sleeve. "Sheriff, do you have any news for me? Have you found my husband's killer?"

Brady tugged at his collar. "Maybe. I'm not at liberty to say anything yet, but I will say that we have a strong suspect and hope to be making a formal arrest soon."

Patsy paled. Her hand on Brady's arm trembled. She dropped her hand to her side and took an unsteady step back. "Excuse me," she said, her eyes darting wildly around the baking tent. "I forgot something. I'll be right back." She hurried to the open doorway through which Brady had just entered.

"Patsy," Bea called out from Jeffrey's table, which I noticed was now covered by an Indian tapestry, "where are you going? We're starting the contest in a few minutes."

The nine-time baking contest winner lifted her hand in a distracted wave to the older judge. "This will only take a minute. I won't be gone long, I promise. I forgot something at the house." Patsy darted out of the tent, leaving Bea and Sharon staring after her in astonishment.

"What did I tell you?" Char said, a satisfied expression on her face. "I bet mommy dearest is chasing after Stephen right now. Before you know it, this town will be but a faint memory to the Morris family."

"I thought you said Stephen was cutting the apron strings."

Char sighed. "The poor schlub wanted to, but looks like mom's not going to let him loose without a fight."

Brady's head swiveled from me to Char. He narrowed his eyes. "Would the two of you care to tell me what's going on?"

"Word's out that Stephen Morris has apparently been embezzling from the chamber of commerce," I said. "Naturally, Wilma Sorensen is fanning the rumor flames, saying Stephen did his old man in before his crime came to light." I flicked my eyes to Char. "Your girlfriend here is convinced Stephen's doing a runner," I said, using one of my favorite BBC mystery terms.

"A runner?" The non-anglophile Brady lifted his eyebrows.

"Making a run for it."

"If you ask me, mother and son are making a quick getaway even as we speak," Char said.

"We'll see about that," said Brady. He pulled out his cell to call Augie, but as he did, Stephen's voice sounded outside the tent.

"My apologies for the delay, everyone," he said. "The contest will be starting in another minute or two. We appreciate your patience." Stephen reentered the tent. "So sorry about that," he said in his smooth salesman voice. "I had some urgent business that couldn't wait. Shall we get started?" He looked around. "Where's my mother?"

Patsy rushed back inside the tent, her face flushed with exertion from the dash to her house two doors away. "Here I am, son. I'm sorry. I'm ready now," she said in a resolute tone. She patted Stephen's arm.

Brady and Char departed to join the rest of the audience as the three judges began making their rounds. They started at Sophie's table.

"How cute is that?" Bea said. "I love Mickey and Minnie."

Each judge took a taste of Sophie's cherry cobbler, topped with vanilla ice cream that she had brought in her Yeti cooler.

"Mmm," Bea said, as she savored her bite. "This is absolutely delicious. Not too sweet, with a nice crunch."

"Scrumptious," Sharon agreed.

Stephen took a second bite, then delivered a slow smile to Sophie. "I have to say, that is the *best* cherry cobbler I've ever had." He gave her the Paul Hollywood handshake.

Sophie flushed at his praise.

The three judges moved on to Barbara's blueberry cobbler, which they pronounced equally delicious.

"I can tell this is going to be a close contest," Stephen said with a chuckle.

Sharon, Bea, and Stephen then moved en masse to Jeffrey's tapestry-clad table, decorated simply with a jade plant in a terra-cotta flowerpot and a sprig of huckleberry. As the judges tasted the lone male contestant's blackberry-and-huckleberry gluten-free entry, I pulled the whipped cream from my cooler bag and stirred it, ready to spoon it onto my peach cobbler as soon as the judges arrived. While I waited, my mind wandered to Stephen's and Patsy's mutual rushed departures from the tent earlier.

What was that *all about, anyway?*

Maybe Stephen raced to the chamber to eliminate evidence of his cooking the books.

Nah, my logical side interjected. *That would have taken longer than five minutes.*

And Patsy said she forgot something, but when she came back, her hands were empty . . .

Bea Andersen's cheerful voice interrupted my wonderings. "Okay, Teddie, your turn. Are you ready for us?"

"Sure," I said to the three judges ringing my table. "Let me put on the whipped cream, and we're good to go."

"Are those cherries around the edge?" Stephen asked.

"Yep. I thought it would be a nice contrast against the peaches."

"Nice touch," Bea said.

Sharon cut into the cobbler and placed three bite-sized portions with whipped cream onto the paper plates I'd provided. Then the judges dug in.

"Yum," Bea said. "Those peaches are delicious, and the cherries are a nice addition."

"Definitely," Sharon said.

"I think I need another bite before I can decide," Stephen teased. He cut a larger bite and added a dollop of whipped cream. When he finished chewing, Stephen held out his hand to me, offering the coveted Paul Hollywood handshake.

As we shook hands, suddenly I heard an odd wheezing sound from across the tent, followed by a heavy thud.

The judges whirled around as one, and as they did, I saw that Patsy had fallen to the ground and was clutching her throat.

Stephen raced over and dropped to his knees beside his gasping mother. "Mom, where's your EpiPen?" he yelled.

I dashed behind Patsy's table and grabbed the older woman's purse, dumping the contents on the table and searching frantically through the jumble. I raised desperate eyes to Sharon and Bea. "There's no EpiPen here."

Sharon called 911 as Bea ran to the tent doorway and yelled, "Sheriff! Get in here ASAP!"

Jeffrey raced over to the fallen woman with his backpack. He flung it to the ground at Patsy's feet and lifted her legs onto the backpack as I heard Barbara in the background yelling to the crowd in the park, "Does anyone have an EpiPen?"

Patsy continued to wheeze. Her eyes locked on Stephen. "I love you, son," she gasped hoarsely. Then she passed out.

Brady rushed into the tent, followed by Char, and immediately began administering CPR to the unconscious Patsy. Augie joined him.

"Get back, everyone," Char said. "Give them some room."

"What's she allergic to?" Augie asked Stephen.

"Shellfish and penicillin," he said in a panicky voice. "She made lobster for me last night, but she didn't eat any—she had chicken."

Sophie appeared beside me, shaking, as she stared in shock at Patsy. "Oh my gosh, oh my gosh." Her breathing quickened, and she began to hyperventilate.

I put my arm around her and moved my young neighbor away from the sight of Patsy and Brady on the ground. "Sophie, slow your breathing," I said. "Take it easy." I pinched one of her nostrils. "Breathe through your nose, Sophie."

Sharon joined us and rubbed Sophie's back. "That's it, sweetie," she encouraged. "Nice and easy. There you go."

As we took care of Sophie, I could hear Brady continuing his ministrations in the background as Stephen pleaded, "Hang in there, Mom. You're going to be fine."

Barbara, Bea, and Jeffrey joined us. Sirens blared nearby. Moments later, pounding feet entered the tent. I glanced up to see our local fire department EMTs take over CPR for Brady.

My fellow contestants and I stayed out of their way and focused on Sophie rather than the EMTs and the noisy and urgent medical actions they were taking to try to save Patsy. Jeffrey talked to Sophie in a low, calming, fatherly voice, and Barbara closed her eyes. I saw her lips moving, and I knew my Catholic friend was offering up prayers for Patsy. I did the same, trying to shut out everything else around me. I don't know how long we prayed, but it seemed like mere moments before Brady's words made my eyes fly open.

"I'm sorry, Stephen," he said, his voice full of regret and compassion. "She's gone."

Slowly I turned to see Brady shove his hand through his hair and expel an exhausted breath as the EMTs gently closed Patsy's eyes.

Stephen stared at Brady and the EMTs in disbelief. "No," he said.

"I'm so sorry," Brady said. The EMTs echoed his apology.

Tears fell from Stephen's eyes. "No," he repeated softly. Then he bent his head and gently stroked his mother's hand. "I love you, Mom," he said.

The fire department EMTs discreetly moved aside to talk to Brady and get the necessary details.

Char squeezed the head judge's shoulder. "I'm so sorry, Stephen," she said softly.

He nodded and continued stroking Patsy's age-spotted hand, his tears splashing onto his mother's hand.

I turned around to meet the shocked eyes of the other two judges and my fellow contestants. Bea's eyes filled, and fat tears rolled down Sophie's face.

"I can't believe it," Sophie said, the tears falling in earnest now. "P-poor Patsy."

Sharon hugged the youngest contestant, who was her daughter's age, and led her outside, but not before I heard Sophie mutter, "This tent is cursed!"

Barbara bent her head and murmured softly, and I knew she was saying prayers for the dead.

As the other two judges gently approached Stephen to express their condolences, I moved on autopilot over to Patsy's table and numbly began putting her personal items back into the interior of her worn white purse.

As I did so, a folded piece of notepaper fluttered to the floor. I picked it up and saw the spidery handwriting. *Read after my death.*

I skimmed the words in the note and gasped. "Brady," I said, "you need to see this."

"Not now, Ted," he said, intent in conversation with Frank Cullen, who must have entered the tent when I was focused on Barbara and Sophie. The two had stepped away from Patsy and Stephen and were engaged in a quiet conversation.

I walked over to Brady and the coroner, paper in hand. "Brady," I said quietly. "You're really going to want to look at this." I handed him the paper.

He quickly scanned the note. His eyes flew up to meet mine. "Suicide?" he whispered. Brady glanced over at Stephen, who was being comforted by Bea.

I nodded. "Keep reading."

As the sheriff read, his mouth tightened into a grim line. Brady straightened his back. Then he told Augie to clear the tent of everyone except Stephen and the coroner.

As the last one to exit, I overheard Brady say to the lone judge in a voice tinged with regret, "I'm sorry to have to tell you this, Stephen, but I'm afraid your mother committed suicide."

"Suicide?" Stephen's voice rose in disbelief. "Why? Why would she do that?"

"Because she killed your father."

Chapter Twenty-One

"*Patsy* killed Lester?" Sharon said as we gathered around my kitchen table half an hour later. "I can't believe it."

"I can," Char said, taking a bite of peach cobbler. "Lester was a pig."

"Well, we all know that," Sharon said, "but Patsy seemed so broken up about his death."

"She was a good actress," I said. "She had everyone fooled." I sipped my coffee. "I guess that's why she pointed the finger at me and Sophie—to divert attention from herself." I shook my head. "I can't believe I never thought of Patsy. It often turns out to be the spouse. You always check out the husband or wife first. I should know that. I write murder mysteries." I expelled a sigh. "Maybe I need to switch genres."

"You could always write bodice rippers," Char teased. "That would be right up your alley. All that purple prose and heaving bosoms."

I stuck my tongue out at her.

"Don't you dare change genres," Sharon said. "I love your Kate and Kallie mysteries. I'm dying to read *Suffocating in Soufflé*."

"Which, by the way, I need to get back to in a few days." I forked up some peach cobbler. "Now that Lake Potawatomi's latest murder has been solved, I'm looking forward to returning to the world of fictional murders."

"What I don't understand," Sharon mused aloud, "is why Patsy waited until the day of the contest to fess up to her husband's murder. Why didn't she do it sooner? What prompted her to confess today of all days—after she killed herself?"

"Patsy figured an arrest was imminent," I said. "When Brady came to the tent, she asked him for the latest news on Lester's murder. Brady told her he had a strong suspect and planned to make a formal arrest soon."

"Little did Patsy know Brady was talking about Angel, not her," Char murmured.

"That's right," I said. "With all this going on, I almost forgot about Angel. Guess she'll be back at the club tonight dancing for dollars again."

"Or not," Char said, with a knowing smile. "Rumor has it that the Candy Club may be going belly-up soon. The cops have been working on a joint undercover investigation, checking on complaints of drug dealing and more than just dancing happening at the club. They've been trying to find someone to corroborate this illegal activity and provide the necessary specifics they need to bring charges and close the club down, but they couldn't get anyone to go on the record. Until recently."

"Candy is not going to be happy being forced into early retirement," I said.

"I understand there're some lovely concrete retirement communities with all the amenities," Char said with a wicked grin. "Group activities, daily exercise, and three gourmet meals a day. What more could a retired exotic dancer want?"

"Patsy Morris knew she'd never make it out of one of those retirement communities," I said. "The very thought of prison terrified her. She wrote that in her suicide note. That's why she took the only way out she could see."

Although Patsy hadn't liked me and had done a good job of pointing the finger of suspicion at me and Sophie for her husband's murder, which had sent me in several different directions and taken up a lot of my time and energy trying to disprove her accusation, I didn't hate Patsy. I certainly didn't want her dead.

"What else did her suicide note say?" Sharon asked.

"Patsy wrote that Lester was a liar and a philanderer who cheated on her their entire marriage. She only stayed married to him because of her son, the real love of her life. She told Stephen she should have listened to him and divorced Les years ago. She asked Stephen to forgive her and said it had been a privilege and the greatest joy of her life to be his mother."

Sharon sniffled. "Poor Stephen. To lose both parents in one week. So tragic. And then to find out his mother murdered his father in cold blood? How awful. I don't know how he's going to cope with that," she said, "especially on his own. Stephen's all alone now. Too bad he's not married, or at least in a relationship. If he had a girlfriend, she could help him through this."

"His friends can help," I said. "I'm sure they'll be there for him."

"I don't know that Stephen has any friends," Char said thoughtfully. "I've never seen him hanging out with anyone.

He always came in the bookstore by himself. I think he's more the loner type. But back to Patsy's suicide note." Char tilted her head at me. "Did she say why she killed Lester now? After all those years of his cheating and humiliating her, what finally pushed her over the edge to whack him now?"

"Patsy said the last straw was finding out Les was"—I paused for dramatic effect—"a thief. She wrote that Lester had been stealing from the chamber of commerce for years, but recently he had been found out and was now trying to pin the blame on Stephen. She wouldn't stand for that. Patsy insisted her son would never steal and that Lester was the thief in the family."

Char let out a long, low whistle. "Whoa." Then she raised her hands in the air and applauded. "Great move, Mom, protecting your son with your final act and throwing your creepy husband under the bus instead."

"Exactly what I thought," I said. "With Lester dead, he can't turn Stephen in for embezzlement."

"But wait." A wrinkle formed between Sharon's brows. "I'm confused. So Lester's the embezzler now, not Stephen?"

"According to Patsy," I said. "Whether the rest of the chamber, the fraud investigators, and the feds buy that or not is another story. But that's not my problem."

I heard a familiar car pull into the driveway and glanced out the window. Mom's Lexus.

Now that, *however, is my problem. And one I need to fix. Time to make amends.* I squared my shoulders, cut two pieces of cobbler and put them in small dessert bowls, filled two mugs of coffee, and set the food and drinks on the vintage, hand-painted floral green toleware metal serving tray with pink cottage roses that I'd scored from a thrift store.

"Can you guys let yourselves out? I'll talk to you later." I puffed out a breath, lifting up my bangs. "Wish me luck." I picked up the tray and headed over to the lion's den.

I knocked on my mother's door.

"Who is it?" she called through the closed door.

"Your daughter." I raised my voice. "With humble pie."

Mom opened the door and regarded me warily. As always, Claire St. John looked flawlessly put-together from head to toe. Today she wore a sleeveless navy-blue shift, loosely belted, that fell to her calves. Flat T-strap sandals highlighted her perfect pedicure. I did notice something different, however. Instead of her usual classic gold or silver jewelry, an artsy enamel cloisonné pendant of swirling blues and silver hung around her neck.

"Nice necklace," I said, lifting the tray. "I brought your favorite—peach cobbler."

Mom opened the door wider and stepped aside to let me enter.

I headed to her minimalist gray galley kitchen and set the tray down on the spartan white quartz counter top. Then I took a deep breath and turned to face my mother. "Let me say this straight out. I'm sorry I hurt you, Mom. I'm sorry I confronted you in the park and accused you of having an affair with a married man. I should have known better. That's not your style." I puffed out a breath. "I hope you can forgive me and we can start afresh. I know we're totally different people, but you're my mother and I'd like to get to know you better.

The real you. The you I saw in the art gallery." I raised my hands, palms out. "Only with clothes on," I said slyly.

"I knew that sculpture would embarrass you," Mom said, her contoured cheeks reddening. "That's why I asked Jeffrey to keep it under wraps for now, until I could explain and tell you about it."

"It didn't embarrass me at all, Mom. It's beautiful," I said quietly. "*Beauty* is the perfect name for it. I'm proud that my seventy-three-year-old mother had the guts to show the world that beauty is timeless and age is irrelevant. And I'm also proud that my mom will be forever immortalized in a work of art, like a modern-day Venus de Milo. But with arms."

Tears slipped down my mother's face. They were followed by a waterfall that gushed down her face as she began to sob. Great, shuddering sobs shook her whole body.

"What? What did I say?" I shot her an anxious look. "I'm sorry. I keep saying the wrong thing. I came over to make things better, not worse."

Mom held up her hand in a stop motion and shook her head as the tears continued to snake down her face. "You didn't make things worse, Teddie," she said. "It's simply that I'm all verklempt."

I did the only thing I knew to do. I hugged her. Mom's never been a big hugger, unlike my dad, who loved to hug. Dad was affectionate, while Mom's always been more detached and aloof. Her hugs have always been brief, and perfunctory at best. But this time when I hugged her, she clung to me like she never wanted to let go.

Eventually, however, she did. We were both getting hot and sweaty, and her chunky enamel pendant was poking into my concave chest and imprinting on it. Mom stepped back, grabbed a tissue, and blew her nose. Loudly. She managed a weak smile.

"I brought coffee," I said, "but I think we could both do with a nice, cold glass of water instead."

"Forget that." She opened her skinny stainless-steel fridge and yanked out a bottle of white wine. "I think wine is the perfect accompaniment to peach cobbler, don't you?"

"Yes, I do. Especially that sweet Moscato. Bring it on."

She filled two wineglasses and headed for the living room, me bringing up the rear with the cobbler. As we sat down on her contemporary, narrow gray couch, my eyes were caught by the massive square painting on the opposite wall. It had to be at least six feet wide.

"Wow," I said. "Did you do that?"

She nodded shyly. "Do you like it?"

"I love it! I like the one that's hanging at the studio, but that one's only got three colors. This one is a riot of color." I stared, mesmerized by the swirls and drips of pulsing red, yellow, fuchsia, cobalt, turquoise, lime, coral, teal, orange, and chartreuse. "It's amazing."

"I call it *Teddie*," she said.

And then Mom and I talked, really talked, for probably the first time in our lives. She told me that she'd loved modern art ever since she was a young girl and saw Jackson Pollock and Mark Rothko's works on a field trip to the Art Institute of Chicago. She determined to be an artist like them someday.

But her wealthy, traditional midwestern parents laughed at the idea and said those kinds of paintings weren't really art—a kindergartener could have done them. They told their daughter, a teen in the early 1960s, that what she really needed to focus on was making herself pretty enough to find a good husband. Appearance was everything.

And my mom listened. Although she began studying art in college—"I was even an artist's model," she told me, "pretty daring for me"—she gave it up when she fell in love with my dad, married, and then got pregnant. "Real life," she said wryly.

"It's never too late to pursue your passions, Mom," I said. "I'm glad you're painting and doing what you love again. An artist needs to create. It looks like I need to thank Jeffrey for reawakening those artistic passions."

"Jeffrey and I are just friends," she said, and I think she almost believed it.

Chapter Twenty-Two

I Skyped with Tavish the next morning to give him the scoop and fill him in on all that had happened since we last talked, which was a lot.

"I'm happy to hear the murder has been solved," he said. "I was rather worried you might run afoul of another crazed killer. I'm sure Brady's relieved as well to close the books on this case and get everything back to normal."

"We all are," I said. Then I told Tavish about yesterday and my mother's rekindled interest in art as well as our reconciliation.

"I'm happy you and your mum have made amends and are getting closer," he said.

"Baby steps."

"Tell me more about this Jeffrey she's seeing," Tavish said. "On the surface, he doesn't seem like Claire's type."

"I know, right? If you'd have told me my mother would ever be interested in a hippie with a ponytail and Birkenstocks, I'd have said you were crazy. Jeffrey's very nice—laid-back and incredibly talented. He's an amazing artist. He and Mom got to know each other when she was taking a couple art classes at the collective. Apparently they love a lot of the same modern artists. Mom mentioned that she'd briefly been an artist's model in college, and Jeffrey asked if she would pose for him. She said she turned him down at first and he accepted that, didn't push her or pressure her. As she got to know him better, though, she said she felt more comfortable and reconsidered. Mom said she was still a bit hesitant because of her age and what people would think, but Jeffrey said what really mattered was what *she* thought. Apparently he quoted David Bowie, who said, 'Aging is an extraordinary process where you become the person you always should have been.' And that sealed the deal."

"Bowie was the master of self-invention and reinvention," Tavish said. "So are Claire and Jeffrey actually dating then?"

"I'm not sure. Mom says they're 'just friends,' but she blushed when she said it. I think their friendship is beginning to blossom into something more."

"Good for Claire." He sent me a gentle smile from across the pond. "And how do you feel about that?"

"I'm actually delighted," I said, and I realized I meant it. "I'd never have put those two together in a million years, but I really like Jeffrey. I think he's good for my mom. I had no idea she was such a good painter. I'll text you some photos of her work," I said. "It's brilliant."

We chatted for a few more minutes about his family and the progress of his novel and agreed to talk again tomorrow.

After I logged off, I decided to make some comfort food to take over to Stephen Morris. I recalled Patsy saying in the past how she'd always kept her son stocked with a steady supply of baked goods and how he especially enjoyed her quick breads for breakfast in the morning. Since I had some overripe bananas, I figured I'd make banana bread. There's nothing like warm banana bread and butter in the morning—the ultimate breakfast comfort food.

I pulled out the banana bread recipe from my rosemaling recipe box. When I saw the crumb cake recipe right behind it, I decided to make that as well. Grandma got this classic breakfast cake recipe from a transplanted New Yorker friend of hers whom she'd met at a Daughters of Norway event—it was one of my dad's favorites. He used to say, "Crumb cake is better than coffee cake, because there's a lot more crumb topping."

I opened my baking cupboard and removed sugar, flour, baking powder, baking soda, salt, and vanilla. Then I grabbed eggs, butter, and milk from the fridge. I'd make the banana bread first, since it would take longer. As I mashed the bananas, I relived the events of the day before. I still couldn't believe Patsy was dead—and that she'd killed herself so publicly.

Maybe with Les gone, Patsy knew she no longer had a lock on the first-place trophy and she offed herself rather than face the ignominy of not winning and being number one anymore.

I slapped my inner snark. *That's a terrible thing to even think! No, I think Brady forced her hand. When she heard him say an arrest was imminent, she knew she had to act fast, so she ran home and ate the leftover lobster.*

Frank Cullen had found the denuded lobster tail sitting out on the kitchen counter when he and Brady took Stephen home yesterday. The coroner had also discovered the empty bottle of Lester's penicillin tablets tipped on its side next to the lobster. Patsy had clearly been determined to make her suicide stick and didn't want to leave anything to chance, Char had told me on the phone when she called last night to share this insider tidbit.

My best friend had also told me—confidentially—that even though Patsy insisted in her suicide note that Lester was the one who had embezzled monies from the chamber rather than Stephen, an outside fraud investigator from Racine would be coming to town next week to begin a full investigation of the chamber's finances.

I sighed as I sifted the flour, salt, baking powder, and baking soda together. I hoped Les Morris would turn out to have been the thief. Otherwise Stephen's troubles were only beginning. I beat the butter and sugar together and added the mashed bananas and beat them until they were combined. Then I beat the eggs in one at a time. Finally, I stirred the vanilla and milk into the mixture. I poured the batter into several loaf pans and stuck them in the oven.

I had doubled the recipe so I could take some banana bread over to Jeffrey and Astrid at the art studio as well as to Brady and Augie, who'd had a stressful time lately dealing with the deaths of two of Lake Potawatomi's leading citizens. I also made a couple loaves for my Musketeer pals, knowing that if Sharon and Char found out I'd made banana bread and not given them any, I'd be in trouble.

While the bread baked, I decided to take Gracie for a long walk. I hadn't been spending as much time with her lately as I normally did, what with Lester's murder, my mom's mystery man, and the baking contest occupying most of my attention. I grabbed her leash from the hook by the back door. "Gracie-girl, want to go for walkies?"

She jumped up from her dog bed and scampered across the checkerboard floor to my side.

I clipped on her leash, and we set off at a brisk pace down the sidewalk. We'd barely gone thirty feet when Joanne LaPoint waved us over from her front yard.

"Oh my gosh, Teddie," she said. "Wasn't yesterday horrible? I still can't believe Patsy Morris killed herself. And murdered her husband. What a shock. Poor Stephen. From the way Patsy always talked, I thought she adored Les." Joanne made a face. "Although I never understood how she could."

Gracie strained at the leash and yipped.

Come on, Mom. I thought this walk was supposed to be all about me.

"Sorry, Joanne, I have to go. The alpha female in my house insists." We jogged down the block and rounded the corner, startling Cindy Torkilsen, who was about to turn onto our street. The funeral-home and salon owner's hand flew up to her chest.

"Oh my goodness, Teddie, you gave me a fright. I've been a bundle of nerves ever since the contest yesterday. I still can't believe Patsy Morris killed herself in the baking tent! What was she thinking? Our grandkids were in the park picnicking with us when it happened. What if they'd seen her body? That would have been awful."

"I agree." Gracie tugged on the leash. "I'm sorry, Cindy, I can't stop and chat. This little girl really needs her exercise."

I puffed out a sigh as my Eskie and I continued our walk. *I should have known Patsy's suicide and confession would be the talk of the town. Maybe we can escape all the neighbors by going to the park.*

Gracie and I trotted down the street and cut over to enter the park from the back end, where dozens of maple trees stood sentinel. The red and silver maples would be changing their leaves in a couple months to brilliant shades of crimson and gold for fall. As I strolled through the park, allowing Gracie to leisurely sniff the mail her other canine friends had left behind, I enjoyed the coolness of the August day. It wasn't nearly as hot and humid as it had been earlier in the week. As we rounded a curve in the pathway, the gazebo and baking tent came into sight, along with Barbara Christensen walking Taffy.

Gracie let out a joyous bark at the sight of her puppy friend and dragged me over to the excited, yipping mini goldendoodle.

"We have to stop meeting like this," Barbara said with a smile as she watched the two dogs greet each other happily.

"Either that or schedule an actual playdate."

"Good idea." She sat down on a nearby bench, and I joined her while our dogs frolicked together. Barbara passed her hand across her face, and I noticed the dark circles under her eyes. "I had a hard time sleeping last night," she said. "I kept seeing poor Patsy struggling to breathe." She shuddered. "I still can't believe what happened. It's all so terrible." She looked at the tent and shivered. "I don't think I can ever go back in there again. I have a feeling this will be the end of the baking contest for good."

"Maybe not for good," I said, patting her arm. "But definitely this year. I don't imagine any of us want to return to the tent. I know Sophie doesn't."

A familiar annoying voice pierced the air.

"I always thought Patsy was putting on an act about her marriage," Wilma Sorensen said as she came into view from behind the vinyl baking tent with a couple of her senior-citizen pals, "but to actually murder him beggars belief."

"I wonder if Stephen will move into his parents' Victorian now," Beverly Price said. "It would make sense—it's paid off and he wouldn't have a mortgage."

"I don't think it's really his style," Kathy Henderson said. "It's too old-fashioned for him. And I can't imagine Stephen would feel comfortable living in the same house where his mother ate the remains of his lobster dinner to deliberately kill herself."

"I saw someone offering Stephen some *comfort* last night, on my nightly walk." Wilma smirked. "I needed to get more steps in, so I changed my route and walked all the way down to the end of Main Street, where the art studio is, you know?"

Her enraptured audience nodded.

"As I passed by, I saw Stephen and some woman pressed up against the side wall of the warehouse way at the back in a dark corner," she said. "I couldn't tell who the woman was for sure, since she was in the shadows, but I recognized Stephen immediately from those silly Hawaiian shirts he always wears," Wilma said. She paused as if struggling to remember. "You know, now that I think about it and replay it in my mind again," she said, with mounting conviction, "I think the woman with Stephen was that Cheryl Martin—the bottle blonde who always wears those tight gym clothes. Can you believe it? On the very night Stephen's poor mother killed herself. Poor Patsy would turn in her grave if she knew."

As Barbara and I exchanged disbelieving looks, the trio of gossiping women moved beyond the gazebo and headed toward the park exit.

"Unbelievable," Barbara said, shaking her head in disgust. "Someone really needs to slap that Wilma silly one day."'

Yes, they do. And if I hadn't had banana bread in the oven just then calling my name, I would have done so with relish.

* * *

An hour and a half later I drove over to Stephen Morris's Craftsman-style house on Durand with a loaf of banana bread, a container of crumb cake, and a sympathy card. As I got out of my Bug, I noticed Cheryl Martin approaching Stephen's walkway with a grocery bag, a card, and a book.

"Hi, Cheryl," I said as she joined me in front of the house. "Looks like we both had the same idea." I held up the banana bread and crumb cake.

She grinned. "Sort of. Except I don't cook or bake, so I brought rotisserie chicken, salad in a bag, and store-bought Bundt cake. I knew Stephen wouldn't feel like cooking, so I wanted to make sure he had some food."

"What's the book?" I squinted to read the title without my readers.

"Joan Didion's *The Year of Magical Thinking.* We read this in book club a couple years ago, and it really helped me with the loss of my mother."

"That's so thoughtful," I said. "I'm sure Stephen will appreciate it."

"What he'll really appreciate at a time like this is good booze and some of my down-home comfort food," a familiar voice said.

We turned around to see Colleen Murphy in her skinny jeans and ubiquitous white T-shirt holding an open box with a bottle of Johnnie Walker Red and several foil-covered containers of food wafting incredible smells.

"That smells delicious, Colleen," I said. "What did you make?"

"My specialty: chicken-fried steak, mashed potatoes, fried okra, and biscuits and gravy." She licked her lips. "Best comfort food around. And pecan pie for dessert, of course."

"I didn't know you were from the South," Cheryl said. "That's a quintessentially southern-fried meal."

Colleen's eyes narrowed. "I'm not from the South. I'm from Michigan, but my Texas granny raised me after my folks died and taught me how to cook southern-style."

"She also gave you a little of her accent," I said with a smile. "I think I detected a touch of Texas twang there."

Stephen's front door opened, and he stepped out on the porch, looking like hell. He had on the same clothes he'd been wearing yesterday, except the Hawaiian shirt was badly rumpled and buttoned crookedly, his salt-and-pepper hair was sticking straight up, his face was grizzly with stubble, and his eyes were bloodshot. "What can I do for you, ladies?" he asked in a dull monotone.

"We brought you something to eat, Stephen," Cheryl said gently.

"I know it's probably the last thing you feel like doing right now," Colleen added, "but you need to eat. Your mother would want you to eat."

Stephen stared at her. Then he burst into tears. "I can't believe she's gone. Mom was always there."

* * *

"Then what did you do?" Char asked over the phone.

I'd Facetimed the other two Musketeers when I got home from Stephen's house and put them on speakerphone to share the latest.

"I gave him a hug, set my offering on the front-porch table, and left Stephen in the quite capable hands of the two single women who can fight over who gets to take care of him."

"Well, Stephen's quite a catch now," Sharon said. "With his parents both gone, he'll likely inherit everything."

"Which he won't be able to enjoy if he's doing time for embezzlement," Char added.

"Depends on how much he embezzled," I said. "*If* he was in fact the embezzler and not his dad. And what kind of sentence he'd get. I was researching embezzlement to use as a possible plot line in my next book, and prison sentences can range anywhere from twenty months to twenty years."

Sharon snorted. "Twenty months is nothing, not when there's a big payoff involved. It will be interesting to see which of Stephen's wannabe girlfriends hangs in the longest."

"There's always the possibility Colleen and Cheryl are not the least bit interested in Stephen romantically," I said. "They could have simply been extending kindness and compassion to a man who just lost his mother."

"Right." Char rolled her eyes. "Didn't you say our favorite tattletale Wilma saw Stephen making out with Cheryl in the dark last night?"

"Wilma wasn't entirely certain it was Cheryl."

"But naturally she's spread that rumor all over town by now," Sharon said.

"People like to have something to talk about," Char said. "I'm sure glad Wilma never saw Teddie and me in our exotic-dancer outfits."

"What do you mean, *Teddie*?" I asked. "*I* never dressed like a sexy dancer. I wore my favorite jeans and a tank top—an outfit I plan to take to England on vacation with me, as a matter of fact."

We talked about Tavish and my upcoming vacation and caught up on Sharon's twins, who were getting ready to enter their last year of college. Char informed us that Augie had gone over to see Sophie last night because he knew how freaked out she was over Patsy's death. The two twentysomethings had talked for hours and were having their official first date tomorrow night.

"Yes!" I said, doing a fist pump.

After I hung up, I opened up *Suffocating in Soufflé* on my laptop and started reading it to begin the final editing process. Three hours later I took a break to feed Gracie and have some dinner. Then I snuggled on the couch with my canine daughter to binge-watch more *Downton Abbey*.

Chapter Twenty-Three

The next morning, while I was scrolling through Facebook and enjoying a cup of coffee and a piece of banana bread, a light knock sounded at my back door. I opened it to see my mother standing there holding a small gift bag in her hand.

At least I thought it was my mother. The woman standing before me wore a paint-spattered T-shirt, denim capris, Toms canvas slip-ons, no jewelry, and not a speck of makeup. She looked fresh-faced and natural. As natural as you can look with Botox.

I stared at her. "Mom?"

She giggled like a schoolgirl. "Yes, it's me. Are you going to invite me in?"

Since when do you need an invitation? You've always walked right in.

"Sure," I said, dazed. "Come on in. Do you want some coffee?"

"No thanks." Mom bent down and ruffled the back of Gracie's neck. "Good morning, Gracie. How are you on this glorious day?"

Gracie sent me a side eye. *Mom, what's going on?*

I verbalized my canine daughter's question. "Mom, what's going on?"

"A couple things." She extended the gift bag. "First, I have a present for you. I was going to save it for your birthday next month, but I couldn't wait. Go ahead, open it."

I sat back down, and Mom sat across the table from me, eyes sparkling with anticipation. I reached into the bag and pulled out a flat jewelry box from a high-end jeweler in Milwaukee. My heart sank. *Not expensive jewelry.* Mom knows it's not my thing. I've told her over the years that gold and fancy gemstones are not my style. I prefer simple silver like my Celtic knot earrings or funky costume jewelry. She was so excited, though, that I pretended to be too.

I opened the box and gasped. Nestled inside was a miniature replica of a vintage black-and-silver Royal typewriter on a silver chain. A tiny diamond winked from the middle of the number keys. Slowly I lifted out the chain and examined the little typewriter.

"Do you like it?" Mom asked anxiously.

"Like it?" Tears sprang to my eyes. "I love it. It's absolutely perfect."

"I know you don't like precious gems," she rushed out, "but the diamond is from my engagement ring. Since your father always said your writing shines bright like a diamond, I hoped you wouldn't mind."

"Mind?" I stared at her, the tears now slipping down my cheeks. "That makes it all the more meaningful." I looked at her bare left hand, "But you loved your engagement ring. Why would you get rid of it?"

"I did love my engagement ring," she said softly. "That ring was on my finger for more than fifty years." Mom looked down at her left hand and rubbed her thumb over the pale strip of skin where her ring used to live. "But things change. I'm starting a new chapter of my life now. I had a jeweler fashion the larger diamonds into earrings for me, but I wanted us both to have a remembrance of the symbol of your father's love."

Then it clicked into place. "Wait," I said. "The hot guy in the park with the Italian leather shoes—he was the jeweler, right?"

"Yes. I couldn't tell you who he was, or it would have spoiled the surprise."

Shame swept over me like one of my hot flashes. "I'm sorry, Mom." I stood up and hugged her tight. "Thank you," I said softly. "This is the best gift I've ever gotten. I'll treasure it always."

Then Mom and I cried together, remembering Dad.

I brushed the tears away. "You said there were a couple things you wanted to tell me. What's the next one?"

Her eyes sparkled. "I've finished my painting for next week's fund raiser—I just need to add a final touch. It's over at the studio. Would you like to see it?"

"Love to. If it's anything like the one in your living room, people will be fighting to buy it."

Mom drove us to the warehouse, talking all the way. "No one else should be there this early, so we'll have the place to ourselves. Jeffrey went to Racine last night to meet with a new artist, and Astrid's off on one of her day-long wildlife jaunts. Cheryl's probably still sleeping—she's not a morning person."

Reminds me of someone else I know. I glanced at my phone to check the time—8:15. *Although clearly that someone I know is changing.*

My mother chattered on, talking about next week's fund raiser and how they hoped it would raise a lot of money for the collective. The excitement fairly shimmered off of her. Once we arrived, she unlocked the abstract stained-glass door with her key—"Jeffrey gave me an extra key, since I'm always here," she explained—and we entered the light-filled studio. "It's over here on the side," Mom said.

And then she screamed. My eyes locked on the horrible sight above us, and I screamed too.

Stephen Morris dangled from the thick wooden beam across the high ceiling, Colleen's heavy shawl of many colors stretched tight around his neck. The shawl I loved and had planned to buy.

Chapter Twenty-Four

Brady read Stephen's typed suicide note, shoved his hand through his hair, and spat out an expletive. Stephen confessed that *he* had killed Lester, not his mother. He admitted he had been embezzling funds from the chamber, his father had found out and was going to turn him in, and so he had killed Les in the park after "his skanky dancer" left, then told his mother what he'd done. Patsy was afraid the police were closing in on her son, so she killed herself and took the blame for Lester's murder. Stephen wrote that his mom had sacrificed everything for him her entire life—culminating in the ultimate sacrifice: giving up her life for her son. He said he couldn't live with the guilt of his mother's suicide and didn't want to live in a world without her.

Mom and I huddled in a corner of the studio together, trembling, eyes averted from the awful sight, having given our statements to a grim Brady. No, we hadn't seen anyone. No, we hadn't touched anything besides the front door. Yes, the studio was locked up tight when we arrived. What time was that? Eight-fifteen. Blah, blah, blah.

Frank Cullen entered the warehouse, black coroner's bag in hand, and looked up at Stephen's lifeless body and the raised scissor lift next to him. He shook his head sadly. "That family is cursed."

Augie drove us home in Mom's car while Brady and Frank stayed to work the suicide scene. As Augie pulled up in front of Mom's cottage, I noticed my two Musketeers waiting for me on the back steps. Numbly, Mom and I exited the car.

"What the actual hell?" Char burst out. She gave me a fierce hug as Sharon embraced my mother. "I can't believe Stephen killed himself. How did he even get up to that beam? That thing must be at least twenty feet high."

"He used the scissor lift," Mom said dully. "All the artists do to access the beam to hang art exhibits."

"But Stephen wasn't an artist," Sharon said. "How did he know about this lift thingy?"

"He stopped by recently to talk to Jeffrey about the fund raiser," Mom said. "When he arrived, Cheryl and Astrid were standing on the aerial platform hanging Cheryl's mosaic chandelier. Stephen said that looked like fun, so once they finished and came back down, Astrid hopped off and Stephen hopped on. Cheryl showed Stephen how the lift worked—he was fascinated by it. Thought it was a great *toy*." She shuddered and gave me a haunted look. "He even joked that he'd like to get one for his office."

"I think we need to stop talking about this now," I said. "Let's all go inside and have a cup of tea."

"Sorry, but I need to get back to the sheriff," Augie said. The young deputy squeezed my shoulder as he left. "Hang in there." He jogged down the driveway.

Sharon and Char made small talk with my mom as I made tea and warmed up banana bread. As the four of us sat around the kitchen table drinking tea, to distract my mother, I pulled out the jewelry box and proudly showed my Musketeer pals the silver pendant Mom had given me earlier.

"Oh my gosh," Sharon squealed when she saw the typewriter. "That is beautiful and *so* Teddie."

Mom flushed with pleasure.

Char gave her a thumbs-up. "You done good, Claire."

My Musketeer pals peppered my mother with questions.

A tentative knock interrupted us. I opened the back door to a shell-shocked Cheryl Martin. "Is Claire here?" she asked in a dazed voice. "Is it true about Stephen?"

I led her inside. Cheryl stared at my mom in disbelief. "I can't believe it. I just saw him yesterday." She burst into tears.

Mom jumped up and hugged her. "It's okay. It's okay." She rubbed her friend's back. "It's an awful shock, I know."

Cheryl exhaled a quivering breath. "Stephen was such a sweet guy. You and Teddie found him?" she asked.

Mom nodded.

"Is it true he used the scissor lift?"

"Yes."

Cheryl's eyes filled again. "I'm the one who showed him how to use that damn thing! It's my fault."

"It's not your fault," Mom said. She gripped Cheryl's hand in hers. "You couldn't have known Stephen would do what he did. None of us could." She expelled a sad sigh. "If Stephen hadn't used the lift, he would have found another way to kill himself. He was riddled with guilt over his mother's death."

"I know," Cheryl said. "That's what he kept saying to Colleen and me yesterday."

"How long did you stay at Stephen's after I left?" I asked.

"Only about half an hour, forty-five minutes," she said, with a wry grimace. "It was obvious, even in the midst of his grief, that Stephen and Colleen were attracted to each other, and third wheel is a role I have never played." Cheryl blew her nose with a tissue Mom handed her. "When I left, the two of them were drinking Johnnie Walker Red." Her eyes widened. "Oh my gosh. I wonder if anyone's let Colleen know. She's bound to be devastated. I have a feeling she was hoping she and Stephen would get together. Poor Colleen."

"Poor Stephen," Sharon said sadly. "And poor Patsy. We all know Lester was a jerk, and honestly, I don't know of anyone who mourns his demise, but now the entire Morris family is gone. Dead. Every last one of them."

* * *

That night, after an emotionally draining day of everyone and their brother calling or dropping by, wanting to talk about Stephen's suicide, I lay in bed, unable to sleep. I kept seeing Stephen Morris's dead body hanging from the beam. Finally, at two thirty, I got out of bed and made a cup of chamomile tea. I took my tea and a piece of crumb cake into the living room. Something I'd heard recently had been niggling at the back of my mind, evoking a wisp of a memory from time past. *What is it?* I frowned and tried to recall, but the memory hovered just out of reach.

Absently, I pulled out some of my dad's old scrapbooks from the bookcase and started paging through them. Dad had been a collector and a sentimentalist. He kept everything, much to my minimalist mother's chagrin. When he passed, Mom wanted to toss out his dusty old scrapbooks, but I saved them from the trash heap. Dad kept clippings from the *Lake Potawatomi Times* and pasted them into his myriad scrapbooks. Anytime one of his friends' or his family members' names made it into the newspaper, he'd paste the clipping into his scrapbook—"to look at in my old age when my memory starts going," he would tease.

I continued paging through the scrapbooks as I sipped my tea, taking a trip down memory lane. I smiled at the proud, gap-toothed photo of me winning the spelling bee in fourth grade. Another faded newspaper photo showed Mom modeling bell-bottomed pants and platform shoes at the 1973 Junior League fashion show. I grinned at the photo of Grandma Florence and Astrid tying for first place for the greatest number of fish caught in one day. Then there was the clipping of Dad winning "Best Bratwurst" at the annual town barbecue. I turned the page and froze. I pulled out my readers and looked closer at the old photo. Then I read the article, and the memory came back into sharp focus.

As I pulled on my black jeans, tunic, and Skechers, Gracie sat up and wagged her tail. She stood on her hind legs and did her *please* routine, pawing at the air with her front feet.

"Sorry, girl. Not this time. It's too late, and Mommy needs to be very quiet. I won't be long. I need to check something out." I grabbed my phone and pepper spray, slipped from the house, and headed down the street.

When I arrived at my destination, the house was dark and still, like every other house on the block. With one notable difference. In this section of town, the houses were older and smaller and didn't have garages. Every house on the block had a car parked in the driveway. Except this one. I crept to the side of the dark house and peeked in a window. The curtains were tightly closed, and I couldn't see anything. I crept over to the next window, where I had better luck, finding a small gap at the bottom of the curtains. Taking a deep breath and saying a prayer, I turned on my phone light and shined it through the gap. What I saw confirmed my suspicions. Someone had left in a hurry.

Am I too late?

I sped over to the art warehouse, where I was relieved to see a car out front with a stained-glass lamp, pillows, and bedding shoved in the back seat. The passenger seat was crammed full of Hefty trash bags of stuff and a small suitcase. Quietly, I tried the front door of the studio. In the artist's haste to get away, they'd left it unlocked. I turned the handle and slipped inside on my rubber-soled Skechers. A faint light and a rustling from the back greeted me. I crept forward noiselessly and saw a dark shape shoving things into a garbage bag.

"Hello, Colleen," I said, snapping on the light by Astrid's canvas. "Or should I say Bobbi?"

Colleen whirled around. "Teddie!" She placed her hand on her chest. "You scared me. What are you doing here?"

"I could ask you that same question."

"I stopped by to pick up a few things. I realized I'd left behind a whole bag of yarn that I need for my next project." She gave me a weak smile. "I have what I need now, though, so I'll be going."

"Going *where* is the question," I said. "Back to Michigan? Or Texas? Or most likely a brand-new state, I'm guessing."

"I don't know what you're talking about," Colleen said. "I'm going home. I told you." She hoisted the garbage bag. "I forgot my yarn, but I've got it now, so I'm heading home to bed."

"Cut the innocent act," I said. "I *know*, Bobbi. If you were heading home to bed, why is your car out front jam full of bedding and suitcases?" I fixed my eyes steadily on the yarn shop owner and former beautician. "You killed Lester Morris, didn't you," I said quietly.

Colleen dropped the trash bag to the ground with a sly smile. "You're damn right, I killed him, and I'd do it again in a heartbeat. Les Morris ruined my life. I had a sweet deal going here with my beauty shop, but I lost everything because of him." She sent me a curious glance. "How'd you figure out who I was? I don't look anything like Bobbi Turner anymore. I made sure of that when I set my plan in motion years ago," she said. "I lost seventy-five pounds, changed my hair, my eye color, my accent, and the way I dressed." Colleen's eyes flicked to the blue butterfly on her chest. "I even got a tattoo."

"When you said, 'Nothing beats down-home comfort food,' with that slight Texas twang, it triggered a memory. You said the exact same thing eleven years ago when you won the cooking contest." My hand closed around the pepper spray in my pocket. "I remember, because my dad's lasagna, garlic bread, and lemon-sugar cookies came in second that year. You beat him with your chicken-fried steak, biscuits and gravy, fried okra, and pecan pie. The same southern-fried comfort-food meal you brought to Stephen."

Colleen rolled her eyes. "Stephen. What a loser. Such a mama's boy. Lousy in the sack too."

"You and Stephen were sleeping together?"

"Sure. All part of the plan to kill his old man," she said. "Stephen whined all the time about how much he hated his dad and wished he were dead. He'd say over and over, 'One of these days, I'm going to kill that SOB,' but when it came right down to it, he couldn't do it, so I whacked Lester instead." Colleen smirked. "With your rolling pin, no less. Thanks for that, by the way. Made a great weapon."

"But Stephen confessed to killing his father in his suicide note."

"I know." She gave me an evil smile. "I thought the 'skanky dancer' bit was a nice touch."

Oh. My. God. Stephen didn't kill himself. Colleen killed him *too.*

"But the best line was when Stephen said he didn't want to live in a world without his mother," Colleen continued, raising her palm to her head and giving a theatrical swoon. "Pure poetry. Maybe for my next job I should be a writer."

"Stephen didn't commit suicide." I said out loud what I already knew.

She snorted. "Stephen was too much of a wuss to kill himself. And he weighed a ton. Thank God for the lift." Colleen winked. "I'm guessing you don't want to buy that pretty shawl from me now, huh?"

"You're insane," I said, surreptitiously removing the pepper spray from my pocket. "Did you kill Patsy too?"

"I was going to, but she beat me to it." She brushed off the palms of her hands. "And now my work is done here. Well, almost." Colleen grabbed a knitting needle from her bag and lunged at me.

I jerked to the side and pepper-sprayed her full in the face.

She dropped the needle and clutched her eyes, cursing at me and scrabbling around for something to grab. Her hand closed around one of Cheryl's mosaic vases and she struck out blindly with it, grazing my arm.

"Get away from her, you bitch," my mother, sounding remarkably like Sigourney Weaver, yelled from behind me.

Chapter Twenty-Five

"Teddie, Teddie, Teddie." On the screen before me, Tavish dropped his head in his hands and shook it from side to side. "What is it about you that attracts mad killers?"

"I must emit some distinctive pheromone that draws them to me like moths to a flame." I shrugged. "At least this time I wasn't the intended murder target."

"No, only the unexpected side effect of a psychopath who murdered two members of a family and had actually been planning for years to murder the entire family in a revenge killing against her former lover Lester. Do I have that right?"

"You're missing a couple things." I explained that Colleen-slash-Bobbi's initial long-term plan had been to make Stephen Morris fall in love with her and do her bidding—including sell his father a large life insurance policy and embezzle funds from the chamber of commerce, where Stephen was the treasurer. Stephen did both those things.

The next part of Colleen's plan was to get Stephen to bump off Lester, then secretly marry her without Patsy's knowledge. As Stephen's wife, Colleen would share in Stephen's portion of his inheritance. Colleen next planned to murder Patsy so Stephen would receive the full insurance amount. After a suitable period had passed, Colleen would then murder her devoted husband and have everything she wanted—the destruction of the entire family of the man who wronged her, plus a ton of money she would inherit as the lone Morris survivor.

However, Lester's unexpected dalliance with Angel and his bringing her to Lake Potawatomi had hastened the timing of Lester's murder when Colleen realized that Lester's latest mistress was the perfect murder suspect. And when she saw my rolling pin in the tent that night, Colleen had decided that using it as the murder weapon rather than the knife she'd brought might cast suspicion on me as well, which would be a nice diversionary tactic. After Lester's death, however, Patsy stuck to her son like glue, and Colleen and Stephen couldn't sneak away to get married. Then Patsy killed herself to protect her son, and Stephen fell to pieces and became a liability. At that point, Colleen realized she'd have to shelve the insurance money part of her plan and get rid of Stephen before he cracked and revealed everything to the cops. She already had the money Stephen had embezzled for her, and this way she would still get her revenge on Lester and his family and could skip town with no one the wiser.

"It sounds like a bloody soap opera," Tavish said.

"Too right. Thank God that soap opera has now ended and the villain is in jail," I said. "Now I must dash and get this cake over to Sharon and Jim's."

He stuck out his lower lip in a pout. "I wish I was there to enjoy one of your luscious cakes."

"Me too. But I promise I'll make you whatever cakes you want once I get to England."

* * *

I transported my chocolate creation over to the Lake House and set it up in the kitchen, shooing Sharon and Jim out beforehand so they wouldn't get the full effect until I wheeled it into the dining room. The intricate multilayered cake had been meant to be my showstopper entry on the final day of the baking contest. Once the contest fell apart after the demise of the entire Morris family, however, I'd sighed and said, "So much for the fancy chocolate cake I'd planned."

My sweet-toothed best friend had pouted and given me a plaintive look. "No. Say it isn't so. I really wanted to see—and eat—this special cake you've been practicing making for weeks."

"Me too." Brady had licked his lips. "Your cakes are the best, Ted. My mouth's been watering for this chocolate cake you've been teasing us about ever since the contest started. I know it would have blown all the other entries out of the water. Can't you still make it for your friends? Please?"

"Pretty please, bestie," Char had pleaded. "If you do, we'll even buy you a first-place trophy."

"All right. Stop begging. You all are pitiful."

At last the cake was put together and ready to be judged and consumed. I wheeled my showstopper into the dining room, where Sharon, Jim, Char, Brady, and Augie were waiting expectantly.

Sharon clapped. "Yay! It's a wedding cake."

A cascade of fresh white and orange roses tumbled down the front of the four round graduated layers of chocolate cake with a hint of orange flavor. Orange and white orchids rested on the top cake layer, completing the elegant picture.

"Looks good, Ted," Brady said, "but the proof is in the pudding. Let's see how it tastes."

"You got it." I held out the cake knife to my best friend. "Char, would you do the honors, please, and cut the first piece?"

"Yah, you betcha," she said, getting up from her seat and approaching the cake.

Brady sent me an anxious look, but I ignored him.

"Start here," I instructed Char, pointing to the right of the fresh flowers at the bottom layer.

She cut a large piece of cake and put it on a plate, carried it over to her boyfriend, and gave him a kiss. "Here you go, babe. I know you're champing at the bit to taste this, so go ahead and take the first bite."

He looked at me uncertainly.

I winked at him. "Go ahead, Brady. It's fine."

Brady stabbed his fork into the cake and hit something hard.

"What the heck's in that cake?" Jim asked. "Sounds like a rock."

Brady shot me a desperate look.

"Jim Hansen, are you saying my cake is hard as a rock?" I teased. "Go ahead, Sheriff, carry on."

Brady gingerly stuck his fork back into the cake and slowly lifted out a Saran-wrapped ring box on his fork.

Char dropped to her knees, grabbed the box, opened it, and said, "Brady Wells, man of mine, sexiest sheriff around, and love of my life, would you marry me?"

Brady stared at her. There was a pregnant pause. Then he threw back his head and roared.

Char scowled. "What's so funny?"

I quickly cut a second piece of cake and passed it over to Char. "Here, bestie, this is for you."

She gave me a weird look. "I don't want any damn cake."

"Humor me. Take a bite."

Char stabbed her fork into the piece of cake and hit something hard. Her eyes shot to me, then Brady.

"Go ahead. See what it is."

She slowly removed a Saran-wrapped ring box.

Brady, still laughing helplessly, dropped to his knees and said, "Char Jorgensen, love of my life, sparring partner, and occasional pain in the ass, would you marry me?"

The whole room erupted in laughter.

Recipes

Classic Cherry Pie

Recipe courtesy of Connie Weichert

Filling

1 cup sugar
¼ cup all-purpose flour
¼ teaspoon salt
½ cup juice from cherries
3 cups drained, canned, pitted tart red cherries*
1 tablespoon soft butter
4 drops almond extract
10 drops red food coloring

In a large saucepan, combine the sugar, flour, and salt; stir in cherry juice. Cook and stir over medium heat until thick. Remove from the heat and add cherries, butter, almond extract, and food coloring. Let stand while you make the pastry.

Pastry

3 cups all-purpose flour
1½ teaspoons salt
1 cup shortening*
Ice water

Combine flour and salt in a medium bowl. Using a pastry blender, cut in the shortening until it is very fine—pea-sized or smaller. (If you don't have a pastry blender, it's fine to use two table knives to cut the shortening into the flour.) Make a hole in the middle of the flour mixture and start adding the ice water by tablespoonfuls. Put some ice water in and mix with a fork. Continue to add ice water and mix until the mixture starts to hold together.

This is a little tricky, but it really is the key to making tender, flaky pie crust: If it is too wet, the crust will be tough and gluey. If it is too dry, it will not hold together. That's why it's important to add the ice water by the tablespoon. It needs to hold together enough to form a ball of dough and be rolled out. Do not overwork or knead—it will be tough as cardboard if you do.

Assembly and Baking

Divide the dough into two balls, one slightly larger than the other. Grease and flour a 9-inch pie tin. Roll out the bigger half of the dough and fill the bottom of your tin, then add your filling.

Roll out the remaining dough. Use a clean ruler to make a lattice top crust, cutting strips about half an inch wide, ideally with a pastry cutter with a fluted edge. You can use a knife or pizza cutter to cut the lattice, which gives it a straight edge, but the pastry cutter makes the lattice look more decorative.

With a pastry brush (or your fingers), apply a little ice water to the lip of the bottom crust to make it sticky enough to hold the lattice. Lay one strip over one way onto the filling and then turn the pie at a 90-degree angle and lay the second strip that way, repeating the process over and over until the top of the pie has a lattice on it. If you're going for extra-special decoration, lift the strips as you go, putting the "weaving" strip over one and under the next so that the pie has a woven, lattice top. Cut off the excess pieces of the strips around the edge and fold the bottom crust over, using a little more ice water if necessary to seal it, and crimp the edge. It's not complicated, just time-consuming, and quite beautiful when done.

Bake in a preheated 450-degree oven for 10 minutes. Reduce heat to 350 degrees and bake 40 to 45 minutes longer.

*This recipe calls for "canned" cherries, using the traditional definition of canning. Wisconsin is cherry country, so it's not hard finding them. Wherever you live, don't try making this with fresh cherries; it's not going to turn out half as well. And yes, I know shortening isn't good for you, but butter/margarine doesn't work as well. And let's be honest—if you were going to eat only healthy foods, would you really be having pie?

Peanut-Butter Blossoms

This recipe also calls for shortening. Yeah, we know it's not the best for you, but there's not much of it, and it's necessary to get the desired texture. These cookies are intended to be a treat, not an entire meal.

Ingredients

¼ cup shortening
¼ cup butter
½ cup creamy peanut butter (regular, not the natural or "old-fashioned" kind)
½ cup granulated sugar
½ cup densely packed brown sugar
1 egg
2 teaspoons vanilla
1¼ cups flour
½ teaspoon baking powder
1 teaspoon baking soda
¼ teaspoon salt
1 bag Hershey's kisses (unwrapped)
⅓ cup extra granulated sugar for rolling

Instructions

Be sure to unwrap the kisses before you start on the rest of the cookies. (This step takes longer than you'd think.)

Preheat oven to 375 degrees. Cream together shortening, butter, peanut butter, and sugars thoroughly until smooth. Beat in egg and vanilla. Sift flour into a separate, medium-sized bowl. Add the baking powder, soda, and salt. Stir with a hand whisk (or large fork) to mix all the dry ingredients. Slowly add the flour mix into the peanut-butter mixture, beating until incorporated. Place remaining sugar into an empty pie tin (or use the now-empty bowl from the flour mixture) and set aside. Roll dough in 1¼–inch balls (I use a small melon scooper to form the balls, then roll them in my hands). Roll balls of dough in bowl of extra sugar. Place sugared dough balls 3 inches apart on parchment-lined baking sheet (do not flatten).

Bake 9 to 10 minutes. Remove cookies from oven and add a Hershey's kiss to the top of each cookie. Push down gently. We want to fuse the kiss onto the cookie, so return the sheet of cookies into the oven for about 8 to 10 seconds. Be careful not to melt the kiss!

Remove from oven and immediately transfer cookies to baking rack to cool. Resist the temptation to eat the cookies right away, since the chocolate will be hot. Once the cookies are completely cooled and the chocolate is firm, it's fine to stack them in your desired storage container.

Tip: Reuse the parchment from baking as a liner between layers. This will help keep the shape of the kisses.

Makes about 3 dozen cookies.

Crumb Cake

Recipe courtesy of Michael Johnson

Cake

¾ cup baker's sugar
¼ cup soft butter
1 egg
½ cup buttermilk
1½ cups flour
2 teaspoons baking powder
½ teaspoon salt

Preheat oven to 350 degrees and grease and flour a 10 × 15–inch cake pan. (Tip: I often serve this right out of the cake pan, since it's so much easier. If you plan to remove the whole cake, a little extra prep of the pan will help tremendously. After you grease the pan but before adding the flour, line the bottom of the pan with parchment paper. Lightly grease the top of the parchment. Then, if you like, flour the sides of the pan.)

Mix sugar, butter, and egg together until smooth. Stir in the buttermilk.

In a separate bowl, sift together the flour, baking powder, and salt. (If you don't have a sifter, it's okay to use a fine-mesh strainer.)

Add the dry mixture to the wet and mix fully incorporated. Set aside while you make the topping.

Topping

½ cup sugar
½ cup brown sugar
⅔ cup flour
½ teaspoon cinnamon
½ cup soft butter

Combine all ingredients into a bowl and mix well until crumbly. Set aside.

Assembly and Baking

Spread cake batter into the cake pan, smoothing with a spatula. Sprinkle the crumbly topping evenly over the batter mixture, using a tablespoon (or your fingers), and pop it into the preheated oven. Bake 12 minutes, then rotate pan and bake an additional 5 minutes.

Remove from oven. After cake has cooled, sprinkle top with powdered sugar.

Peach Cobbler (with Cherries on Top)

Recipe courtesy of Michael Johnson

Ingredients

4 cups fresh peaches, peeled and sliced*
1 tablespoon lemon juice
¼ cup baker's sugar
3 tablespoons butter, cut into bits
¾ cup flour
½ cup sugar
¼ teaspoon salt
¼ teaspoon cinnamon
¼ cup butter
½ cup cherries, pitted and quartered

Directions

Slice peaches into greased 9 × 12–inch baking dish. Sprinkle with lemon juice, then baker's sugar, then dot with bits of butter. Place fruit in 375-degree oven to heat while mixing topping.

Sift flour, sugar, salt, and cinnamon together. Cut in ¼ cup butter with fork or pastry cutter until it is like coarse cornmeal. (Yes, you could use your food processor to mix the topping, but it's such a small amount I'd rather mix it manually and save cleanup of the processor blades and bowl. It's totally up to you which you prefer.)

Spread topping over hot peaches and decorate with the quartered cherries randomly on the top of the cobbler. Bake in 375-degree oven for 25 minutes or until golden brown.

Serve warm or cold, with or without whipped cream.

*To easily peel the peaches, put the whole peach in almost-boiling water for 30 seconds. Then immediately cool under cold water. Peel will slip right off.

Banana Bread

Ingredients

Cooking spray
2 cups unbleached white pastry flour
1 teaspoon salt
1 teaspoon baking powder
1 teaspoon baking soda
½ cup butter, softened
1 cup sugar
3 ripe bananas, mashed
2 large eggs
1 teaspoon vanilla extract
¼ teaspoon butter extract
1 tablespoon milk

Preheat oven to 325 degrees. Coat a 9 × 4–inch loaf pan with cooking spray (or, if you want to give as gifts, spray seven mini-loaf aluminum pans instead).

Sift flour, salt, baking powder, and baking soda together in a bowl, then set aside. If you don't have a sifter, a medium-mesh strainer works as well.

Using the whisk attachment with your standing mixer, beat butter and sugar until smooth and sugar dissolves. Add mashed bananas and beat until combined. Beat eggs into the butter mixture one at a time, fully blending each egg before adding the next. Stir vanilla extract, butter extract, and milk into the mixture until incorporated.

Swap the whisk for the beater attachment on your mixer. Stir flour mixture into banana mixture until just incorporated, scraping the sides of the bowl as necessary.

Pour batter into prepared loaf pan(s). Tap pans on the counter to release any air pockets.

Bake in preheated oven for approximately 1 hour and 10 minutes or until a toothpick inserted in the center comes out clean. Let the bread rest in the pan for 15 to 20 minutes before removing.

Serve as is, or, for an extra-decadent down-home comfort-food taste, spread butter atop your slice of warm banana bread.

Heaven.

Everything but the Kitchen Sink Cookies (aka Sinkers)

1½ cups all-purpose flour
1 teaspoon baking soda
1 teaspoon baking powder
1 teaspoon salt
1 cup butter
1 cup brown sugar
1 cup granulated sugar
2 eggs
2 teaspoons vanilla
5 cups of "stuff":
    1 cup oatmeal
    1 cup chocolate chips
    1 cup butterscotch chips
    1 cup coconut flakes
    1 cup Raisin Bran (or Rice Krispies)
Optional: ¾ cup chopped pecans

Depending on your preferences, you can substitute Rice Krispies for Raisin Bran and use either mini M&M's or raisins in place of the butterscotch chips. If you're not a fan of coconut, consider using a cup of peanut butter in place of the coconut flakes. (Basically, I use whatever I have in the kitchen that day.)

Instructions

Preheat oven to 350 degrees.

In a medium bowl, sift flour, baking soda, baking powder, and salt.

In a separate large bowl, cream together butter, brown sugar, and granulated sugar until fluffy (usually about 5 minutes). Add eggs and vanilla. Combine well.

Add flour mixture to wet ingredients and stir until just combined. Then add "stuff" and stir by hand to combine.

Place parchment paper on cookie sheets and use a melon baller to scoop slightly rounded dough onto the sheets—10 cookies per sheet.

Bake 12 to 14 minutes. Remove when edges turn golden brown (cookies will finish cooking after being removed from the oven—this gives you a crunchy outside and a nice, soft inside).

Makes about 40 cookies.

Chippy Chunk Cookies

Ingredients

2 sticks unsalted butter (room temperature)
¾ cup sugar
¾ cup brown sugar
2 cups flour
1 teaspoon baking soda
1 teaspoon baking powder
2 teaspoons kosher salt (or 1 teaspoon regular)
2 eggs
2 teaspoons vanilla
2½ cups oats
12 ounces (one bag) semisweet chocolate chips
8 ounces milk-chocolate candy bars, chopped into different-sized chunks (use however many bars it takes to get 8 ounces)

Instructions

Combine butter and sugars on low speed, then cream together at medium speed for 5 minutes. In a separate bowl, sift flour, baking soda, baking powder, and salt. If you don't have a sifter, it's fine to use a fine-mesh wire strainer. If some of the salt crystals don't go through the sifter/strainer, that's okay; stir them into the mix.

Add eggs and vanilla to the butter/sugar and mix until combined.

On low speed, add flour mixture and stir until just incorporated. Do not overmix.

Stir in oats until incorporated.

Add chocolate and stir by hand. (Tip: Keep the mixing bowl locked into the mixer to hold it in place while you stir. The dough will be very thick.)

Refrigerate dough overnight. (If you're in a hurry, refrigerate dough for at least 4 hours. If planning ahead, it's fine to refrigerate dough for up to 3 days.)

Use parchment paper to line cookie sheets.

Bake at 375 degrees for 6 to 7 minutes or until light brown around the edges. (Heads up: These are temperamental cookies, but well worth it. There are seconds between raw and overbaked cookies. They'll get brown after they're taken out of the oven.) Remove from oven and allow to cool a bit before transferring to a wire rack.

Quick, grab a glass of milk, 'cause these cookies are heavenly while warm.

Grandpa's Favorite Chocolate Cake a l'Orange (aka Char and Brady's Proposal Cake)

This is an old-fashioned recipe that's been updated with modern techniques. Hint: It helps tremendously to prepare items ahead of time for this recipe, including measuring out the ingredients into small prep bowls. Also, Dutch-processed cocoa powder is a must. Quality makes all the difference, so go with the best stuff you can get.

Ingredients

4 ounces unsweetened chocolate, chopped coarse
½ cup boiling water
¼ cup unsweetened Dutch-processed cocoa powder
2 cups white sugar, divided (½ cup and 1½ cups)
2 cups all-purpose flour
2 teaspoons baking soda
1 teaspoon baking powder
1 teaspoon salt
1 cup buttermilk
2 teaspoons vanilla extract
2 tablespoons orange juice (about ½ fresh orange)
1 tablespoon grated orange zest (about 1 medium orange)
½ teaspoon orange extract

4 eggs and 2 large yolks, room temperature
1 cup (2 cubes) unsalted butter, softened

Directions

Prep three 9-inch round cake pans: Cut out parchment-paper circles to fit in the pans. Spray pans with coconut or canola oil spray, line with parchment paper, then give another quick spray on top on the parchment. (Oil beneath the parchment helps it stay in place.)

Preheat oven to 350 degrees.

Boil more than enough water in a teakettle so that it's boiling when you measure out the ½ cup needed for this recipe. Prepare a double boiler (or use a glass mixing bowl that fits into a saucepan without touching the bottom of the pan). Add water to the bottom pan, making sure the water does not touch the upper pan/bowl, and turn heat on medium-low. Add the chopped chocolate and cocoa powder into the upper pan/bowl and add the ½ cup of boiling water. Stir until chocolate is melted. Add ½ cup of sugar and stir until glossy (1 to 2 minutes). Remove top pan/bowl from double boiler and allow it to cool.

In a medium bowl, whisk flour, baking soda, baking powder, and salt.

In a small bowl, combine buttermilk, vanilla, orange juice, and orange zest.

Using a standing mixer, whisk eggs and yolks on medium-low speed until combined. Add remaining sugar and whip on high speed until fluffy (2 to 3 minutes).

Switch to paddle attachment. Add chocolate mixture to egg mixture. Mix on medium speed for about 45 seconds. While mixer is still on, add butter 1 tablespoon-sized chunk at a time, allowing about 10 seconds between each chunk.

Alternate adding flour mixture and buttermilk mixture in five small batches: Start with about a third of the flour, then add about half the buttermilk, then another third of the flour, then the remaining buttermilk, and end with the remaining flour. Mix each until just incorporated before adding the next batch.

Mix on low speed for about 15 seconds until everything is thoroughly combined.

Pour into prepared pans. Bake 22 to 28 minutes, rotating pans about halfway through. Bake until toothpick comes out with a few moist crumbs. Do not overbake, or the cake will be dry.

Cool for about 10 minutes before removing cakes from pans. Continue to cool completely on wire racks.

Orange-Chocolate Buttercream Icing

Ingredients

½ cup (1 cube) butter, room temperature
4 cups (1 box) confectioner's sugar
4 tablespoons unsweetened Dutch-processed cocoa powder
⅛ teaspoon salt
¼ cup buttermilk plus more as needed
2 teaspoons vanilla extract
½ teaspoon orange extract

Directions

Mix butter until it's light and fluffy.

In a separate bowl, whisk confectioner's sugar, cocoa powder, and salt.

Slowly add sugar/cocoa mix to butter and mix for 1 to 2 minutes, scraping bowl as needed.

Add ¼ cup buttermilk, vanilla, and orange extract.

Add additional buttermilk, 1 tablespoon at a time, until icing is spreadable.

Lick the beater, then frost the cake.

Acknowledgments

Writing during the initial time of COVID-19 was . . . challenging. As all of us responded to and tried to cope with a crazy, frightening, once-in-a-lifetime deadly pandemic that no one understood or knew enough about, it was difficult to focus or concentrate. I've never struggled with anxiety before, but suddenly my anxiety level went off the charts. I couldn't write or even read any books (my favorite pastime) during those first six to eight weeks. Thankfully, after those first anxiety-filled months, I found my footing again and developed a new, safe rhythm of how to live and work during the coronavirus. Returning to Lake Potawatomi was a joy and a safe and delightful haven during this stressful time.

Thank you to my agent, Chip MacGregor, for your continued support and for putting me together with Crooked Lane. I am grateful to my fabulous and clever editor, Faith Black Ross, the hardworking and intrepid Melissa Rechter, Madeline Rathle, Rachel Keith, and the great Crooked Lane team. (Thanks again, Rob Fiore, for another killer cover!)

I'm also grateful to my friends and early readers Marian Hitchings and Cheryl Harris for their feedback on an initial draft, with a special thanks to Cheryl for vetting the pole-fitness dancing parts for accuracy. Any mistakes are my own. Additional thanks to Cathy Elliott, Dave Meurer, Annette Smith, and ("Team Laura") Kujubu. Deep gratitude to my first reader, longtime journalism friend, and editor-pal Kim Orendor for her speed and willingness to read chapters, answer questions, and provide encouragement. I owe you, Kimmie. (And I can't wait to read your first book!)

Heartfelt gratitude to dear friends Dave and Dale Meurer for once again opening up their lovely home (pre-COVID) to me for a desperately needed writing getaway and for thoroughly spoiling me the entire time I was there with delicious food, cups of steaming-hot PG Tips, and yummy shortbread and other goodies. Every writer needs a Dave and Dale Meurer in their life.

A special shout-out to the kind and generous Zoe Quinton for allowing me to nervously bounce off a new-ending idea at the eleventh hour and confirming that yes, it works. (One of these days, I'll make it to Santa Cruz to buy you that drink.) Finally, thanks to Michael for being the head baker of the Cozy Bakery and to our friends who sampled the Cozy Bakery's delicious treats (and failures), with special thanks to Connie Weichert and Michael Johnson for allowing me to use their family recipes.